DEATH ON THE ISLE

DEATH ON THE ISLE

M.H. ECCLESTON

An Aries Book

First published in the UK in 2022 by Head of Zeus
This paperback edition first published in 2023 by Head of Zeus,
part of Bloomsbury Publishing Plc

975312468

A catalogue record for this book is available from
the British Library.

ISBN (PB): 9781803280394
ISBN (E): 9781803280370

Typeset by Divaddict Publishing Solutions Ltd

Printed and bound in Great Britain by
CPI Group (UK) Ltd, Croydon CR0 4YY

Head of Zeus Ltd
First Floor East
5–8 Hardwick Street
London EC1R 4RG

WWW.HEADOFZEUS.COM

For Mum and Dad

The End

Astrid stumbled back, felt a sharp stab of pain as her head hit the wooden seat of the dinghy, and she rolled over the side.

The coldness clamped around her.

Swim.

Her limbs didn't respond.

Swim.

Please.

Swim…

The weight of her clothes was pulling her down. One last breath. Drag in as much air as she could.

Then the water sealed around her. She was on her back, looking up at the surface. A hazy glow through the fog. The dinghy to her right. How long did she have?

Thirty seconds.

Someone her age. Her fitness. That's what Jane had said. Then the air in her lungs would rush out. The saltwater rush in. Suffocating her.

Twenty-five.

Was this it? Here?

Your life was supposed to flash before your eyes. All those

moments that mattered crushed into a hyper-speed video. But there was only sadness, as burning as the cold water.

Twenty.

For the whole of her life, she'd only truly loved one person. And they'd loved her. Not her husband. Or boyfriends. Or friends. It was her father – just her father.

She saw him now. A single image. Was that what you were given?

He was holding her hand. The first day at primary school. She walked ahead to the classroom door, then turned and ran back to him. His arms folded around her. He kissed her forehead – told her it was going to be alright. He'd always be there.

Now she'd never see him again.

Ten.

The pain gripped her chest.

Her head pounded.

The dinghy drifted over the light.

Swim. NOW!

Her legs jerked. Then kicked. Arms swept down by her sides. Working together. Finally… climbing up through the water. Her head about to explode.

One

last

surge…

And she broke the surface. Ssssucked in air like an inward scream. Gasped. Again and again, until her lungs stopped hurting.

Treading water, she slowly spun round. The fog was still hanging over the water. She could only see ten feet ahead of her. The dinghy was now to her left. She made a few slow, strong kicks towards it. The Isle of Wight was less than a mile away, somewhere out there in the mist. Too far to swim.

She'd have to get back onto the yacht... and deal with both of them there.

One

It was nearly the end of July, over three months since she'd moved down to Hanbury. The summer had been – everyone seemed to agree – one of the best for years. Long cloudless days. Gentle breezes. No rain. Only Dolly had complained, about having to keep watering the window boxes outside the Angler's Arms. For everyone else, it had been the dream British summer.

Astrid sat in a foldaway chair on the boardwalk, a late-morning coffee tucked into the armrest. There was more shade here, up against the high rushes. The water out in the estuary was glassy. *Smooth and mirror-like* – Force 0 on the Beaufort wind scale. She'd read it in one of books in the cabin. There were lines that sounded like poetry.

'Wind felt on face.'

'Vanes begin to move.'

'Whistling in wires.'

Whistling in wires? How beautiful.

Over the summer, Cobb had taught her how to sail. He'd shown her how all the navigation equipment worked. How to read the weather and currents. To tie knots and fish. It felt good to know these things. The secrets and jargon that made her know she was a real sailor. Speed across the water is measured in 'knots'. Ropes are known as 'lines'. Unless they're attached to the sails, then they're 'sheets'. Even if sails look more like sheets than ropes do. Well, who said it had to make sense?

Then there was the Shipping Forecast on BBC Radio 4. After the news bulletins, the announcer would read out the weather reports for stretches of water around Britain. Before she had the boat, it made no sense. She'd only listened because she liked the soothing names.

Malin. Bailey. FitzRoy. Rockall.

They used to sound like names celebrities might give their kids. Now she knew where most of these regions of sea were.

Then she had her own tips for living on a boat. The wind is free – so don't use the engine unless you have to. A wine box is more useful than a bottle. Wine boxes sit squarely on the table. Bottles clank around on the shelves or fall over when the waves get up. Eating cereal at any time of the day is acceptable. Did that make her a sailor, or a slob? She couldn't remember and wasn't bothered either way. *Curlew's Rest* was the best place she'd ever lived. It was all hers and together they owned the sea beneath them.

She had her dear Uncle Henry to thank for that. He'd left her the boat in his will and a chance to find a new life. At times she wondered if she should even thank her ex-husband, Simon, for cheating on her. A strange thought maybe. But it had spurred her to leave London and her old job and discover a whole new life and friends in the country.

Nah, she thought again, he was still a weasel. Her new life was all down to her.

She finished her coffee and got up. It was time to take the boat out. From the clouds out over the bay, she could tell a breeze was picking up. Just as she untied the last line, a man stepped out from the rushes and sauntered towards the jetty. He was wearing jeans and a shiny blue jacket that might have been half of a suit. In his hand was a brown leather briefcase.

'Astrid Swift?' he shouted over.

'That's me.'

'Andy Marriot. H M R C.'

He'd spelt out the initials slowly, as if to make sure she knew how serious his mission was today. Her Majesty's Revenue and Customs. A tax inspector. Not someone you wanted a visit from. Especially on a Sunday.

She threw the line back onto the jetty. Without asking, he put down his briefcase, strode over to the rope, his cowboy boots clacking on the planks, and tied the rope to the post. A good double clove hitch too.

She invited him on board and he hopped up on deck, unfolded a chair and sat down. A bead of sweat had gathered on his sizeable brow. He wiped it away with the back of his hand. 'Niiice...' he drawled, looking around the boat. His hair was silver grey and thinning. What little there was on the top of his head was scraped back into a short ponytail.

'Can I get you a drink, Mr Marriot?'

'No, thanks. I had a couple of Pinot Grigios down at the harbour.'

'I meant tea or coffee. But hey, good for you.'

He was too busy studying the boat. 'Like it – a classic,' he said under his breath.

'Do you sail yourself?' She sat down opposite him.

'Used to as a kid. Had a Laser. Would love to get back into it. Maybe not a sailboat though.' He talked in quick bursts. Bouncing between sentences as if he didn't know how to end them. 'A Sunseeker. That would be the dream. Right? Jacuzzi on the top deck. Ooh...' He wiggled his shoulders at the thought.

'So, Andy, how can I help?' Astrid thought it was probably best to get this over with. Since she stopped being staff at the National Gallery, she hadn't given much thought to how you paid tax. Was being too busy an excuse?

'Well, Astrid,' he said gravely, 'I've recently been through your financial affairs and it's not good.'

'Really?' She sighed.

'I'm kidding.' He burst out laughing, shaking his head at his own joke. 'Just a little ice-breaker there, Astrid.'

'Niiice,' she said.

He crossed his legs, so his jeans rode up, revealing most of his tan cowboy boots. Then he unbuttoned his suit jacket. It had a fuchsia-pink lining. She stared at him.

'I know what you're thinking.'

'Bet you don't.'

'You're thinking, what's a guy like me doing in the tax business? Right?'

Wrong. She was thinking two things. One – he probably pulled that 'you're in trouble with your taxes' joke *every* time. Two – what was his outfit all about? And his hair? It was like a roadkill squirrel, slowly sliding down the back of his head.

'I've done loads of crazy things in my life, Astrid,' he continued. 'Been a DJ in Ibiza... tick. Set up a Mexican street-food restaurant in Cheltenham... tick. Went bankrupt... double tick.'

'Then you got into tax?'

'Yeah, I needed to settle down for my own sake. Although, investigating tax can get you into some pretty crazy situations. Like recently, I've been working on a few big UWOs.'

'UWOs?'

'Unexplained wealth orders. It's the super-rich trying to hide their money. Yachts, supercars, golf courses. They can't explain where they got it, we're gonna take it. That's why I was headhunted to be an inheritance tax assessor.'

'And is that why you're here? To go over my recent inheritance?' Astrid flinched. She couldn't bear to have her beautiful boat taken from her.

Andy picked up her anxiousness. 'Hey, sorry... not your inheritance. You're golden.' He uncrossed his legs again. 'Come on – focus, Andy,' he told himself off. 'Okay, I've been asked to assess the inheritance tax on a big estate on the Isle of Wight. There's a house, a couple of boats, funds and shares. An art collection. That's why I'm here.'

'What kind of art?'

'Maritime art. Nothing after 1900.'

'My expertise is in restoring art. Not valuing it.'

'I know.' He reached down for his briefcase, unzipped it and pulled out a sheet of paper, which he passed over to her. It was a list of artists – some of the most famous painters in their field. Luny, Minderhout, Carmichael. *This could be exciting*, she thought. *Better play it cool*. 'Impressive,' she said flatly.

He carried on talking as Astrid studied the list. Someone else would be doing the valuation. Her job, if she took it, would be to work out the cost of the restoration needed to get the paintings to auction in the best condition. This was called the 'hope value'. And HMRC were hoping it was going to be a lot of cash.

Astrid turned the page. There was another dozen or so paintings on there too. Around forty in all. As she wasn't doing the restoration work it would take around two weeks. Which was perfect. The Sherborne Hall money would run out soon enough and her divorce settlement was a long way off. 'Okay... I might be interested.'

'Splendid.' He then explained the whole story, and the part she would play in it. The bulk of the inheritance was a big seafront property called The Needles' Eye. That's where the art collection was. Both had been owned by a businessman and keen sailor called David Wade. He'd been long divorced when he died in his late seventies. Everything he owned had been left to his only daughter, Celeste, a socialite and environmentalist in her mid-twenties.

Astrid flashed through the maths. There was a much younger mother then, which pointed to serious money. No judgement. That's just how it usually went.

The consultancy fee was excellent. Triple her usual rate to reflect, as Andy said, the urgency of the job. 'We need to get this done ASAP Rocky.'

'ASAP Rocky?'

'You know... like the rapper.'

'If you say so,' said Astrid.

He opened his jacket out straight to one side. Like

old-fashioned spivs do when they sell stolen watches in black-and-white movies. He took a fountain pen from a pocket in the pink lining and handed it to her. Then he pulled out two copies of a contract from his briefcase. She signed them quickly, because it was another chance to spend time with some amazing art. And if she gave herself time to mull it over, she'd back out for all the wrong reasons. Because she liked it here on the boat, with Cobb.

Astrid made a note of the contact details. She was to call Celeste, who'd arrange to let her into the house.

Andy took his copy of the contract and said, 'You're working for the Queen now. Nobody can stop you in your duties. If they try, then show them this.' He handed her a letter that had HMRC at the top, with a gold-embossed crown. 'It's the kind of headed notepaper that says, "Back off, Buster".' He got up and made a little kung fu chopping move with his hands.

'Thanks, I'll keep that in mind.' She folded up the letter into a neat square and slipped it into the pocket of her hiking trousers. Then she followed him off the boat to the lane. He'd taken off his jacket and slung it over his shoulder, hooking it with one finger. 'Do you have any more questions?'

'Why did you choose me?'

'Ah, yeah. I was at the press event at Sherborne Hall. I went to see how much that Constable was worth. For the record.' He winked. 'Then you exposed it as a fake in front of your husband. And I said to myself – hey, Andy. That's ballsy. Someone we can trust. So, when this job came up, I thought of you.'

'I'm flattered.'

'And you probably need the money.'

He half-smiled. As if to say there was a good Andy and a bad one. That's how she read it. 'And how would you know?'

'I checked your files. Noticed that you've hopped over from PAYE to self-employment. It's a steep drop in income.'

'That's considerate of you, Andy. But I'll be taking this job because of the art, not my finances, thanks.'

'That's the spirit.' He kicked the heel of his boot on the path, scuffing up a puff of dust. 'Right, well, I better skedaddle. Good luck on the Isle.' And off he went down the lane, as pleased as any tax officer could possibly be. To be fair, he should be pleased. He'd won her over. An investigator for the Queen – that had a certain air of authority.

Two

Over the next day and a half, Astrid got ready for her trip to the Isle of Wight. She made sure the boat's water tanks were topped up and the batteries were fully charged. Lashed the mountain bike on the deck. Bought plenty of supplies – lots of tins of chopped tomatoes and pulses, dried pasta, good-quality dark chocolate, biscuits (mostly shortbread fingers), long-life milk and spare batteries for torches. Just in case there wasn't a decent shop near Yarmouth Harbour, the nearest marina to The Needles' Eye.

She also bought a hiking map of the Isle of Wight and a sailing chart for the waters around it. The island was a rough diamond shape. Slightly flattened, as if it were a square of fudge that had been pinched and squashed down between a forefinger and thumb.

The largest coastal town was Cowes. It was on the northernmost point of the island, facing out over a wide strait between the island and the mainland called The Solent. Yarmouth was much smaller, out on the western point at the mouth of the River Yar. Another mile and the headland tapered away in the sea, ending with a string of broken crags known as The Needles. Maybe, wondered Astrid, that was why the house was called The Needles' Eye? Because it had a view out to these rocks. It wouldn't be inspired by the biblical saying. After all, a rich man wasn't going to remind themselves how hard it was to get into the kingdom of heaven.

Astrid spent an hour or so planning the sailing route across to Yarmouth from Hanbury. It would take half a day. She rang her best friend Kath to tell her she was going to be away for a while, and they arranged to meet in the Angler's Arms. A few early evening drinks to send her off.

A few weeks back, Astrid had offered Kath all her designer dresses, seeing as she was only wearing sailing and hiking gear these days. Kath hadn't taken any of them because, she said, she never went anywhere that 'fancy'. So, Astrid had dropped them in at the animal charity shop in town instead. They both agreed that an old donkey's needs were greater than Kath's. But 'only just', Astrid had said. Which was followed by beer spray and hoots of laughter.

Kath had accepted Astrid's Chanel parfum. She loved it. Said it smelt like Febreze 'but classier'. Astrid was pleased to give it away. The fragrance would always remind her of how she defended herself against Emily on the ledge at Sherborne Hall. There had been only a few news reports of Emily and Cressida trying to steal the Constable. And none of them had mentioned Astrid, which was a relief. The whole episode, it seemed, was behind her.

The two of them were sitting opposite each other on one of the tables outside the Angler's Arms. Both had a fresh pint of Badger's in their hands. Astrid sluiced down a couple of inches.

Kath shook her head. 'The Isle of Wight – I can't believe it.'

'It's not another planet, Kath.'

'It is a bit.' She sucked her lips. 'Another world – trapped in time. When a plane goes over, they all rush inside and bolt their doors. Very odd place.'

'I thought you'd never been there?'

'I haven't. It's just what I've heard. From people who've been.' She shivered. 'The ones who came back, that is.'

'Kath, I know you're just trying to put me off. But I have to go.'

'Busted.'

Astrid pushed her hand out over the table and Kath gripped it. 'Don't worry, I'll be back in a couple of weeks.'

They chatted for about an hour, until the sun dipped below the ridge of hills beyond the river. It was time to go. Astrid had an early start in the morning, to catch the first tide. Kath sensed the goodbyes were coming and reached down for a plastic shopping bag at her feet.

'A few leaving presents for you, Astrid.'

'Aww... how sweet of you, Kath,' Astrid said, opening the bag. She rummaged around and brought out the items one by one. First was a grey T-shirt with a cartoon of a round smiling character with pigtails, the words *Little Miss Know-It-All* arched over its head. 'That's very funny. Thanks, Kath.'

'I found it on the beach. When everyone leaves to go home, I have a little scout about to see what I can find. You know... before the metal detector lot turn up. They're vultures, Astrid... vultures.'

Next was a small Chinese embroidered silk purse that was empty apart from a scoop of sand in the corner.

'That's lovely,' said Astrid.

'There was a fiver in there when I found it. Which I spent, of course – you're not exactly going to hand it in, are you? Police have got better things to do.' Kath reached into the bag again and brought out the last item. 'Don't worry, I didn't find this on the beach.' She handed over a small deodorant spray.

Astrid took it and read the side slowly. 'Forty-eight hours guaranteed protection.'

'Good, eh?'

'Forty-eight hours.' Astrid paused. 'I'm just thinking… under what circumstances would you not be having a wash in two days?'

'Music festival, maybe? Power cut?'

'But what if it was longer than forty-eight hours? Like, three days?'

'Dunno. Spray some more on?'

'Really? Like, add another forty-eight hours?'

'Guess so.'

'Then why not keep going? Never wash again?'

'That's not a bad idea.'

They both burst out laughing. 'Anyway,' said Astrid when they'd calmed down. 'You really didn't need to spend money on deodorant for me.'

'I didn't. It was just lying around in my bathroom. I've only used it a couple of times and I thought you might like it.'

Anyone else, and she would have handed it back. But this was Kath, the greatest friend anyone could wish for. Sitting there, in the tie-dye T-shirt shirt she'd worn nearly every day this summer. Grinning like a fool. Astrid popped the deodorant in her bag and smiled. 'Thank you... That's very kind.'

They finished their drinks, gathered their things and gave each other a hug. Then Kath said, 'Is Cobb upset you're leaving him?'

'Cobb?' Astrid grimaced.

Kath stared at her. 'Astrid? Have you not told him?'

'Not yet.'

'Why not?'

Astrid wasn't sure why she hadn't told Cobb. Or deep down she was, but didn't want to deal with the truth. Her time with Cobb had been wonderful. They'd seen each other every day. Staying up on the deck at night talking. Or reading poems to each other. Falling into each other's arms below deck. It had all been so perfect. So unreal.

She walked down the lane towards the boat in the last glow of the day. The plants on either side were beginning to yellow and dry. The stalks of the cow parsley had turned to thin sticks that rattled in the wind. July, the last truly warm and dreamy month of summer. Before the wind at night carried a chill like a scent and the year was looking back. The end of something glorious. Maybe she and Cobb were just for this one summer.

She pushed open the door of the boatyard. Cobb never locked it. Sheepdip, the dog Uncle Henry had left her, was curled up in his basket in the kitchen. No doubt exhausted from a long day ferreting around in the undergrowth. He greeted her with a raised ear, then closed his eyes again. Cobb was in a chair out on the decking by the river, a book in his hand. He saw her and put the book down. Read her expression.

'You okay?'

'Was it that obvious?'

She stood on the decking and explained about the new job and how she'd be leaving the next day on the first tide. He said he was pleased for her. That he'd miss her, but two weeks would 'fly by', and when he said that she flinched slightly, and she knew that he'd noticed. And that she'd avoided eye contact with him since she walked in.

She sat down in a chair next to him and looked out over the water, which was flat calm. Waiting to find the right way of saying it. But Cobb got there first.

'Are we okay?' He stressed the 'we'.

She wanted to tell him that everything was fine. That they'd carry on as they were when she got back from her trip. But that would be putting it off, and it would be tougher to deal with then. 'The thing is, Cobb,' she sighed, 'we've had an amazing time together. You know, I've been so happy, and I can't believe it happened.' She turned to face him. 'It's been so fabulous. Like those big-print books they have in the romance section of the local library.'

'I don't know that section.'

'They have these swoony covers and titles. Ours would be *The Boatyard Owner and the Art Conservator*. It would fly off the shelves.'

'People like those stories then?'

'They do. Because they're an escape from real life.' She took a deep breath. 'What I'm trying to say is – maybe this is supposed to be just a summer romance.'

'"Summer's lease hath all too short a date."'

'Aargh…' She scrunched up her nose and laughed. 'That's so annoying. I have my big-print books and you have Shakespeare's sonnets.'

He brushed the hair from his forehead. He'd let it grow longer over the summer and it suited him – which wasn't helping.

'Listen.' He leant forward and put his hand on her forearm. 'Don't worry. Just be honest with me, Astrid. Then it won't hurt.'

She took an even deeper breath. 'I've just come out of a terrible marriage. Didn't know how terrible it was until I left it. And then I find you and you're amazing. But there's a part of me that's still broken. I don't know what it is. But I can't give you any more until I've fixed it.'

'Have I asked more from you?'

'No, you haven't.'

'Then maybe you're overthinking things as usual, Astrid Swift.'

'Yeah, I've been wondering why I do that so much.' She gave a wry smile.

'Yeah, very good.' He chuckled. Then he reached out and put his hand to her cheek and she didn't turn away. 'Whatever you want, I'm cool with that. I understand – it's just timing, isn't it?'

She nodded. He took his hand away, and she missed the warmth of it.

'Hey, maybe it is a summer thing. But it doesn't make it any less precious, does it?'

She sighed. 'Thanks, Cobb.'

'Thanks?'

'For being you. For letting me be me.' She stood up and took his hand. 'And you know what?' she said. 'If this is a summer thing, then technically it's still the summer. Right?' And she led him back through the kitchen, tiptoeing past Sheepdip and up the ladder to the bedroom.

Three

She got up well before dawn. No alarm. She didn't want to wake Cobb, because they'd said what they needed to the night before.

When she'd left Simon and her apartment in London, it had felt like an escape. With Cobb, she had to drag herself away. They were good for each other – just not right now. In a way, it hurt just as much. It was hard to leave Sheepdip too. But it was better that he stayed. He was an outdoor dog – free to roam. She'd be working over the next two weeks at the house so would have to leave him alone on the boat during the day. They'd see each other soon enough.

Back at the boat, she changed into her sailing gear, made a flask of coffee and went up to the wheelhouse. It was still dark. She switched on the red lamp over the dashboard so she could read the charts. Red light is better than white light in the dark. You don't have to reset your night vision if you look out into the darkness. That was another of the things she'd learnt in the past few weeks.

She laid out the chart and ran her finger over the route she'd plotted the day before. The map had contours marked in shades of blue. The darker the blue, the deeper the sea.

There was a small number on the edge of each patch. This was the depth in metres. There were a few negative numbers, which indicated sand bars and reefs exposed at low tide. Sometimes there were tiny arrows to show the direction of currents.

She ran the boat on the engine until it was well through the deep-water channel at the mouth of Poole Harbour. Light had begun to seep into the day. A slash of pink above the horizon glowed under a creamy bank of clouds. To her starboard was the sandy curve of Shell Bay. Kath's café was out there somewhere. It was six o'clock. She wouldn't be raking up the shutters for hours.

When she'd passed the last marker buoy in the channel, she swung the boat due east, cut the engine and unfurled the mainsail. The wind had picked up, five knots from the south-west. With a helpful tide, she should reach land well before lunch.

Three hours later, the Isle of Wight began to take shape on the horizon, its low green shoulders rising from the sea. For the first time, she saw The Needles. They were three jagged ridges of limestone that loomed out of the water. Astrid gazed at them in wonder. They were magnificent. Ancient. Rock formed in the cupped hands of time. Clawed back into the sea by millions of years of waves and gravity. Past the furthest point was a red-and-white lighthouse.

She checked her chart. The contours swirled tightly through the three rocks. The small arrows that showed the direction of the currents pointed in all directions – like a flight of arrows fired into a hurricane.

The Needles were nearly a mile away, but she could feel

the current pulling the boat to them, as if an unseen hand had gripped the keel. Astrid swung the prow towards the mainland and set a route through deeper waters.

An hour later, she reached the entrance to Yarmouth Harbour. On the west side was a wooden wall of tight beams that shielded the pontoons and boats. To the east, was a concrete slipway. A big blue-and-white ferry with *Wightlink* painted down the side was coming into dock. Just beyond it was a big white hotel with *The George* written in big letters along the sea wall in front of it. Then there was a wooden pier that jutted out 200 yards into the bay.

Astrid lined up at the harbour mouth. A couple of minutes later, a smart grey inflatable drew alongside. A young man with mirrored sunglasses was standing at the helm. He read the name on her boat, checked a clipboard by the helm and shouted, 'You don't have a reservation.'

Astrid shook her head. There were very few times she ever wanted to look feeble, but this was one of them. If they didn't let her into the harbour, where would she go? 'I'm really sorry. I didn't know you had to,' she said. He gawped at her in disbelief. Then, after a bit of thought, he waved at her to follow him, spinning the boat in a neat semicircle and leading the way into the harbour.

The marina was crammed with boats. There were gleaming white single-mast yachts sunk low in the water. Wooden ketches like hers, but in better condition. Big motor cruisers with two or three levels, smart furniture arranged at the front, smoked-glass doors behind that led into dining rooms. Astrid gripped the wheel and slowed down past a line of towering boats. She leant out to check the fenders were hanging evenly down the side of the hull. Grinding along the side of one of these yachts would cost more in repairs than her entire boat.

She followed the inflatable as it turned inland past a row of boats moored up with their sterns facing her. A couple sitting at a round table with an ice bucket in the middle tipped their glasses to her. Another man in an armchair folded down his newspaper and watched her glide past. The harbour was awash with money. And if the boat names were anything to go on – *Current Account*, *A Loan at Sea* – most of it came from banking.

Soon the bigger boats ran out and she arrived in a brackish lagoon. The jetties here were older and worn. The boats were much smaller. All of them sailboats. Some that looked like they hadn't been out to sea for years. The man with the mirrored sunglasses indicated a mooring up in the corner. Told her that the harbour master would be round sometime to sort out the fees. Then he spun off without waving back.

This was the last empty mooring, the furthest point from the entrance to the marina. There was a clear view back up the winding River Yar, the woods on either side of the valley and the high rolling headland.

The river was ten feet wide and barely flowing. The tide had just started to turn from its lowest point. Thin cracked fingers of grey water probed the mudflats either side. A handful of black-and-white birds chittered high notes as they stalked among the sludge and yellow-green samphire. It smelt of kelp and crab shells. 'Yes.' Astrid inhaled. 'This will do nicely.'

She went down below and poured herself the last of the strong coffee from the flask. Then she fixed a bowl of muesli with long-life milk, ate it quickly, and headed out to explore the town.

Four

It was peak summer season and Yarmouth was out to charm its visitors. The buildings were newly painted in pastel colours – blues, yellows, pinks. Lines of bunting criss-crossed the narrow streets. Hanging baskets foamed with bright flowers. And it was working. People filled the alleys and the high street. Couples and families mostly, who stopped every few yards to peer at the window displays of fossils, gemstones and sweets. The usual tourist catnip shops, mixed in with a handful of upmarket interior and clothes stores for the richer locals.

Astrid carried on down the high street and turned a corner into a cobbled square. There was a stocky church at the far end, and a café called The Chatterbox at the entrance to the town pier. Around the square were a dozen shops and three pubs, the largest being The Bugle, a hefty stone coaching inn with a Tudor black-beamed porch over the door.

She was about to cross the square when a man stepped out and blocked her way. He was in his mid-sixties with a comb-over of white hair. A tidy grey moustache hovered under a beakish nose. Everything about him seemed officious. His stiff posture. The smart blue-and-white gingham shirt buttoned up and pressed against his broad chest by the straps of a leather backpack.

'Are you local?' he said, sliding a leaflet from a pile in his hand.

'I'm sort of working here for a bit,' said Astrid.

'That'll do.' He handed her the leaflet. It had a picture of a bike that was crossed out with a red diagonal line. The text was in various fonts, mostly capital letters with plenty of exclamation marks. The phrase 'YARMOUTH SAYS NO!' leapt out.

'I'm alright, thanks.' She handed the leaflet back. He didn't take it.

'The contact details to write to the council are on the back.'

'I'm fine, honestly.' She'd set aside only a small amount of politeness for this man. He was using it up fast. Then she'd be on to the 'just bugger off' fund. She tried to step past him on the pavement, but he swung one of his black brogues out to the side, then slid his other foot to catch it up. It was like a nifty dance move that maybe he'd learnt at a salsa class where he wasn't that welcome. 'I'm late,' said Astrid.

'We have to stop it.'

'Stop what?'

His dark eyes narrowed. 'The cycle lane.'

'The cycle lane?'

He drew in an impatient breath. 'The council want to take out the parking spaces on the high street and replace them with a cycle lane. It will strangle the life out of local business. Mark my words—' he wagged a finger at her '—if the council get their way it will be like the speed bumps on Ventnor Avenue. And we all know how that worked out.'

'Do we?'

'We do. It was madness.'

The man saw another couple approaching and thumbed a leaflet off the top of the stack in his hand. Astrid saw her chance and slipped across the square, and when she was sure he was out of sight, she screwed up the leaflet and put it in the recycling section of the nearest bin.

Astrid meandered through the streets for a while, shaking off the memory of the annoying man in the square. Eventually, she found her way back to the harbour car park and the track upstream to her boat. It was too early to crash out in her bunk, so she decided to keep going on the path up the valley.

The track first skirted round the mudflats. Then it cut west into the swampy ground, changing into a wooden boardwalk that plunged into high reeds. After ten minutes of brisk walking she emerged from the rushes and climbed up through the woods. When she emerged from the trees, there was a fork in the path. The choice was up to the headland or west to the woods on the other side of the valley. There was a wooden sign pointing that way, with the familiar acorn and oak leaf branding of the English Trust. And the words *Abbotsford Manor – ½ mile*.

The sun was still beating down. It might not be a bad idea to get some shade in the woods, she thought. Then a drink from a café at the manor – it was the English Trust so there was bound to be one. She checked her membership card was in her rucksack and took the right fork.

Five

Abbotsford Manor was much smaller than the Sherborne estate. About a quarter of the size. But it was perfect and lovely in its own way. The entrance was through the middle of a long barn. At the other side was a gravel area, and a low wall that circled the manor house. It was two storeys high, with a steep slanting roof of grey stone slabs. There were small square windows that gave away its Tudor heritage, and a collection of gables and tall chimneys, later additions and repairs that hinted at fires, local wars and owners making their mark. Beyond the manor house was a village. It was only a handful of cottages and a church that stood guard over a village green, the sea glistening in the distance. It was all so achingly beautiful. As if it had been stolen from a summer daydream and placed there.

Astrid set off into the gardens to find the café. The deep flower borders exploded with colour. Red and orange lilies nearest the path. Drifts of tall white daisies and blue delphiniums floating above them.

She carried on, through arches cut into the high hedges. Discovering fountains, marble statues, stone benches and grids of shin-high boxes filled with different herbs. Finally, she found a black chalkboard sign advertising the café, and hot and cold drinks. Ice cold, with a bit of luck.

Astrid had no idea which way to go. The sign gave no clue where the café was, and she'd lost her bearings wandering from garden to garden. She picked a gap to her right and arrived at a mosaic square with a stone bench in the corner. There was a woman sitting on the bench, wearing a black dress and high, lace-up black boots. In front of her was a wooden wind-up easel. A wheelchair stood to one side.

Astrid went over. She was just about to ask for directions when she saw the canvas. The painting was startling. Not least because it looked nothing like the scene in front of them. In the centre was a female warrior, buckled into a leather outfit, a heavy glinting sword trailing in the dust. The warrior's other hand gripped a leash that trailed up to the neck of a dragon that was three times her height. Smoke curled from its nostrils. Behind them, the ruins of the manor house smouldered under a leaden sky.

'Oh, that's... erm... darker than I was expecting.' Astrid studied the canvas. 'But it's, you know... it's fantastic.'

The woman looked up. She was young – late teens. Her dress was vintage lace, dyed black. Her lipstick dark purple, the same shade as a streak that ran down one side of her hair. 'Thank you,' she said quietly. 'It's not though. Is it?' She put her brush down on the ledge of the easel. There were silver rings of skulls and spiders on each finger.

'Sorry. I shouldn't have interrupted you when you were painting.' She stepped back. 'But honestly, this is really brilliant.'

'Thank you,' she said, and this time it had conviction.

'I'm into gaming. I like to paint my favourite characters in landscapes. This is Morrigan from *Dragon Age*.'

'Is that right?' Astrid didn't know anything about gaming. Whatever that was. But she knew a lot about composition. She stepped forwards again and studied the painting. Yes, she'd nailed it. There's something called The Rule of Thirds. It's a technique used by all the great masters. The canvas is divided horizontally and vertically by three. The things the artist wants you to notice are placed on the points where the lines cross. But when she explained this to the woman, she shook her head. 'Have I?' she said, making eye contact just long enough for Astrid to see she had greenish-hazel eyes.

'Yes. You definitely have.'

The girl shrugged. 'I never knew. I mean, I just paint.'

'Well, you've got a natural talent for it. Trust me – I'm an art conservator and I've spent a lot of time with masterpieces.' She thrust out her hand. 'My name's Astrid.'

The young woman reached up and shook her hand. 'I'm Wren.'

'Nice name.'

'Like the bird. My dad's precious little bird.' There was a sourness to the way she said it. As if this wasn't a compliment she liked. There was a canvas bag hanging from the armrest of her wheelchair. She started packing her watercolour box and brushes into it. 'I better get going. He's picking me up in about twenty minutes.' She unclipped the pegs that held the canvas in place and rolled it up. 'Listen. If you're an expert on art, you should come and meet the others.'

'Others?'

'Yeah – there's four of us. We're a little art club. Mr Rigby, the estate manager, he lets us use the potting shed as a studio. And we get to display our paintings in the reception area. In case anyone wants to buy one.'

'Okay,' said Astrid. 'I'll drop by sometime.'

'No, no,' protested Wren. 'They're all here now.'

'Now?' It was a kind offer, thought Astrid. But she was tired, and thirsty. 'Thanks, but I better get going.' She smiled, feeling the dryness on her lips. Then she saw how disappointed Wren was. 'Could I get a glass of water there?'

'Sure.'

'Right then.' Astrid picked up Wren's easel. 'Lead the way.'

Six

The potting shed was tucked up against a beech hedge on a level tier about a hundred yards from the entrance. It was twenty feet long and made from blackened wooden boards. There were two simple windows either side of the door, and a pitched tin roof.

Inside, it was just as humble. Wooden planks on the floor. An iron stove in the corner. A sideboard under rows of shelves that were filled with pots of paints and varnishes.

There were three other people in the room. Two men sitting in battered leather armchairs, and a woman standing by the far wall. 'Hi, everyone.' Astrid made a vague waving gesture to all of them.

Wren edged round her towards the sink. 'This is Astrid. She's an expert in fine art. We could learn a thing or two.'

The man next to Astrid got to his feet. He was slim, with a smart black jacket, short silver-grey hair and darting blue eyes. 'What a pleasure. My name is Kabir.' He took a canvas chair from the corner and dusted it with the back of his hand. Then he placed it next to Astrid. 'We could do with an expert round here.'

'Thanks,' she said, sitting down. 'I'm not really an expert

at painting though. My job is in art conservation. But I have a background in fine art.'

'Fine art?' scoffed the other man. 'You won't find much of that round here.' He laughed again, creases forming under his reddish cheeks, which were only a few shades lighter than the football shirt he was wearing. 'No offence.'

'None taken,' said Kabir, smiling. 'I've just retired, Astrid. A long career as a GP. Painting is my new hobby.'

'We're all amateurs,' said the other man, his thick, hairy arms hanging over the sides of the chair. 'Except Wren. She's amazing.' The man reached for a thermos flask at his feet and topped up a silver mug. 'Honestly – I don't know how you do it, Wren.'

'Thanks, Frank,' said Wren from the sink, where she was filling a glass with water.

All this time, the woman by the wall had been shifting from foot to foot, waiting to be introduced.

Kabir turned to her. 'And this is Annabelle, who is over on the island for the summer.'

She had on a white sweatshirt with black hooped stripes. A blue scarf knotted at her neck. The whole 'Picasso on a studio photo shoot' vibe. Her brunette hair was tied up in a bun, held in place with a yellow HB pencil – to keep up the arty theme. 'My husband and I have a summer place here in Yarmouth. Our main home is in London.'

'Oh, London,' said Astrid. 'That's where I used to live.'

'Really… whereabouts?' said Annabelle, playing with the corner of her scarf.

'I used to have an apartment on the South Bank.'

Annabelle glanced at Frank, to make sure he'd seen that

she had something in common with Astrid. 'Wow... that's great. We have a town house in Bloomsbury. It's such a good central location for all the...'

'I've got a London joke for you.' Frank wasn't going to let this develop. 'You hear about the man who taught his dog to play the trumpet on the Underground?' He paused, gathering himself for the punchline. 'He got from Barking to Tooting in under an hour.'

Astrid, Kabir and Wren burst out laughing. Annabelle didn't join in. She folded her arms, a vinegary expression fixed on her face. 'Frank's the joker of the group,' she said. 'You'll get used to him.'

Wren came forward and gave Astrid the glass of water. She thanked her, then drank it as fast and as politely as she could. When she'd gasped down the last inch, Wren took the glass and went back to refill it.

'Yeah,' said Frank, 'well, I have a chalet up on the cliffs at Totland.'

'Chalet?' Annabelle turned to Astrid. 'Sounds so exotic, doesn't it? So Swiss. But it's really only a static caravan.'

'Well—' Frank sucked his lips '—if it wasn't for all these rich mainlanders coming in, us locals could afford the houses round here.'

'Listen,' Kabir said, fending off what was a brewing argument, 'let's not go on about ourselves, shall we. Let's hear a bit more about your job, Astrid.'

Everyone was so interested in what she did. She sometimes wondered why. To other people, art conservation sounded so mysterious. If they only knew the painstaking work involved. The hours and hours of cleaning and picking away varnish.

Wren brought her the second glass of water. She drank it more slowly this time, stopping to tell them about her job and the new contract at The Needles' Eye. They seemed impressed, which wasn't why she'd told them. 'So then,' she said, happy to change the subject, 'what sort of painting do you all do?'

Kabir went back to his seat and held up a nearly finished watercolour of the house and gardens. It was colourful and sunny. The sort of scene you could find on a postcard on the way in. 'I know.' He shrugged. 'It's a bit boring. But I'm just starting.'

'No, no,' protested Astrid. 'It's great. You know, and it's just my opinion…' She put her empty glass down. 'Next time, you could find something to focus on in the foreground. Certain flowers in the beds, maybe. Give us glimpses of the manor house through the foliage.'

'Good advice, thanks,' said Kabir.

'This is the sort of thing I like to do.' Annabelle stood up and presented her painting, which was the size of a large greetings card. It was a watercolour of a riverbank. There was a stand of bulrushes, which parted in the middle to reveal a bright blue stream. A kingfisher, wings outstretched, had been placed directly at the centre of the picture. 'I like to include a bird in flight somewhere. It ties…' she mimed making a knot '…the landscape with nature.'

Frank craned round to get a better look. 'Um,' he humphed. 'What are the chances of catching a kingfisher flying right slap bang in the middle of a picture?'

'You know, Frank, this composition is very popular online.' She nodded to Astrid. 'I have an Etsy shop. The kingfishers sell very well.'

Astrid noticed that Wren was stifling a giggle.

Annabelle hadn't finished. 'And, Frank, when are we expecting your masterpiece? You've yet to paint anything.'

Frank grinned. Nothing Annabelle said seemed to make a dent. 'All in good time, Annabelle. I'm just waiting for my muse to strike.'

'Is that right?' sniffed Annabelle. 'And what time do the pubs open round here?'

'Listen.' Kabir stepped between them. 'I have a wonderful idea, Astrid. Why don't you join our art club? Most of us are here in the afternoon, so if you get some time off you can just hang out. Give us some advice on our painting.'

Astrid hesitated. She wasn't sure how much free time she'd have in the next two weeks. And she didn't want to let them down. Then she saw Wren who had her hands clasped together as if she was praying. So, Astrid agreed. It would be good to get to know some new people on the island, she thought. 'But I'm only here for a couple of weeks,' she added.

'That's fine,' said Kabir. 'It will be nice to have your company for as long as you're here.'

The decision for her to join the Abbotsford Art Club, as they described themselves, lifted the mood in the potting shed. Frank and Annabelle even stopped sniping at each other. Everyone started to pack up. Wren was the first to leave and Astrid said her goodbyes a couple of minutes later, promising to be back soon.

On the way out, she found the café near the entrance. It was a smart wooden shack on wheels, with a shiny corrugated-iron roof and a dark-green awning. In front of it, a few round tables had been arranged in the gravel. She'd seen off her thirst, but was now hungry, so she grabbed a muffin and a coffee to pep her up for the walk back to the boat. It was almost five thirty – closing time. She sat at one of the tables and watched the last of the visitors trail to the exit.

In the car park in front of the reception barn, Wren tracked over to a beat-up black minivan, and the driver, her father presumably, came out to see her. Although he was too far away for Astrid to hear what he said, it was clear he was telling Wren off. He checked his watch. Put his hands out, palms up, and mouthed something that made Wren look down at the gravel. Then he helped her get into the passenger seat, stowed her wheelchair in the boot and drove off.

Seven

Astrid woke to the sensation of the boat lifting gently from the mud and scraping the side of the mooring. She'd turned in early the night before. It had been a tiring day and she needed to be fresh for what would be her first day working at The Needles' Eye. She'd arranged to meet Celeste Wade at the gates of her late father's house at ten o'clock. That would give her a bit of time to get some stuff done. Tidy the boat up, wrestle a few emails into the delete bin and write a note to her father in Spain.

This would be the third time she'd written to him this summer. Her first two letters had gone unanswered, which, even for him, was odd. He'd usually get round to dashing off a postcard. She'd arranged to have her post forwarded from her old London address to Hanbury so she would have received anything he'd sent.

She wrote the letter – a quick update on her new job – and told him to send her a note in reply. Just to say he was okay. Then she picked up her black work case for the first time in months and headed out.

* * *

The Needles' Eye was on the far side of the town, a hundred yards up the coast from the town pier. Astrid took the most direct route. Across the harbour car park, down the high street – stopping for stamps at the post office – then a short wiggle down the backstreets to a high-walled alley that ran down the side of the house to the water. Halfway down the alley was an iron gate in the wall. It was locked with a padlock and a heavy chain. Astrid peered through the bars. There was a big white house at the end of a wide drive. Three storeys, the first propped with a row of white pillars. The second and third had wrap-around balconies. It had its shoulder to the gate, chest puffed out, facing the sea – like a barrel-chested opera singer squaring up to their audience.

At ten o'clock on the dot, a woman emerged from the side door of the house and came over to the gate. This had to be Celeste Wade. She was tall – almost six foot – with an almond-shaped face and long honey-coloured hair. And she was beautiful, thought Astrid. To describe her like this in a book, say, would be a problem these days. But it was just a fact. Like the fact she was dressed in a white-and-black polka-dot shift dress, with a large sailcloth bag over her shoulder. She looked like a young Julie Christie. With the same natural manner that suggested she didn't know she was beautiful or care either way.

She had a rose gold smartphone pressed against her ear. 'Uh, huh… orchids. No, we can't. They'll be imported. The air miles are terrible,' she drawled with an accent that hinted at an expensive education. 'Hang on.' She took her phone from her ear and swished her hair over her shoulder. 'Astrid?'

Astrid nodded.

Celeste clamped the phone back to her ear and dug out a set of keys from her bag. 'Uh, huh… vegan canapés. No sushi. The caterers know that though.' She unlocked the gate and smiled apologetically, as if she was trying as hard as she could to wrap up the phone conversation. Then she gestured for Astrid to follow her to the house.

They walked down the drive, Astrid keeping back a few paces. There wasn't much of a garden at the front of the house, just a short lawn that ran up to a deep stone wall by the waterline. Behind the house, from what she could make out, the gardens were more generous. Deep flowerbeds were crossed by grass paths. Beyond, was an orchard that blended into a wood of beech trees.

Celeste rang off the call and dropped her phone in her bag. 'Sorry about that.'

Astrid stopped to take in the gardens. 'It's really lovely back here.'

'I don't spend any time in the gardens, to be honest.' Celeste's phone rang in her bag. 'If I was staying, I'd have it completely rewilded with native species. Sorry—' she reached into her bag '—I should get that.'

Celeste answered the call and kept up a conversation as they went into the house and climbed two flights of stairs to a short landing without any windows. 'Uhh… honestly.' She slipped her phone in her bag again. 'Cowes Week… it's just insane.' She whirled her finger near her temple.

'Cowes Week?' said Astrid. 'What's that?'

Celeste stood there, stunned. 'Are you serious?'

'Um… yeah. What's Cowes Week?'

'It's only the most famous sailing festival in the world. Astrid was then given a quick summary of Cowes Week. It was seven days of yacht racing, starting on Saturday, in three days' time. That, thought Astrid, would explain why it was so hard to get a mooring in the harbour.

The island, as Celeste explained, would be heaving with 'celebrities and high-worth individuals'. Celeste's eyebrows arched when she said this. She ran an environmental charity and was keen to make some influential contacts.

Astrid waited for her to wind up her speech, then put her work case down and said, 'I just want to say, I'm sorry about your loss. I gather your father was an extraordinary man.'

Celeste pursed her lips. 'That's so kind.' Her voice cracked. She reached into her bag and found a clear plastic bottle of water, loosened the top and took a sip. 'Yes, he was an incredible man. As you are about to see.' She conjured a weak smile. Then she went over to the door and pushed it open.

The room was around fifty feet long, running the entire upper floor, with floor-to-ceiling windows looking out over the Solent. It was as full as an end-of-pier museum. On the walls were dozens of oil paintings, hung so close you could barely make out the wood panelling behind them. Arranged around the room were carved ships' figureheads of mermaids and gods, models of yachts in glass cabinets, ships' wheels, brass bells, telescopes, compasses and varnished wooden rudders.

In the middle of the room was a long walnut table polished to such a sheen it reflected the roof above. She looked up and saw sailing pennants draped over the beams. A canoe made from sealskins hung high in the rafters. Astrid circled the table and came back to Celeste, who was still by the door. 'He was quite the collector, wasn't he?'

'Oh, yes. He certainly was.' She took a careful step forward, arms crossed, as if there was something about the room that made her uncomfortable. The memories of her father must still be raw, thought Astrid. 'He bought the house after selling his business in East Cowes,' Celeste continued. 'Wade Nautical Instruments.' Celeste's voice rose for the last sentence, as if asking a question.

'Sorry, I haven't heard of it.'

'It was a well-known company... on the Isle of Wight, at least.' She scanned the room. 'He loved everything about sailing and maritime history. When he was too ill to go out on the water, he'd sit up here in his "lookout", as he called it, watching the boats in the bay.'

Astrid gazed out of the bank of windows. It was breathtaking. There was a panoramic view from the eastern tip of the island to The Needles on the western point. There must have been two hundred boats and yachts bobbing on the water between.

'So, Astrid... I've been so busy, I didn't check why you're here. I just got the call from HMRC that you were coming.'

Astrid told her what she'd been asked to do. To write a report on the restoration work needed to get the art into the best shape for sale. So HMRC could work out its peak price.

'I don't understand?' said Celeste. 'Why can't they value the paintings now?'

'It's about potential. It doesn't matter if you keep them

or sell them without any restoration. They call it the hope value, apparently.'

Celeste shrugged. 'Okay. I mean, I'll just be glad to sell them off and move on. I'm not that bothered about money.'

Astrid took a closer look at the paintings on the walls. They were all of sailing scenes and naval battles. 'And all the art is here in this room?'

'Yes, I think everything of any value has been brought up here.' Her phone was buzzing in her bag, and Astrid could see she was itching to pick it up.

'Listen, you're super busy. Why don't you leave me to it?'

'Sure.' Celeste reached into her bag and handed over another set of keys. 'You can come and go whenever you like. The lights are on timer switches, so they come on in the evening if you're working late.'

'Timer switches?'

'It's a big empty house, so you want it to look occupied. We're on the waterfront so anyone could dock up and start nosing around.'

'And nobody else will be coming in here?'

Celeste sneaked a glance at her phone as it rang off. 'Um... no. There was a gardener, but we no longer required his services.'

'Right.'

'So, you have the place to yourself. Just close the curtains when you leave.'

Before Celeste left, Astrid managed to tease out a bit more about her environmental charity. It was all about stopping plastic getting into the sea. There was, apparently, far too much of it there already. Swirling around. Breaking down into tinier and tinier pieces. Cowes Week was, Celeste explained, her chance to raise awareness in the sailing community, as well as snag some big business sponsors for other local projects she had – beach cleans and marine sanctuaries. If that meant, Celeste said with a hint of revulsion, 'getting into bed with big business, then so be it.'

Astrid listened to what was a well-rehearsed spiel. Impressive, nonetheless. Then Celeste took another call. Astrid mimed her goodbyes and watched her glide out of the far door.

The room was perfectly quiet. For the first time, she noticed a leather rocking chair by the window. Celeste's father must have sat there in his last years, cloaked in sailing memories, surrounded by his treasures.

Astrid opened her work case and found a folded-up linen dust sheet. She unfurled it and cast it over one end of the long walnut table. Best not damage the antiques. Setting her work case on the table, she brought out her notebook and magnifying glass and laid them down for later.

Then, she took a quick tour of the paintings. There wasn't a single painting set on dry land. Maybe the odd sliver of shore in the foreground – smugglers unloading a boat under moonlight, or a rocky outcrop dashed by waves. But most of the canvases were of sea and sky with the weather in every mood from serene to murderous. Dinghies becalmed on a summer's day to galleons cresting waves as sharp and white as icebergs.

She checked a signature. Keith Shackleton, a relative of the explorer Ernest. A painting of deep blue troughs in the

Antarctic. An albatross scudded across the waves, its wing tip inches from the foam.

Another name. This was Hendrik van Minderhout – 1632–1696, according to a small gold plaque below a whaling scene. In the centre of the picture was a sailor in a rowing boat, harpoon aimed at a breaching whale. And what a whale. It was huge – dome-headed, glistening. An arc of water spouting between bent harpoons bristling from its inky head. Its jaws open, ready to swallow the rowing boat. This was a beast that sailors would talk about in hushed tones, below decks and in harbour taverns lit by the oil from its flesh.

Then there were the naval battles that made up about half of the paintings. All the major skirmishes involving the British Navy were covered. Her favourite was a stirring scene of the Battle of the Nile by Thomas Luny, a prolific artist who turned in over three thousand paintings, even though his hands were crippled by arthritis.

The largest canvas was of the Battle of Trafalgar. Dated 1820, and by another Thomas – Thomas Buttersworth, a sailor-turned-painter who fought in the Napoleonic Wars. You could tell he'd been in the thick of battle from the energy on the canvas and the detail of the ships. At the centre of the painting was Nelson's warship *Victory* locked in battle at close range with the French *Redoutable*. Clouds of cannon smoke billowed between the two flanks of the ships.

Next to the *Victory* was the *Temeraire*, sails holed and tattered. Later, Turner would paint the *Temeraire* being towed to the ship-breaking yards on the Thames under a gold-infused sunset. Nelson was long dead. Killed by a musket ball on the deck of the *Victory*.

In all, there were around forty paintings, nearly all by well-known artists. Even without a Turner, it had to be one of the finest maritime collections in the world. Eighteenth and nineteenth-century, mostly. Steeped in patriotism, when Britannia ruled the waves. Her father would have loved this place. He and David Wade would have got on like a house on fire. She could see them up here – sharing a toast to Queen and country.

Astrid spent the rest of the day logging the paintings. She noted down names, dates, dimensions. It was relaxing work. Blissful – a reminder why she loved this job. She had her own private gallery and nobody to bother her.

She was so absorbed in her work she didn't notice the time. It was four o'clock before her hunger pangs dragged her out of her thoughts. It felt like a good time to call it a day. She tidied up, drew the curtains and set out to find a bite to eat.

Eight

Back in the town, she weighed up the food options. It was still busy at The Bugle and all the tables were taken up outside the pubs. So that was out. Then she noticed a long queue heading into an alley, which was promising, but it turned out it led to the counter of an ice-cream parlour called Scoops.

She was about to move on to the high street when she remembered The Chatterbox Café by the entrance to the pier. Luckily enough, it had some spare tables.

Astrid sat down and waited a couple of minutes, happy to just watch the tourists heading out along the pier. There was a donations box with a £1 suggestion written on it, which everyone ignored. It was mostly families. Parents shambling to the rail for a photo as their kids ran ahead, clear plastic buckets with orange crab lines inside. She was enjoying the people-watching so much she hadn't checked the menu before the young waitress appeared.

'You know what you want?' The waitress flipped a stray strand of blonde hair behind her ear. The rest of it was tied up in two pigtails.

'What do you recommend?' Astrid was too hungry to be fussy.

'McDonald's.' The waitress laughed.

'Hah!' Astrid checked the name tag on her white polo shirt. 'That's very funny, Melody.'

'Thanks.'

'This a summer job for you?'

'Sort of. I'm gonna hang on for a couple of weeks. Get some money for a trip to Majorca and a bit of weed.' Melody giggled again. Then she checked over her shoulder. 'Between you and me, they think I'm staying on.'

'Not a word.' Astrid winked. Why did people open up to her these days? She was glad they did, though. Since Simon was gone – long gone – she realised she liked people.

'Actually,' said Melody, 'the food's really good here. Especially the crab sandwich.'

Astrid pointed down the pier. There were a bunch of kids with buckets on the left rail, about twenty yards from the entrance. 'Is it the same crabs they catch here?'

'No, no… those crabs are shore crabs. They're too small to eat.'

They watched as three small boys hurried down the pier and stopped on the right rail, opposite the other gang of kids. They started unwrapping their lines. One had a pack of bacon, which he tore open.

Melody said, 'You know… those kids will have better luck on the other side. That's where the crabs are. There are some rocks and weeds down there that they like. They'll catch nothing.'

'That right?'

'Yeah, I watch them all the time. I'll have a word with them in a minute.' She collected up the menu and headed in.

Astrid sat back and watched the three boys. They dropped their buckets over the side on a line, and dragged them up again, full of water. Next, they opened the small white net bag on the end of the orange line. Stuffed a strip of bacon in. Tightened it up again and lowered it down over the edge of the rail into the water.

Right on the end of the pier, about two hundred yards away, was a blue-and-white painted hut. A shelter from rough weather. In the middle of the pier, a couple of anglers were sitting on boxes, eyeing the tips of their fishing rods that hung over the deep water. Back to the three boys. One of them was yanking up the line, hand over hand. He'd caught something. An olive-coloured crab was hanging on by one claw to the net. The boy yelped with excitement, held it over the bucket and jiggled it into the water.

The other kid got on his knees and watched the crab swimming round in circles. Then there was a cry from his friend. The line was pulled up and another crab, about the same size, was hauled over the rail. For the next few minutes, the three boys couldn't go wrong. Crab after crab was dragged up to the surface. The bucket was filling up quickly. There was more crab than water in there. One of the boys lowered a fresh bucket down and filled it up. Melody's theory that the right side of the pier wasn't much good for crabbing was proving to be wrong.

Some other kids on the left had noticed the boys' good fortune. A couple of younger girls came over and slung their lines out to either side of them. And they had instant luck. Soon all the other kids, about a dozen of them, were jostling to get close to the hot spot.

There were plenty of crabs to go round. Lines were dropped and instantly pulled up, sometimes with two or three crustaceans hanging off. In the fishing frenzy, a few crabs missed buckets and skittered off, sliding into the gaps between the planks and dropping into the sea. Then one of the kid's lines got snagged. He was about thirteen, with ginger hair. He strained to loosen it from the bottom of the seabed. But it wouldn't budge. His father, a bodybuilder type, wandered over to give him a hand. Even he struggled. The orange nylon line dug into the palms of his hands as he slowly hauled up whatever the line was latched on to below the surface.

'Come on,' the father shouted, leaning back, heaving the line up a step at a time. He was almost at the other rail, so he didn't see whatever had now breached the surface. The kids did, and gasped.

'Jeez, what the...' The ginger boy's jaw fell. All the kids retreated from the rail. Then they slowly edged forward. Open-mouthed.

A couple went over to see what they were looking at. They turned away and hurried off down the pier. All the kids had got over the first shock of what they'd seen, and were now hopping up and down, clapping their hands and cheering.

Astrid got up slowly from her seat, without thinking. She broke into a quick walk through the entrance of the pier. Some other people from the café were ahead of her. By the time she reached the rail, there was a horseshoe of onlookers in front of her.

A single scream split the air.

A teenage girl had pushed to the front and was leaning

over the rail, staring into the water. Astrid squeezed in next to her and saw what everyone was looking at. It was the body of a man. The upper half at least, held in position by the taut orange line. Arms floating out either side.

Astrid could make out a blue gingham shirt. The straps of a leather backpack. But not the face. It was covered in crabs. A seething mass of shells and pincers obscured any features.

The father with the orange line wound in hand over hand, until he saw what he'd snagged. 'Holy…' His voice trailed off, the line slipping between his fingers. The body slowly sunk back to the depths.

Melody was by Astrid's shoulder. 'That was unbelievable,' she said.

'It sure was.'

Then she looked at Astrid and grimaced. 'So… you still want that crab sandwich?'

Nine

Back at the boat, Astrid filled a glass of red from the wine box. She wouldn't normally drink this early, but she needed a glass of wine or two to settle her nerves. It wasn't every day you saw a body dragged up from the seabed. Especially not someone she had only bumped into the day before. The same shirt and leather backpack. It had to be the person who'd given her the leaflet on the corner of the town square. So, who was he?

She booted up the laptop and latched onto the Wi-Fi from the harbour office. It was a good signal, and she quickly had a name from a simple search of the words 'Yarmouth', 'cycle lane' and 'furious'.

Victor Leech was a seventy-one-year-old retiree and 'community campaigner'. That's how he was described in the *Isle of Wight Courier*, which had much to thank Mr Leech for. Over the years, he'd filled countless pages for them. He was always available for a photo shoot – kneeling down next to potholes in the road, pointing at CCTV cameras. Always on hand to offer an outraged quote about the local council's plans. Particularly when it came to road changes.

The most current story was Victor's battle against plans

for a cycle lane on Yarmouth's high street. There was a picture of him handing out leaflets on the same corner she'd met him. The same outfit, same shiny black brogues. The same stern expression. To Victor, the scheme 'was the thin end of the wedge'. Although what the rest of the wedge looked like was unclear.

Half an hour's scrolling later, and it was obvious that everything the council had planned to do in changing Yarmouth's roads, from Safe School Streets to speed bumps, had been met by fierce resistance from Victor.

It also seemed like a lot of people agreed with his views. There were plenty of pictures of him standing at the front of crowds of protestors, all with home-made placards. Or handing in thick petitions over on the steps of the Town Hall. Victor Leech had been something of a local celebrity. If not Yarmouth's only celebrity.

Astrid refilled her glass, went back to the laptop and quickly became distracted by an article entitled 'Dog Dumped in Sainsbury's Car Park'. Which could mean two things, of course. A dog had been abandoned in the car park. Or it had taken a crap there. Either way, it wasn't much of a story. If that made it into the *Isle of Wight Courier*, you could see how they were grateful to get a call from Victor about the council's latest 'fiasco'.

Astrid searched around for a bit longer and found a couple more bits of information on Leech. He was a retired chartered surveyor who'd lived on the island all his life. He shared a house with his wife, Cynthia, on Merrivale Road (there was no number available), a cul-de-sac overlooking the bay east of the town.

After the next glass of red, she spiralled off elsewhere on the internet, ending up on Marks and Spencer's online store and doing a bit of very early Christmas shopping – which was a sign to get some fresh air. She emptied the 'Luxury Chocolate Yule Log – serves 12' from her virtual shopping basket, shut the laptop, and went up on deck with a fresh glass.

The tide was almost completely out. The last of the brackish water was draining out of the fingers in the mudflats. She sat in a chair and watched it sucking and popping at the damp air until there were only a few inches of water in the side channels.

How had Victor Leech ended up in the same water, not four hundred yards from here? She'd seen exactly where he'd come out – just under the pier. But where had he gone in? And why? It was none of her business – she knew that. But to be fair, the last time she'd snooped around, it had worked out in the end. She stretched her legs and took a swig of wine. Thinking about it – she had pretty much solved the murders at Sherborne Hall single-handedly. If it hadn't been for her, Cressida would have got away with it and the fake Constable would be the star attraction of the English Trust's latest exhibition. Hiding in plain sight.

She must have a talent for this kind of thing. And if she could get to the bottom of Victor's death, then it might be a comfort to Victor's widow, even if Cynthia – poor Cynthia – didn't know that's what she was at this moment. In fact, thought Astrid, it was her duty to investigate. It wasn't just the wine that was giving Astrid a warm feeling. It was a sense that she was about to do the right thing.

The red ensign was hanging twisted over the rail of the boat. She reached out without getting up from her chair and unfurled it, draping it over the rail.

'That's it. Get it all shipshape,' came a voice from the pontoon.

Astrid turned to see a tall man, six foot two at least, peering down at her. His thumbs were tucked into black trousers below a matching V-neck jumper – white shirt and tie beneath.

'I'm Jim McKee, the harbour master,' he said brightly. He had a craggy face, hooded blue eyes and a thatch of sandy hair that was swept back over his ears. He brought his hand up to his forehead, shielding his eyes from the sun. It looked like he was saluting badly. 'You mind if I come aboard?'

'Of course. I'm Astrid.' She got up unsteadily from her chair.

Jim stepped nimbly over the rails. His trousers were tucked into a pair of green cut-off wellies. He surveyed the boat, nodding appreciatively. 'Where did you sail in from?'

'Poole Harbour.'

'I've got to say, you were lucky to get a mooring. With Cowes Week coming up.'

'I know. I had no idea.'

'No idea?' He blinked in amazement. First Celeste, now this guy, thought Astrid. Was it such a crime to not know about a flippin' sailing festival?

He gestured to a spare fold-out chair. Astrid nodded and he opened it, brushed the canvas with the back of his hand and sat down. 'We've been booked up for months. You only got this mooring because we had a last-minute cancellation.'

'Bit of luck then.' She got up. 'You fancy some wine?' She raised her empty glass to him.

'No, no. I'm on duty.' He held up his hand. 'Not a good idea.'

For him maybe, thought Astrid. She was enjoying herself – happy to have some company on the boat. She went below, got another refill – her last one, she promised herself – and returned to her chair.

'Well, welcome to the Isle of Wight.'

'Cheers.' Astrid raised her glass and a bit of wine sloshed onto her trousers. 'Oops a daisy.'

'Right, then… um.' Jim watched her rubbing at the red wine mark with the back of her sleeve. 'So, Astrid, do you know anything about the island?'

'Not much. Someone told me you still have black-and-white televisions, but they were trying to put me off coming here.'

'Don't worry. We've had colour television for years.' He drew his chair nearer to her. 'Okay then, here's a few fun facts for you.'

Astrid put her glass in the pocket in the armrest and squared her feet on the deck to steady herself. The wine was really kicking in now. 'Let's hear them then, Jim.'

'Okay… did you know that the Isle of Wight is the smallest county in England?' She noticed he spoke louder than most people. Maybe, she thought, it was from shouting at boats against the wind. 'But only when the tide is in,' he continued. 'When it's out, it's Rutland County.'

'Uh, that's incredible,' she said enthusiastically. He carried on reeling off more facts, as if he were a tour guide on his first shift. Facts like there were on average one thousand nine hundred and twenty-three hours of sunshine a year on the island. And there were more than twenty-one times the number of visitors to the island every year than there were residents.

'Crikey,' she said. *Crikey?*

Those people born and bred on the island were known as 'caulkheads' – after the job of caulking, or sealing the planks in wooden boats. He chuckled between sentences, rolling up his laughs like crashing waves. After about ten minutes, Astrid felt Jim was sufficiently relaxed to ease the conversation over to what was still on her mind – the watery end of Victor Leech. She may not get another chance.

Astrid pointed over the marina to the pier. It was deserted. It must have been closed off by the police. There was an ambulance parked up on the slipway. 'Soo... I noticed the pier was closed off earlier. Has there been an accident?'

'Yes, I'm afraid so,' Jim said gravely.

'Really, what happened?' All innocent.

'Well.' He hesitated. 'Unfortunately, I can't tell you. I spoke to the police and they want to keep it confidential.'

'Oh, right.' She smiled. 'But don't you have the authority to investigate? As the harbour master?'

'I have certain powers, yes.'

'Like what?'

He puffed his chest out slightly. 'I have the powers to investigate or detain a vessel,' he said sombrely. Plus, I can caution and arrest anyone within the tidal range of the harbour.'

'Does that cover the pier?'

'Technically, I suppose it does.' He got up from his chair. 'Right, I better carry on with my rounds. Drop into the office when you get a chance and we'll settle up. We have piping hot showers, and Kettle Chips in our "Cabin Essentials" shop.' It was back to the cheery, welcoming Jim. He stepped over the rail and set off down the boardwalk.

'Wait... Jim.' She got up and hurdled clumsily over the rail. This was his patch – he would know every boat. Every current. If anyone could work out what had happened to Victor Leech, it was him. And he was getting away. She scurried after him, catching him up where the boardwalk reached the path. 'Mr McKee.'

He stopped in his tracks. 'Sorry, I really can't say any more.'

She stood there, not sure what to say next. The wine sluiced around in her stomach, warming her chest. Thawing what might just be her most brilliant idea. 'Jim.' She reached into her trouser pocket and pulled out the folded letter that Andy Marriot had given to her. 'I hate to pull rank on you, but I'm actually on assignment for the HMRC. A big case.'

'Oh, I see,' he whispered.

She unfolded the letter and held it up in front of him. But not long enough for him to see much more than the royal crown logo.

'Why didn't you say?'

'I just thought I'd see if you were someone I can trust.' She folded the paper and tucked it back in her pocket. 'And now I'm sure I can.'

'Thank you... erm. Can you tell me your full name?'

'Astrid Swift.'

'Is there a title? Detective?'

'No, Astrid is fine. Let's not get too formal.' She paused. 'So, the police are saying Victor's death is an accident.'

'Victor Leech. Yes, that's who they say it was.' His eyes flashed. He was now completely convinced. 'The police think it's a tragic drowning.'

'I get it.' She put on an American accent. 'It's a sunny day, the harbours are open and people are having a fantastic time,' she slurred. This was a misquote from *Jaws*, one of her favourite films. It had sprung to mind and she'd just blurted it out. That was the thing about spending most of your time on your own. The conversation brakes were rusty. Hitting that wine box wasn't helping.

'I don't understand.'

'It's what the mayor in *Jaws* says to avoid scaring the tourists away. You know, when the shark starts eating people. Do you know what I'm saying?'

'Not really.'

Astrid thought for a moment. What was she saying? Oh, yeah. 'The thing is, Jim, it's Cowes Week. There's a lot at stake for local businesses. This town doesn't need bad publicity right now.'

'You did know about Cowes Week?' He put his hand to his mouth to hold back a gasp.

'Of course. Who wouldn't?' she snorted, a little too loud.

Jim glanced anxiously up the boardwalk towards the car park. There was nobody around and he relaxed again. 'You think Victor's death was no accident?'

'We don't know that yet.' Astrid rubbed her chin. 'All I'm

saying is the police might not want to look too hard to find the truth.' She was feeding him the bait, and he was taking it.

'But the Hampshire Police—' his eyes widened '—they're one of the best forces in the country.'

'Yeah, they're great guys. A tribute to the institution of policing.' She was sure that wasn't even a real phrase. But Jim didn't seem to notice. 'Remember, it's the people at the top who make the decisions. No names, Jim.'

'Of course.'

'And they would prefer to keep this under wraps. The reputation of the whole island is at stake.' She was definitely past the point of no return now.

'Have you spoken to them?'

'The police? Er… no. It's too complicated. That's the nature of UWOs.'

'UWOs?' Jim looked nonplussed.

'Unexplained wealth orders. Huge wealth makes people behave very badly. Trust me.'

'I will.' He sighed. 'I definitely will.'

Jim might be just about the most trusting person Astrid had ever met. Or the most gullible. As they walked together to the harbour office, it was obvious he was in no doubt she was working for an authority higher than him, even higher than the police. When he reached the automatic doors at the entrance, he stopped and earnestly laid out his plan. He knew a few people in the force, and he was going to discreetly ask around. Do some investigating of his own.

'You have those powers, Jim. Let's use them,' said Astrid, crunching her fist as if the facts of the case were in there getting squeezed. She could see he liked the idea because she caught him making the same gesture with his hand. He leant in. 'I've got to say... the old battered yacht. It's a good cover, Astrid.'

'Oh, right. Glad you think so.' Astrid scratched her nose to hide a smile.

On the way back to her boat, the wine setting her legs on a slaloming route, Astrid began to think that stringing Jim along had been a smart move. A very smart move. She wouldn't be able to get any information from the police herself. But he could. He could discreetly ask around. Be an extra radar... beacon... whatever, in the harbour.

This was worth one more nightcap. Strangle one last glass of red out of that silver wine box bag. No doubt about it. It had been one of her most brilliant ideas.

Ten

Astrid was woken by her hangover. It felt like something was scraping inside of her skull with a rusty teaspoon. There was a throbbing thought in there too – lying to Jim had been a terrible idea. A really terrible idea. What had she been thinking? He had powers of... what was it? Arrest? That was it – he would throw her in jail if he found out she was just an art conservator. At least out of the harbour. Yes, she would definitely have to avoid him for the next week or so.

She got up and slowly ambled to the sink, trying to keep her head steady so as not to annoy what was carving around in there. It turned out that when you got down to the last bit of a wine box bag, there's more in there than you think. If you wring it out hard enough. Two glasses, at least. She got out a tin mug, filled it with water and dropped in a Berocca tablet from the cupboard. Then she put her hand over the mug because the fizzing was tuning in to the drilling sensation at her temples.

She drank it down, then polished off two more glasses of water. Checked her phone. There was an email from another huge mistake in her life – her ex-husband, Simon. She stuck out her lower lip and made a low gurgling noise that sounded a bit like 'blurgh, blurgh, blurgh...'

Yes, she thought. It was childish. But it was something she automatically did now when she saw his name on her phone.

The email had *'Plans for the apartment'* in the subject line. She read the rest, one hand on the countertop to steady herself. Apparently, as property prices in London were on the move upwards, it would be 'madness' to sell the flat right now. Simon was suggesting they keep the place on until prices flattened out. Maybe take on a tenant. Everything else was sorted out but this, the last sticking point in the divorce, then she was free. This could just be his way of keeping her in his life, she thought. If so, she wasn't interested.

She switched off her phone and went back to bed until she felt human enough (roughly 10.15 a.m.) to go out into the world.

Eleven

Astrid went back to The Needles' Eye and spent a solid four hours in the lookout making more detailed notes about the art collection. Most of the paintings were in good shape. Better than you would expect for maritime oil paintings.

Collectors tended to be merchants, naval officers, sailors... people with a love of the sea that kept them not too far from the coast, where their paintings would be cracked and shocked by the salty air. From the labels on the back, David Wade's paintings had mostly come from galleries in Europe and the US. And with the heavily curtained room, they'd fared well. They wouldn't need much renovation to bring them to peak condition.

Astrid decided to call it a day with the notes and explore the house. Just to make sure there wasn't anything of value tucked away, despite what Celeste had said. She'd been excited to have a nose around since she'd arrived.

She put on her rucksack and started to investigate the first floor. All the rooms were bedrooms – three for guests, a master suite at the far end of the house. The furniture had been covered with white sheets, the curtains drawn. She turned on lights, scanning each of the rooms from the doorway.

The cold had seeped into the walls of the house. Wallpaper was beginning to peel at the seams. There were no paintings anywhere, so she carried on down the stairs.

On the ground floor she wandered through a big kitchen at the front of the house. It had Shaker-style units and rows of copper-bottomed pans hanging above an island counter. There was also a formal dining room. A library crammed with leather-bound books, and a cosy lounge with well-padded maroon sofas. It was all homely enough, if a bit dated. A *Country Life* magazine cover from the mid 1990s with not much freshening up since.

At the far end of the house were two other rooms, which were locked. Then finally, she found David Wade's office, which looked out over the back gardens. The furniture included a writing desk, a swivel chair, a filing cabinet and two stand-up shelves, which were empty. Everything had been hastily cleared away into cardboard boxes that were arranged on the carpet.

Over by the desk was the first painting she'd seen since leaving the lookout. It was of a rowing boat not far from the shore. Two blonde children were on-board, each gripping an oar. Had this been painted from a photo? She looked closer. The children were very similar, a couple of years apart. Six and eight, at a guess.

Astrid hooked the painting down from the wall and put it on the writing desk. It was unsigned. Fairly well painted. This was a stock family portrait. She studied the girls. The one on the right had blonde hair, an almond-shaped face. It was almost definitely Celeste. The other girl though… a friend? She leant in, gently tracing the shape of the face with her finger. It was the same as the young Celeste's. A sister then. If so, how had she not known this? Because there was no reason for her to ask.

Around the younger girl, the colours of paint jarred. She tipped the frame in the light from the ceiling lampshade. Yes, there was a patch in the shape of the number '7'. The upper bar ran above the younger girl's head, then hinged over her left shoulder, separating the two girls until it hit the boards of the boat. It seemed like a later repair. But she needed to be sure.

She hurried up to the lookout. Rifling through her work case, she found a UV light torch. It was black, the size and shape of a box of cook's matches. She brought it back down to the office and went over to the window to draw the curtains. Far out by the edge of the wood she thought she saw something move. A fleeting shadow passing behind a tree trunk.

She scrunched her eyes. After staring closely at paintings for hours, sometimes it took a while for her eyes to adjust to longer distances. When she looked out across the garden again, the shadow had gone. If it had even been there in the first place.

She drew the curtains tightly and switched the overhead light off. Then she brought out the UV light and turned it on. The room filled with a soft bluish glow. At the desk, she hovered the light over the portrait. Her hunch was right. It was a repair. Under UV light, fresher paint appears darker. The '7' shape was the newer oil paint used to restore some damage.

Astrid put the UV light in her rucksack and went back to

draw the curtains. Then she returned to the desk and flipped the painting over. To get a good look at the canvas, she worked the stretcher keys loose and prised out the backing board. Now she could see the damage. It had been a deep tear. Along its length, the restorer, whoever they were, had glued small strips of canvas, like the webbing plasters they use for deep cuts. To draw the scar together.

Using the magnifying glass, she could see that there was more to this scar. The elbow of the rip was a deep gouge made by something sharp. The fibres of the canvas had been cleanly cut. The rest of the broken fibres were frayed, indicating that a hard ripping action had torn them apart.

Astrid's breathing quickened. There was something about this damage. There had been violence in it. First, the stab of a sharp object. A knife? Next, fingers had been worked into the corner, pulling and tearing the canvas down. Ruining the painting – in sheer anger. She turned the frame over and studied the two children again. They were angelic. Two kids innocently enjoying a bright summer's day. What rage, what hate, had made someone do this? Maybe there was a reasonable explanation. Right now, she couldn't think of it.

Twelve

A few hours focusing on the deep blues and greys of the paintings had worked a treat. By the time she got back to the boat, her hangover had almost gone. No more wine for a week. That's what she told herself. And this time she meant it.

Below deck, she made a mug of strong coffee, which livened her up even more. Five days then. No more wine for five days, she thought, her resolve evaporating. She got out her phone and punched in 'Celeste Wade' and 'sister'. Ten minutes later she had the whole story, told by a series of news outlets. And it was a tragedy.

Celeste once had a sister – Harlow. She was a couple of years younger. A sailing prodigy who was tipped to be the next female racing champion. The pride of the island. But three years ago, the night before one of Cowes Week's biggest yacht races – a competition she was tipped to win – she disappeared off the face of the earth.

She'd gone out on her boat, *Whitecaps*, the evening before the race and was never seen again. The last sighting of her and her boat was rounding The Needles. Three weeks later, Harlow was officially declared missing at sea. There was a picture of her father, dressed in a black suit at her memorial a month later. It was a shot taken from some distance as he came out of the church. His face was pale and drawn. He seemed crushed by grief. Angry that this private moment had been stolen by a press photographer.

She scrolled away from the story with a pang of guilt. Maybe she wouldn't have been so excited about snooping around the house if she'd known about the family tragedy. And poor Celeste – to lose her sister. It would have taken great strength to pull herself together. Throwing herself into her charity work must have given her a purpose in life.

Astrid decided she'd give her own sister, Clare, a call soon. More pangs of guilt. She'd let things slip between them over the years. But at least she was around to make amends.

It was half past three. There was still time to get up to Abbotsford Manor. See if any of her art club were around to lift her mood. She put on a light waterproof. A few grey clouds had gathered up on the headland. Then she locked up, unlashed the mountain bike on the deck, hauled it over the rail and teetered off down the jetty.

By the time she parked her bike at the entrance, a cool drizzle had set in. She hurried to the potting shed. Frank, as usual, was lounging in the corner leather chair. Annabelle and Wren were behind their easels. They all greeted her cheerily as she hung her coat up on the pegs by the door and took out her sketch pad.

Then Annabelle continued with what had clearly been, so far, a tetchy conversation between herself and Frank. 'So,

Frank...' said Annabelle, not looking away from her canvas, 'you think you know what women want?'

He smacked his lips. 'Sure do.'

'Go on then, please enlighten us.'

'Well, from my three decades in the building trade...' He hooked his leg over the armrest of the chair and wove his fingers together. 'A woman wants a downstairs loo with a four-and-a-half litre flush. A white Vauxhall Astra on the forecourt. And a bit of "how's yer father" at a time of their choosing.' He looked to Wren. 'Sorry about the language.'

'Don't mind me.' Wren carried on with her painting.

'Really, Frank,' groaned Annabelle. 'And that's according to the man who's been married three times?'

'I have indeed. That's how I know – from bitter experience.' He rolled his eyes to the ceiling. 'Woman are like hurricanes. Do you know why?'

'I shudder to think,' said Annabelle.

'Okay...' He drew in a breath. 'When they arrive, they're all wild and exciting. And when they leave, they take your house and car.' He roared with laughter for about twenty seconds, while Annabelle shook her head and dabbed angrily at her painting, which appeared to be an otter swimming in a reflected sunset. 'What sexist nonsense,' she said under her breath.

Astrid decided to keep out of it. She turned a new page on her drawing pad and took out a pencil from her bag. 'Do you mind if I sketch you, Frank?'

'Knock yerself out, Astrid.' He sat back in his chair, still snickering at his joke.

The door swung open, and Kabir trudged in, collar up,

his hair wet and matted to his forehead. In his hand was a canvas. The colours had run in the rain, gathering in a muddy stain at the bottom of the picture. He propped it up against the wall and stood back. 'You know, that might even be an improvement,' he said dejectedly.

'Don't worry, Kabir,' said Astrid, 'you'll paint an even better one.'

'Thanks.' Kabir went to the sideboard, switched on the kettle and dried his face and hands with a tea towel.

Annabelle brought out a metal tin from her bag and took off the lid. Inside was a grid of sticky-looking cake. 'Here.' She handed Kabir the tin. 'Grab yourself a flapjack. I baked them myself. It's a Delia Smith recipe. You can't go wrong with Delia.'

Kabir took a square of flapjack from the tin and offered them around to the others. Wren and Astrid picked out a piece each. Frank got up and took the tin, balanced it on his lap and pinched out the largest slice. 'Do they have nuts in, Annabelle?'

'Are you allergic to nuts, Frank?' she replied.

'Yes.'

'In which case, I can't remember.'

Frank put the piece back on the plate and wiped his hands on his trousers. Annabelle added some detail to the otter, smiling to herself.

The conversation drifted along for a while. They talked about their artwork and the fact nobody had sold anything in the reception area. Astrid carried on sketching Frank. He was a good subject. He had a characterful face that creased and reddened every time he laughed. Which was often. Hogarth wouldn't have had to exaggerate much, she thought. Then the rain stopped beating on the tin roof and there was some discussion about heading out for the last hour of decent light.

But they were all too comfortable, and the flapjack was too good to leave. Even Frank said he'd 'risk it' and ate a piece slowly, stopping now and then to take his pulse. Then, when he'd finished, he sucked his fingers clean and said with barely concealed glee, 'You hear that old Victor Leech fell in the drink?'

They had. It was only twenty-four hours since Victor had been hauled out onto dry land, but word had got out, one way or another. Annabelle had been informed on her summer holiday WhatsApp group. Wren said her dad had been walking past the entrance to the pier and a police officer had told him. Kabir overheard the receptionist at the sports centre mention it. And Frank had heard about it in the pub. It was big news in Yarmouth. The only news. Victor Leech was a famous fixture on the high street – handing out leaflets about his latest campaign. Rain or shine.

Astrid kept a straight face as she listened to what they knew. Filing away any useful bits of information. The others mistook her expression as confusion.

'Sorry, Astrid,' said Kabir. 'You probably have no idea who we're talking about.'

'Well, actually…' There was no way she couldn't tell them what she knew. So, she did. Everything. How she'd bumped into Leech in the town square. How the day after, she'd been at The Chatterbox Café and seen the commotion on the pier. She spared no detail in describing how he was hauled out of the water, covered in crabs.

At this point, Wren put her brush down and shouted, 'Shut up... Leech was eaten by crabs?'

'Not exactly, Wren,' Astrid corrected her. 'The cause of death was probably drowning. The crabs arrived later.'

Frank sat through the story, drumming his fingers on the armrest, drinking it all in. Annabelle was even more enthralled. She shuddered theatrically, then asked a series of rapid-fire questions. What had Victor's mood been like the day before he died? Could Astrid tell how long he'd been in the water? Did she take photos?

It turned out that she was a huge fan of forensic TV dramas. Only this week she'd 'devoured' season eight of *Silent Witness* on box set, because there wasn't a strong enough Wi-Fi signal at their summer house. Which surprised Astrid. It didn't fit with the Etsy shop and Delia flapjack. But hey, she thought, everybody needs a hobby.

Only Kabir kept quiet throughout Astrid's account. When she'd finished answering Annabelle's questions, he raised his finger. 'Actually, Victor Leech was one of my patients.'

'Oooh, go on then,' said Annabelle. 'What's your theory? He had a heart attack and fell off the pier? Right?'

Kabir shook his head. 'No, no... that would be asking me to reveal confidential patient information. Which would be entirely unethical.'

'Sorry,' said Annabelle.

'If, of course, I was still a practising doctor,' he continued. 'But I'm retired now.' He stepped forward to the front of the group. 'Mr Leech was in pretty good shape for his age. Most of my patients are of a similar vintage, shall we say. They're rattling with statins and omega-3 pills. Not Leech. He only came in now and then to show off how well he was. So, no. I can't see him having a heart attack.'

Annabelle's mind was working overtime. 'Could you have a word with the coroner?'

'Sorry, Annabelle, how do you mean?' said Kabir.

'They assign a coroner for suspicious deaths,' she replied. 'You could ask to look at their report?'

Kabir didn't look convinced. 'Well, I was just his GP, so I doubt it.'

As Astrid looked up from her sketch pad at Frank, she saw him quietly repeat the word 'suspicious'. It was what everyone was thinking, and now Annabelle had said it there was no putting it away. Astrid was relieved that she wasn't the only one to see his death that way. Part of her was still wondering if she was being overly suspicious. The wine clouding her judgement. But they were all stone-cold sober now. And they were all right – healthy people don't just wash up in shallow water under a pier.

The light was fading in the shed. They all began to gather their things. Astrid closed her sketch pad and tucked it into her rucksack. She said her goodbyes, bathing in thanks for bringing some juicy gossip into the shed. Frank showed her to the door and followed her out to her bike.

'Hey, Astrid. You busy tomorrow night?'

'No, I don't think so.'

'Great – I've got a guest ticket to the opening party for Cowes Week. It's at Northwood House. Big stately home. Free booze. Very posh.'

'You don't have to sell it to me. It sounds great. Count me in.'

'Good stuff. It's not a date or anything. No monkey business. I just had a spare ticket because a mate of mine is in charge of the catering and I, well... I couldn't think of anyone else.'

'Well, I'm glad you did. Although...' she paused '...I've got to say – it doesn't sound like your kind of thing, Frank. I have you down as a real ale and darts man.'

He laughed as they carried on through the arch in the barn to the car park. 'Yeah, well, the thing is, I'm hoping to meet a hero of mine there.'

'Who's that?'

'Gabriel Tranter.' That's all he said, as if the name itself was explanation enough.

Astrid shook her head.

'Gabriel Tranter.'

'It's still a no.'

'Okay. Tranter is, like, the Isle of Wight's most famous person. He's a business genius. He set up Mistral Industries. And he's loaded – superyachts, houses, everything.' Frank's face was reddening again. 'You should read his book, *Get What You Want: The 67 Secrets to Success*. It will blow your mind.'

Astrid unlocked her bike, listening politely. Frank, the most down-to-earth person she'd met for a long time, was star-struck by Tranter. His idol had been, he said, responsible for all his recent success. Since he'd read *Get What You Want* around five years ago, his building business had gone from strength to strength. He'd moved from doing jobs outside houses that Astrid had never heard of – 'pointing', 'block paving' – to mysterious jobs inside houses – 'grouting', 'dormer lofts' – and now had an annual turnover that almost made him feel guilty about not paying tax.

'That book changed me,' said Frank. 'I didn't work harder. I worked better.' Which Astrid thought had to be a motivational quote from the book. 'I owe Tranter big time. And I want to thank him personally if he shows up tomorrow night.'

'You surprise me, Frank,' she said. 'I didn't think you'd go for all that self-help stuff.'

'You haven't met him, Astrid.' Frank sighed. 'You'll see.'

They arranged to meet the next day at the ticket office of the Wightlink ferry to the east of the harbour. Eight o'clock. They'd pick up a taxi to Cowes from the rank out front. Astrid was beginning to look forward to it. If only to say she'd experienced one of Cowes Week's big social events.

Instead of heading back down the valley, she pushed the bike up to the headland. The rain clouds had drifted off down the coast and it was warm again. She aimed the bike east, down the grass path to the coast. There were a few more hours before it got dark. Might as well make the most of the long summer evenings.

Twenty minutes of freewheeling – feet off the pedals, the rush of warm air riffling her hair – and she arrived at a small town tucked into a cove called Freshwater Bay. A sandy beach wrapped round a bite of cloudy blue water. She found a pizza van on the boardwalk, grabbed a small Margherita and sat on the sand. As she ate it, she thought about what the others had said about Victor Leech.

She was glad she'd shared her story with them. Pleased they agreed – his death was very dubious. Someone must have finished him off a reason. And she had to find out who that was. When she'd woken up this morning, after her wine and lying to Jim spree, she'd promised to mind her own business.

But there were unanswered questions. And if anyone could find out the answers, it was her. She had the skills, the forensic kit and, with the art group – the backup if she needed it.

A seagull landed on a nearby post and fixed her with a yellow eye. She finished off the last crust of pizza and dusted her hands, holding them up to show the bird there was nothing left for it to eat. But it stayed where it was, just staring at her. For some reason that made her feel a bit lost. Empty inside, even though she'd just eaten.

Was that why she was so interested in investigating what happened to Victor? And the slashed painting at The Needles' Eye? Because – and the thought was painful to hold on to – because she was lonely. She'd suddenly ended four years of marriage and then moved on quickly to Cobb. Too quickly maybe. Now, sitting on this beach, she'd never felt more alone in the world. Kath in Hanbury, her own family split up around Britain and Spain, and out of touch.

'Come on, Astrid,' she muttered quietly to herself. 'We've never felt sorry for ourselves, and we're not starting now.' If the investigation was just a distraction, she thought. To keep her mind off other things. So be it. Solving a murder might be the best distraction of all. She got up and the seagull flew off to bother someone else.

***

It was almost dark by the time she reached the boardwalk across the mudflats. The sky was bruised deep grey. She got off the bike, in case she lost her bearings and wheeled off into the marsh. Then she stood perfectly still, fenced in by the bulrushes on either side. Certain she was being followed before she heard the footsteps behind her.

As she'd taken the fork in the path down to the river, she'd caught something in the corner of her eye. A figure stepped slowly out from the woods. Tall. Baseball cap. A dark jacket zipped up high over the chin. It was too dark to make out their features.

They could have taken the path back up to the gardens. But they hadn't. They'd peeled down to the river and now they weren't far behind her. Too far back to be visible in the dark. She knew they were there – watching her. She felt a tightness of her shoulders. A prickle on the skin above her collar.

She carried on pushing the bike over the wooden slats, one hand on the crossbar, the other on the handlebar. A bat twisted and turned in the air. Like a black spark, fizzing off into the still night. She could hear her own breathing.

Was she over-reacting?

Because it was dark?

Maybe she should hold her ground?

Her mind was racing.

About forty yards into the reeds, the boardwalk angled diagonally to her right. She hurried round the corner, then halted and turned back. That's when she heard the footsteps on the boards behind her. The creaks slowed, then stopped before they reached the corner. 'Hullo!' she called back.

No answer.

Astrid carried on, almost breaking into a run. Not daring to look back. She'd been on this route a couple of times. It seemed much longer now, even though she was running. Could she dump the bike and hide in the reeds? Another bad idea. The mud might be waist-high, then she'd be stuck. At the mercy of whoever was following her.

Eventually, the boardwalk emerged from the reeds and she was back on dry ground. The lights of the town were half a mile ahead. She scrambled onto the bike and pumped the pedals, gaining ten, twenty, thirty yards from the boardwalk before she hit the brakes and swung the bike round.

It was lighter now she was near the town, so she could just make out the figure standing in the opening of the reeds. They were motionless. Hands in pockets. Head down – as if unable to cross a threshold into another world. Vampires were supposed to do that – the old mythological ones. Now she was really losing it.

They faced each other for a few seconds, the figure staring back at her. Then something happened. Something Astrid wasn't expecting.

The person raised their hand, palm forward. They held it there for a moment. Why? To show that they knew they'd been seen? That they didn't care if they had? Then they stepped back a few strides and melted into the darkness.

Astrid didn't go straight back to her boat. If the person carried on following her, they would know where she lived. Instead, she wandered around Yarmouth for a while. The town was busy. People spilled out onto the cobbles from the bars and restaurants. There were fairy lights strung up over the café tables. It was just as pretty at night.

By the time she returned to the boat, she felt a bit better. She was probably just being jumpy in the dark. Whoever had followed her was heading her way into town. They didn't want to spook a stranger in the dark, so they held back. It was nothing more than that.

Thirteen

Merrivale Road was a wide, quiet street that looked out over the sea. On the south side was a steep slope of brambles held back by a chest-high wire fence. On the other side was a row of identical bungalows. They were whitewashed with red-tiled roofs, and neat squares of lawn and paved drives out front. Most of them had posters in the window, saying things like '*Yarmouth says NO to the Bypass!*' and '*Facts Not Lies*'. This was definitely the right place.

It was early – just after nine o'clock. Someone once told Astrid that if you're going to do something you don't want to do, do it quick. Then it's over sooner. So she'd got up quickly and walked straight over here. In case she changed her mind.

Halfway along the road she found an elderly woman crouched over a bed of geraniums. She was nipping off the dead flowers and popping them into a council recycling bag. Astrid asked her if she knew Victor Leech.

'Oh, Victor. Yes,' she said, rising slowly to her feet. 'It's awful, isn't it?'

'It is,' agreed Astrid.

'What a dreadful way to go – drowning. I was doing aquarobics for seniors at the leisure centre this morning and

I couldn't think of anything else. The poor, poor man.' The woman seemed close to tears. 'Now what are we going to do about the bypass?'

'Bypass?'

'Yes, if it goes through, it will delay ambulances. That's what Victor said. We'll be trapped and then what?' The woman talked in a steady, urgent stream. About how Victor had fought for his neighbours. How he'd taken on the council on their behalf.

Astrid nodded along, waiting to find a gap to ask where his house was. But another white-haired woman glided in with a tartan shopping trolley on wheels and joined the eulogy. 'Victor was a living saint,' she said.

'He was,' said the first woman.

'Victor was the only person who stood up for us. I have a carer come in three days a week. How would they reach me if the council built the bypass?'

Astrid looked down the street. It continued down to the junction of the next road, which then carried on into town. There seemed no reason why anyone couldn't get to them by car. Or why bike lanes or speed bumps, or any of the things Victor campaigned about would make their lives worse.

Why had they all believed him? Astrid noticed a couple of small yew trees by the fence. They were stunted and twisted by the wind. Then she got it.

Up here, in the summer, it was lovely. Come winter, though... when the grandkids that had been unloaded for the holidays were back at school. When the north winds carried the sea fret over scalded lawns and the double glazing rattled. When it felt like they'd been left stranded on the high-water mark. Then – there was Victor. Knocking on doors. Giving them a lift into town. Always there for a chat and a bitter warning about the horror of some new development in the name of progress. To them, he was a local hero.

Astrid eventually extracted Victor's house number from the two women – 76 – and headed off. It was one of the largest bungalows on the road. Painted white, pebble-dashed, with a large bay window to the side of a smart red door. To one side of the tile path was a slab of well-kept lawn. To the other, a neat border of bedding plants, then a concrete drive with a maroon estate car parked on it.

The door had a glass panel in the upper part. There were three cards stuck up from the inside. A sketch of an owl below the words 'Neighbourhood Watch'. A silhouette of a guard dog – 'This house is alarmed'. And a postcard of the Pope. Although Astrid wasn't sure which one. With their mitres on, they all looked the same. She felt a ripple of guilt for thinking that. Still, she was about to do something much worse – squeeze some information out of a woman whose husband had just died.

Her finger hovered over the doorbell. Before she could press it, a woman came shuffling towards the glass. She was in her early seventies, with grey hair tied back in a bun. Bright eyes set in a moonish face. She opened the door, heaving it over a pile of bills and envelopes on the doormat.

'Hi, Cynthia. I've come to pay my respects,' said Astrid sombrely.

'Please, come in,' said Cynthia blankly.

So far, so good, thought Astrid. She was in. Now she just had to play it cool. Find out what she needed and get out.

Cynthia led the way along the hallway and into a kitchen that looked out on a garden as neat as the one at the front of the house.

'I'll get the tea on.' She reached into an overhead cupboard and brought out a plain teapot. She kept talking as she prepared the tea. Answering her own questions. Finding the ruts of dozens of conversations she must have had in the last day or so about her husband.

Astrid stood by the light socket, trying to look more concerned than nervous.

'Everyone's been so kind. The condolence cards. I have a pile of them in the TV room that high.' She raised her hand to waist height. 'And the flowers. The flowers... just beautiful. I never knew he was so well regarded,' she said, glancing at the sideboard where a dozen bouquets, some with the cellophane still on, had been stuffed into a range of vases and jugs.

'Just gorgeous,' said Astrid.

Cynthia assembled everything – the teapot, two patterned bone china cups and a bowl of sugar cubes – on a metal tray. 'It was all that campaigning he did.'

Astrid nodded. 'He was a busy man.'

'Yes. And he said there was still so much to fight. The cycle lane on the high street. The speed bumps. The bypass – he was very vexed about that. But now...' She stood there, the tea tray rattling. 'It's all so... so...'

'Cruel.'

'Cruel. Yes, terribly cruel.' She checked the tray, happy that everything was there. 'Shall we go into the garden?'

Cynthia put the tray down on a circular metal table on the

patio. The matching metal chairs were to one side. Before Astrid could offer to help, Cynthia picked up the chairs, one in each hand, and set them down round the table. She was stronger than she looked, thought Astrid.

As she served the tea, Cynthia talked about all the arrangements she had to make now Victor was gone – the bills, the insurance, the bank accounts. That had been 'Victor's department'. Part of the shock was having to take over all that admin.

It wasn't until the second cup of tea had been poured out, the sun rising through the branches of a solitary apple tree at the bottom of the garden, that she finally asked Astrid who she was. 'I'm all at sixes and sevens. I've forgotten to ask – how did you know Victor?'

'Sorry, I should have really introduced myself. I'm Astrid Swift.'

'Cynthia.'

'Well, Cynthia.' She paused, gulping down a knot of guilt. 'I helped Victor with some of his leafleting. To stop the cycle lane. Ridiculous things.'

'I suppose. I mean… the campaigning was really his thing. I left him to it.' Cynthia stirred a sugar cube into her tea.

'Oh, I see. I assumed you were both involved.' Astrid tried not to look like she was fishing.

'No, no. It was all Victor. He'd do the posters, the leaflets.' She took a sip of her tea. 'He went down to the council offices in Newport every week, to see if anyone had put in a planning application.'

'Is that right?' The conversation was creeping towards where Astrid wanted it to go. Cynthia's thoughts on how her husband had ended up being crab bait under the local pier. Not that Astrid would phrase it that bluntly. 'So, Cynthia, did Victor say where he was going the night he disappeared?'

'He just said he was going for a stroll,' she said cheerily.

'Did he say where?'

'No.' Cynthia knocked back the rest of her tea.

'Or when he was coming back?'

'No. And Victor being Victor, I knew not to interfere. I just assumed he'd slept in the spare room because he didn't want to wake me up. It was only in the morning that I realised he hadn't come home.'

Astrid gripped her knees under the table. Working out when to time her follow-up question. When Cynthia had drained the last dregs from the teapot into her cup, Astrid said casually, 'And the police... have they told you anything about their inquiries?'

'Not much. They're still piecing it together. They don't know when or where he fell into the water that night. There's no CCTV cameras in the town centre or harbour. It was one of Victor's bugbears. He forced the council to have them all taken out. He hated them. Big Brother gone mad – that's what he said.' She stared down the garden. Already the sun had crept above the highest branches of the apple tree. 'To think, if the cameras were there that night they might have caught his last moments. Maybe even have saved his life. Which, if you think about it is all very...'

'Ironic?'

'No, sad.'

'Sad, that's it.' Astrid made a mental note to stop finishing other people's sentences.

Cynthia shifted in her chair and picked up the teapot. 'Can I get you any more?'

Astrid made a show of looking at her watch. 'That's kind, but I better go.' She had what she wanted.

They both got up and went through to the kitchen. Cynthia stopped by the table and pointed out a bulging black bin liner in the corner. She explained that the bag was full of Victor's old clothes and needed to go to the charity shop on the high street. 'Cynthia... you know, I could take them down to the charity shop for you. Save you a trip.'

'Would you?' She smiled.

'Of course. I'm heading into town now.'

They carried on down the hall in silence, Astrid holding the black bin bag in front of her. When they reached the porch, Cynthia stepped ahead and opened the door for her. They both stood there for a moment, their feet scrunching on the unopened bills. Then Cynthia spoke softly. 'Have you ever lost someone really close to you, Astrid?'

'Really close? No, I haven't.'

'Because I was going to ask something.'

'What's that?'

Cynthia breathed in. 'Is it always so exhilarating?'

It was only when Astrid was well away from the cul-de-sac, sitting on a bench in a park at the bottom of the hill, that Cynthia's answer truly sunk in. 'Exhilarating.' Why would she say something like that? Had she really been pleased that her husband had died? And was it suspicious enough to add her to a list of suspects – a list that, as yet, remained blank?

The more she thought about it, the more appealing the idea was. She soon began to imagine Cynthia following her annoyingly revered husband in his crisp clean gingham shirt, the tedious washing and ironing of which was *her* department, and giving him a hearty shove off the pier.

It had been well worth dropping by. Astrid had learnt one important fact. The police didn't have any footage of Victor's final minutes, because there were no CCTV cameras. Any other town would have. Any other town without their version of Victor Leech.

Then of course she'd picked up something else that could be useful. Victor's clothes. Cynthia had been very keen to offload those, hadn't she? No holding back a couple of things to remind her of him. Astrid lifted the black bag onto her lap and hurriedly opened it up.

The first item she took out was a dark-green blazer. She checked the pockets, but they were empty. As were all the pockets of three pairs of smart trousers that were in there. The rest were shirts and jumpers – half a dozen V-neck sweaters and check shirts, including the blue gingham shirt he was wearing when she bumped into him in the town square. It had been washed and pressed – presumably, it had been returned to her by the police and she'd laundered it – so no clues there.

A woman pushing her toddler in a swing to her right was staring at her as she went through the bin bag. She shook her head in disapproval. Not that Astrid needed the judgement. She knew this was a new low. Rifling through the clothes of a man who had only just died. But if she could find a clue that would solve his disappearance, all would be forgiven. Mrs Leech would be delighted… or arrested. It was hard to predict.

At the bottom of the bag were a pair of shoes. A pair of

shiny black brogues. Victor had been wearing these when she bumped into him in the town square. They were dry. He must have changed out of them before he went for his stroll that evening, and ended up in the water.

She turned them over. The backs of the heels were heavily worn – from all that marching around town. She looked closer. There was a ridge of dried mud stuck into the arch between the heel and the sole. The same for both shoes.

She ran her thumbnail along the ridge of mud, loosening off a triangle of dirt. She held it up. It was a distinctive yellowy-brown – close to the pigment raw sienna. Leonardo da Vinci used it in his underpainting. Applying thin glazes of raw sienna, umber and ochre gave his subject's skin a heavenly glow. Da Vinci was a painter and a geologist. He knew these earth colours contained iron oxide and would darken with time. So, he used them sparingly.

Astrid found a receipt in the Chinese silk purse in her rucksack. She dropped the sample of mud in it, folded it up tightly and put it back.

She decided to drop the clothes off at the dog charity on the high street – Sheepdip could thank her later. The woman behind the counter poked through the bag and nodded approvingly. Astrid then spent a few minutes browsing the tightly packed rails. It was the opening party that evening, and she'd given all her smart clothes to another charity shop in Hanbury. She chose a simple canvas shoulder bag and a black cocktail dress that was almost brand new. This was excellent fashion recycling. Celeste would be proud of her.

The rest of the day was fairly relaxed. Stocking up on

supplies from a small supermarket on the high street that had no name above the door, a leisurely sail around the bay and a snoozy couple of hours in bed to recharge the batteries for the night ahead.

Fourteen

At eight o'clock, Frank wandered up to the Wightlink ferry ticket office, a broad smile on his face. He'd made a big effort. He was wearing a black suit, a starched white shirt and a floppy bow tie in red crushed velvet that sat under his chin like a fat butterfly hiding from the rain.

'Hey, Frank. You look terrific,' said Astrid.

He did a slow circle, then looked her up and down. 'And you scrub up nicely yourself, Astrid.'

'Thank you, Frank.'

There were two ridges on the shoulders of his jacket – a sign that the suit had been hung up on a hanger for a few years at least. She ran her hand over the ridges to smooth them down. 'You look a million dollars,' said Astrid.

'Great, because... you know,' he gabbled, 'if Tranter is there, I want to make a good impression.'

'He's a real hero of yours, isn't he?'

'You've no idea.' He pulled out a book from his inside pocket. The title, *Get What You Want*, was printed above a photo of a man in a black polo-neck jumper and jeans. Jet-black hair and an even tan. The man had his arms crossed and was staring moodily from the cover.

'You mind keeping this in your bag?' said Frank. 'I can get him to sign it.'

'Of course.' Astrid took the copy. It was hardback, the pages so well thumbed that the book fanned out if you didn't squeeze it together. She put it in her bag and they went to the front of the cab rank.

The ride over to the party took about fifteen minutes. Frank chatted excitedly with the driver all the way about Tranter. The driver was also a fan, and attributed all his success to him. Clearly, self-employed men of a certain age on this island saw Tranter as a business guru.

The driver dropped them off at the gates of Northwood House. They walked the rest of the way down a gravel drive, silver buckets with fires in them lighting the way.

A steady stream of guests filed through the main entrance. Mostly couples. Some were in formal dress. Black tie for the men, evening dresses for the women. Astrid's black cocktail dress was a good choice.

Not everyone was sticking to the dress code. A fair few people were in sailing leisure gear. Ralph Lauren polo shirts with the collar up. The odd red gilet. That's the thing about the super-rich, thought Astrid – they don't give a flying toss about the rules.

'Come on then, let's get a few free drinks in,' said Frank, licking his lips.

They wandered in through a grand foyer, then on to the ballroom, where nearly all the guests seemed to be heading. There were a few tables up by the wall, but most people were milling around, chatting energetically. As if they all knew each other. Which was possible.

Frank led Astrid over to a floor-to-ceiling window in the corner. It was next to a door where the waiters and waitresses came out with trays of drinks and canapés. 'This is a good spot.' His eyes were trained on the door. 'You get first dibs on the food and drinks.'

'You've given it some thought, Frank.'

'No such thing as a free lunch, Astrid,' said Frank. A waiter in a black uniform, buttons all the way up the front, drifted out with a black lacquer tray. A dozen full champagne flutes were lined up on it. 'Unless it's at Cowes Week. Then it's all free, if you know the right people.' He reached out to the tray and lifted off two glasses. 'Thanks, mate,' he said to the waiter.

Astrid looked around the grand room lit by a huge chandelier. She hadn't been to a party this glitzy, she thought, since... well, never. 'This is great. Thanks for the invite, Frank.'

'My pleasure.' He handed her a glass. 'Cheers.'

She took a long sip. The bubbles fizzed in her nose, the alcohol veining straight to her brain, unpicking the last knot of tension from the day. 'That's vintage champagne... beautiful.' She thought back to the night before. To what, in her mind, she was now calling the 'wine box night of shame'. 'I better take it easy though, Frank. I had a bit to drink last night.'

'Don't worry. I'll pick up the slack.'

A waitress appeared from the doorway. She was holding a black painting palette, her thumb gripping the tray through the hole. Around it was arranged a selection of canapés.

'Lurvley,' groaned Frank. 'I'm famished.' He reached out and gripped the waitress's thumb. She stood there silently as he tugged at it, a confused expression on both their faces.

'Frank, I think that's actually this lady's thumb.'

Frank looked closely at the tray. 'Oh, yeah. So, it is.' He released his grip. 'Sorry about that – I thought it was a sausage.' He smiled at the waitress, who didn't seem bothered. 'Listen, darlin'. I'll take the tray off you. It'll save you the trip.'

'Sure,' said the waitress.

Frank took the tray and put it on the window ledge.

'This is great,' sighed Astrid. 'Please thank your friend for getting a ticket.'

'Brian… yeah, will do. He's a caulkhead like me. Makes most of his annual income running these Cowes Week bashes.'

Astrid scanned the room. 'I bet he does.' There were flashes of wealth everywhere. Rolex and Cartier watches hanging from wrists. Logos on caps and shirts that suggested they were freebies from exclusive events – the Monaco Grand Prix, Wimbledon, real polo tournaments. This was old money relaxing. Knowing it was in similar company.

'You know who would love this, Frank?' said Astrid.

'Go on.'

'Annabelle. This is just up her street. Mixing with the great and the good of Cowes Week. Did you not think you should have invited her?'

Frank screwed up his nose. 'Nah.'

'Why do you dislike her so much?' But Frank wasn't listening. He was looking over her shoulder at the kitchen door. Waiting for another waiter. 'Come on, Frank, I'm interested.'

'Okay… I'll tell you.' He faced her. 'Because she's a snob.'

'She is, yeah.'

'A massive snob.' He shook his head. 'There was this time I told her about my nephew, who's a barista. You know, he works in a coffee shop.'

'Got it.'

'She thinks I said barrister, so she gets all excited. Wants her daughter to meet him. So I give her his number. And then she finds out he works in Starbucks and gets all weird about it, and doesn't get in touch.'

Astrid laughed. 'Yeah, that's pretty bad.' She paused, wondering if she should tell him. 'The thing is, Frank, not too long ago I was a bit… what shall we say, a bit judgemental of people. And it was because, deep down, I wasn't happy. I just didn't know it then.'

'Hey, I'm sorry to hear that.' He reached out and put his hand on her shoulder.

'No, don't worry. I'm through it.'

'Good for you.'

Frank took his hand away and sent it straight to the canapés.

'I'm just saying – I was a bit snobbish because my life seemed better if I put other people on a lower level in my mind. That might be what's going on with Annabelle. Just a hunch.'

Frank nodded slowly. 'Makes sense. I'll try and go easy on her.'

'Thanks.' She smiled. 'But hey, don't go changing who you are, Frank – because you're pretty great.'

'Thanks, matey.' He crammed the last few canapés into his mouth. 'Now, I'm just going to drain the radiator.'

'Huh?'

'Go to the loo.' He wiped his hands on his trousers, and weaved off into the crowd.

Astrid grabbed another passing glass of champagne and sat down on the broad window ledge. She was glad to be here. Mingling with the super-rich, for once in her life. Free champagne and canapés. A couple standing next to an ice sculpture of a yacht stared at her. Maybe they could tell she wasn't supposed to be here. Best look busy then – have a read of Tranter's book. Act like them – like she didn't give a flying toss.

Gabriel Tranter's book was a mix of his life story and his wisdom on how to become successful in business. The section in the middle, a wedge of glossy photos, showed how it had all paid off. There he was at the helm of huge yachts. Driving low-slung supercars. Climbing out of infinity pools – a sculpted physique that owed much to personal trainers and dieticians.

His family, as the opening chapters outlined, was reasonably well off. Mother a receptionist. Father a businessman who ran a second-hand car dealership in Enfield, in the north of London. He sold up when Gabriel, his only kid, was eight and moved to the Isle of Wight where they both caught the sailing bug.

There were pictures of the young Gabriel with his father on various boats, from wooden dinghies to yachts. The boats got bigger as Gabriel grew up, ending up with a thirty-foot sailboat that won them a few local races.

Astrid carried on speed-reading through the section on his business advice. Each chapter was titled with one of his personal mantras.

'Scared money doesn't make money.' That was about the risks he took with his first software companies.

'Buy the rumour. Sell the news.' That was something to do with cryptocurrencies.

It only took about ten minutes before she'd got the gist of it. It wasn't that complicated. Work out what you want. Then work hard and you might get it. Simple. But you had to know what you wanted – and what Astrid wanted right now was some fresh air.

She got up and made her way through the house, looking for an exit to the gardens. She eventually found herself in a small circular room with white pillars that propped up a blue domed roof. A small skylight caught a disc of the night sky, like the pupil of an eye.

Astrid was about to head out of the door when a shaven-headed man strode into the room and glanced around. He seemed like a boxer – heavy features misshapen by some kind of violence in the past. A ruggedness that didn't match his black designer suit.

He nodded, reassured that only Astrid and a handful of other people were there. Then he stepped aside to let another man through. This man was above average height, but he looked much smaller against his boxer friend. He was wearing dark blue jeans and a simple black T-shirt.

Astrid reached for Frank's book. She turned it over to

check the profile photo on the back. It was him. Same jet-black hair. Same even tan. He was standing in the middle of the room, hands on his hips, nodding appreciatively. As if he was thinking of buying the place.

'Mr Tranter.' Astrid stepped towards him. The boxer blocked her way. Gabriel noticed the book in her hand and told the boxer there was nothing to worry about.

Astrid handed Tranter the book. She felt a rush of pride. Frank was going to be pleased with her for getting his hero's autograph.

The boxer reached into his top pocket, brought out a silver pen and passed it to Tranter, who peeled open the cover. 'So, who do I make it out to?' There was a slight slur in his voice. The hint of an accent she'd heard before on the island. But he'd smothered it with strong vowels that spoke of media voice training.

'Frank.'

'Frank?'

'It's for a friend of mine. He says you changed his life.'

'That's what I love to hear. You know—' he tapped the pen on his bottom lip '—it's why I'm doing this. To give back.' Gabriel signed the second page with a flourish. 'What about you? Did you like the book?'

'Not much,' scoffed Astrid.

He tipped his head to one side and stared at her. 'You've actually read it, right?'

'I skimmed through it.'

He handed the book to her. 'What's your problem with it? And please, be honest. You won't hurt my feelings.'

'Mmm… where to start then.' She slooshed down the last bit

of champagne from her glass. 'Your life story was interesting enough. But the self-help stuff – it's rubbish, isn't it?'

He kept staring at her.

'The idea that we have to be constantly chasing success. Because that's the only thing that will validate us and give us happiness.' She was warming to her theme. 'And a millionaire businessman is going to show the way to do it. I mean… it's nonsense.'

He smiled, completely unfazed. 'Billionaire… but please carry on.'

'And these chapter headings.' She ran through a few pages until she found one. '"Think yourself rich". It's not even possible. I mean, if I could have thought myself how to fly, I'd have saved a taxi fare here.'

'You done?' He crossed his arms.

'No. Everyone's life has its downs, but you've got to work through that yourself. Not follow the rules of a businessman who's retrofitted a mindset around their lucky career, then stuck it in a book and charged… what is it?' She checked the back of the book. '£6.99. But hey… I might be wrong.' Astrid was as surprised as he was about this rant. But it felt completely true. She carried on. 'If you're so rich, Mr Tranter—'

'Gabriel.'

'Whatever.' Swig. 'If you're so rich and money doesn't matter anymore, and it's all about "giving back" then the book would be free. Wouldn't it?'

He shook his head. 'Look,' he said. It was exactly what politicians in interviews on the radio say, thought Astrid. When they want to avoid answering a tough question.

They say 'look', and change the subject, as if it's really the interviewer's fault for asking a dumb question.

'I'm right though?'

'Look,' he said again. 'It seems like you've speed-read over the real message of the book.'

'Have I really?' She tucked Frank's copy in her bag. He would never forgive her if Tranter demanded it back.

'Yes, you have. I'm saying you first need to work out what you want most. Focus on that.' He put his hand to his chest, as if confessing something. 'For me, yes, it is money. But it's not about the zeros at the end of my bank balance. That's a sign that my hard work has paid off.'

The boxer returned after making a slow loop of the room and stood impassively next to Tranter.

'But money doesn't make you happy,' said Astrid.

'Sure. But it's nicer to be crying on a superyacht than a bicycle.'

'Okay, bit cheesy. But I'll give you that one,' said Astrid.

'And yes, I do have a superyacht. Before you ask.' A couple entered the room. They spotted Gabriel and reached for their phones. They held them up and took a couple of pictures. The boxer went over and said something that made them quickly put their phones down.

'I don't know your name,' said Tranter.

'It's Astrid.'

'Astrid, right… do you sail, Astrid?'

'Yes. I have a wooden ketch. A classic.'

'Awesome.' He rubbed his fingers. She noticed there was a ring on his little finger. A square-cut emerald. 'And do you know why I like sailing?'

'The sea biscuits?'

'No. It's because I can control everything in my life. Except two things. The weather is one of them. I'm out there and the tide will change, the wind will turn, and you are at their mercy.'

'Okay, and what's the other thing you can't control?' She hitched her bag higher on her shoulder. 'And please don't let it be what I think it's going to be.'

'Women like you.'

'Ugh... you actually said it.' Astrid made a queasy face. 'If this champagne glass was any bigger, I'd throw up in it.'

Tranter didn't seem to be offended. It was true – being this rich, this powerful, gave people an armour of indifference. 'If you fancy going sailing with me on one of my yachts, then I'd be delighted to have you aboard.' He glanced over to the boxer and nodded. It was a code that they were leaving.

'I'm alright, thanks.'

'Well, if you change your mind.' He clicked his fingers. The boxer reached into his jacket pocket and brought out a white business card. 'It's been good to meet you, Astrid.'

'I'm glad someone enjoyed it,' said Astrid.

Tranter smiled, then wandered to the next room.

The boxer gave her the card and leant over her. 'This is Gabriel's private number.' His voice was deep and raspy, as damaged as his face. 'Don't pass it on,' he growled.

When they'd both gone, Astrid found her way out into the gardens. It was a balmy night. The air smelt of cut grass.

Most people were seated on picnic blankets facing out to the bay, where the mast lights of the boats sparkled like a mist of fireflies. Frank came gambolling over, two more glasses in his hand.

'Definitely last one,' she said, taking the glass.

He apologised for disappearing. He'd bumped into his friend Brian, and they'd got chatting. He sat down next to Astrid and she brought out the book. 'Present for you, Frank.' She handed it over. 'Signed by Gabriel himself.'

His jaw dropped. 'No way. You met him?'

'Yup.'

'And what's he like? Unbelievable, right?'

'Yeah… he's unbelievable.'

Fifteen

It would be good to get on with assessing the art collection. That was the first thought to creep up on her the next morning. There had been too many distractions recently. The mysterious death of Victor Leech, the art club, exploring the town and accidentally drinking too much wine and champagne.

The party at Northwood House had been worth it though. They'd stayed for another couple of hours, chatting on the lawn with Frank, then shared a taxi back to Yarmouth. Frank spent the whole journey gripping Tranter's autobiography in both hands, firing questions at her about his hero. She didn't have the heart to tell him that he'd invited her sailing with him, and she had no intention of going.

He was the cheesiest person she'd ever met – a human fondue. And he was bound to be even more insufferable on board his own luxury yacht. When she'd got back to her boat a text pinged in from him. Some guff about how 'awesome' it had been to meet her, and they should 'catch the wind together real soon'. That was roughly it. She'd speed-read it, then went to bed without bothering to reply.

Astrid got to the lookout at The Needles' Eye around half

past ten. She set out her work tools on the table. Then she surveyed the art collection as if she had just walked into an upmarket gallery. This was something she liked to daydream about. Choosing the paintings as if she were buying them for herself. 'Ahh, Astrid,' the gallery owner in her head said in syrupy tones, 'how lovely to see you again.'

Astrid didn't reply. It was her daydream, and she didn't have to be polite to oily gallery owners. She rubbed her chin, ambling alongside the wall. She stopped in front of a charming busy scene, just off the English coast. A handful of three-mast ships jostled into position as they approached the harbour. On the gold plaque it said, '"Shipping off Dover" by John Wilson Carmichael'.

'It's called "Shipping off Dover",' said the oily voice.

'Thank you, Lawrence, but I'm more than capable of reading a label.'

'I'm sooo sorry.'

Astrid said the next bit aloud. 'Yes, I'll take it. Now put it on my account and have it delivered to the house this evening.'

Okay, the dialogue was a bit creaky, thought Astrid, but she was enjoying herself.

Like much of the rest of the collection, the Carmichael piece was in good condition. There was a patch of paint that had sunk in and become flat and lifeless. It could be easily 'oiled out' by an experienced restorer.

The most badly damaged painting was a small Dutch harbour scene by Willem van de Velde the Younger. The varnish was yellow and badly cracked and needed removing. Astrid teased the tip of a scalpel under the edge of a small scab of varnish, the size of a match head. It cracked loose, revealing a dot of blue sky. It would take a while – a painstaking process she was very glad she wouldn't be doing herself.

She carried on doing tests on the tiniest areas of the paintings. Taking photos and logging everything in her notebook. It was enthralling work and the time flew by.

At just after three o'clock, she was jolted out of her thoughts by the creak of a door downstairs. She put her notebook down and listened as the footsteps crossed the hall and began to climb the stairs towards the door.

She felt a ripple of panic in her chest. After being followed the night before last, she was jumpier than usual. Who would be wandering around the house? She hurried to the door to lock it, but it swung open before she could reach the handle. Celeste was standing there.

'Celeste, it's you.' Astrid breathed out, her heart rate ticking down.

'Hi, Astrid.' Celeste took off her big sunglasses and shook her hair free. She was wearing a long white man's shirt cinched in with a denim belt, her favourite sailcloth bag over her shoulder. 'I didn't mean to scare you.'

'No, I'm fine. I was just miles away.'

'I was taking a walk round the gardens and saw you working up at the window. Thought I'd drop in and see how you're getting on.'

'Making progress – over halfway there.' She went back to the table and started gathering up the tools and putting them in her work case.

Celeste came over. 'Oh, I was going to say.' Celeste rooted

around in her bag and fumbled out her phone. 'I saw a photo of you last night. You're a dark horse, aren't you?'

'Am I?'

Celeste dabbed at the screen of her phone then turned it to Astrid. 'Voila… you and Gabriel. It's all over Instagram.'

The picture showed Astrid and Tranter standing next to each other, a glass of champagne in her hand. She remembered there was a couple next to her who'd taken some photos. They must have posted them online.

'Is Gabriel a friend of yours?' asked Celeste, slipping her phone into her bag.

Astrid told her how she'd bumped into him and they'd got chatting. How he'd signed his autobiography for a friend of hers. Celeste kept up a tense smile throughout.

'Anyway, lucky you,' she said.

Astrid noticed a hint of jealousy in her voice. 'Oh, no,' Astrid laughed. 'I'm not interested in him, like that.'

'Me neither,' protested Celeste. 'He could be very useful for my charity.'

Astrid carried on tidying her things away as Celeste explained a bit more about her charity. She and some local volunteers collected plastic from the shoreline, which was then recycled into different objects – things like sustainable coffee cups, plates and jewellery. Celeste then sold them on her website under her ethical brand 'FBP' – 'Fantastic Beach Plastic'.

'All of our profits are ploughed back into other environmental schemes on the island,' said Celeste, playing with a necklace that appeared to be made of weathered pen tops. 'Like saving the local seagrass meadows.'

Now Astrid was feeling bad. Not only had she been rude to Frank's business idol, but she could also have put in a good word for Celeste. She clipped up her work case. 'You know, Celeste, when I meet people like you – people who try and make the world a better place – I always feel bad that I don't do more.'

Celeste looked her up and down. Astrid had run out of fresh clothes. So, she'd had to throw on the Little Miss Know-It-All T-shirt that Kath had given her. 'I don't know. I think you have strong green values.'

'Do you think so?'

'Yes. I mean your clothes…'

'Huh?'

'This old T-shirt of yours. Most people would have thrown that away a long time ago. Where did you get it?'

'Someone left it on a beach.'

'There you go.' Celeste clapped her hands. 'And the no make-up thing. Hardly any hair products. You are low impact, Astrid.'

The comments had been delivered with such a warm smile it was hard not to take them as a compliment. 'Er… thank you.'

Astrid left her work case under the table and they both walked out of the lookout and down to the ground floor. As they passed David Wade's office, Astrid paused at the door. 'Celeste. Can I ask you something?'

Celeste stopped in her tracks and came back.

'It's about a painting in your father's office.'

'Okay.' She reached for the door handle. 'Let's go in.'

Celeste swung the door open and flicked the light switch.

She stood by the doorway for a moment, looking sadly round the room. Perhaps, thought Astrid, remembering her father working there. Celeste sighed deeply then carried on into the room.

Astrid went round the desk and stood by the portrait on the wall. 'Can you tell me anything about this?'

Celeste took her sailcloth bag from her shoulder and dumped it by the desk. 'Yes – it was a portrait commissioned by my father. I can't remember the name of the artist. They copied a photo of myself and...' Her voice trailed off.

'I'm sorry I asked.'

'No, no. It's fine.' Celeste forced a smile. Then she moved behind the desk, her eyes fixed on the portrait. 'I'm probably eight there. She's a couple of years younger. We both used to sail, but of course, she had the real talent for it.'

So far, Celeste had avoided using her sister's name. It was like she'd reached a knot in a line and couldn't get past it. Astrid brought her finger up to the canvas and gently traced the mark of the repair. 'I noticed that there has been some restoration here.'

'That's very observant of you.'

'It's the art conservator's eye. Do you know anything about this damage?'

'Yes – it was slashed.'

'Slashed?'

'My father... after Harlow disappeared.' Now that she'd said it, her shoulders relaxed slightly. 'You know what happened, Astrid?'

'I do. And I'm so sorry.'

'That's kind – thank you.' She perched on the end of the

desk. 'My father blamed himself for what happened. He wished he'd never taught her to sail. Then pushed her so hard to be a champion yachtswoman. My father was a very driven man and expected high standards from his children.' She reached out and pulled a porcelain pot towards her. It had a blue-and-white Chinese pattern on it, and a bunch of pens poking out. 'Losing Harlow broke him.'

'It wasn't his fault though?'

'No, it wasn't. But you know… grief makes your mind work in strange ways.'

Celeste plucked a gold letter opener from among the pens. It was about five inches long and the exact proportions of a fencing sword. It had a little leather grip and a guard that stopped the fingers slipping onto the blade. 'So, one evening, he was up here drinking on his own. And he slashed the portrait with this.' She waved the letter opener.

'I don't understand.'

'He was trying to cut out the boat. He was angry with himself for giving it to us all those years ago. His biggest regret in his life.' Celeste put the sword back in the pot. Her eyes clouded with tears.

Astrid went round the desk. 'I'm sorry I mentioned it.'

Celeste rubbed her eyes. 'Sorry, it takes me by surprise now and then.'

'Please – don't apologise.' Astrid felt she had intruded too much into Celeste's grief. She stepped back from the painting not knowing what to say next. The air seemed much colder in this room.

Celeste turned to her. 'You know, I'd do anything to have her back.'

'I'm sure you would.'

'We didn't always get on. You know how it is... with sisters.'

Astrid nodded. 'I know.'

'Or just to know what happened to her that night. But hey—' she shivered herself out of her dark mood '—I have to keep looking forward. Keep throwing myself into my environmental work.'

'Then some good can come out of it?'

'Yes, that's it,' she said. Then she reached up and lifted the painting down. She turned it around and leant it against the wall without saying anything. They didn't speak again until they reached the iron gates and said goodbye.

Sixteen

The town was quiet. There were only a handful people wandering down the high street. At The Chatterbox Café, a waiter was collecting the menus and checking the horizon to the south of the town.

Astrid followed his eyeline up towards the headland. A low band of dark cloud hung over the hills. That explained it. The weather was about to turn nasty – the first bad weather since she'd been on the island. She went to the BBC Weather app to make sure. A storm, a big one – two raindrops on a black cloud – was on its way, pushed in by a forty-mile-an-hour wind. Most people had spotted it and headed indoors.

In the marina, a few boat owners were fussing around on deck – retying knots or stowing away the outdoor furniture. Astrid hurried on across the car park, head down. When she was almost at the road, she heard her name being called. Out of the corner of her eye she could see Jim making a beeline for her.

Nearby, next to a bench, was a silver statue of a slug-like animal. It had silver eyes as large and shiny as hubcaps. There was an information board next to it. She went over and started to read it – so she could compose herself in case

Jim was going to talk about her role at HMRC. Which, and she could tell from his quick steps on the cobbles, was going to happen.

'Astrid!'

The sculpture was a scaled-up version of a tiny creature that, over the years, had eaten its way through the wooden pilings in the marina. The statue had been made to celebrate the complete renovation of the harbour.

'Astrid!'

She read on. A TV gardener called Alan Titchmarsh had attended the grand opening. There was a black-and-white photo of him riding the sculpture in 2008.

'Astrid?'

'Hey, sorry, Jim,' she said calmly. 'Didn't see you there.'

'I spotted you from the office. Thought I'd have a word.'

She leant over the board, reading the text for the second time. 'These gribbles sound like they were a menace.'

'Yes, yes… anyway, have you got time to hear my findings about the Leech incident?'

Astrid stopped reading. He'd done some investigating about Leech. This was worth listening to. 'Of course. I've always got time for you, Jim.'

'Right, well…' Jim stared at her Little Miss Know-It-All T-shirt.

'Okay – let's hear what you've found.' Astrid led him to the bench and they both sat down.

'Right, I've been asking around…' He swung round in his seat. 'Sorry, do you not want to take notes?'

A real HMRC agent would probably have a notepad at hand, thought Astrid. All she had in her rucksack was a sketch pad with a drawing of Frank on the first page. Think quick. 'No, no, Jim. It's all up here.' Astrid tapped her temple.

'Very impressive.'

In front of them, a flatbed truck with a steel trailer on the back drove into the car park. It made a U-turn in front of the slipway and backed the trailer down to the water's edge. Jim waited for the driver to switch off the engine.

'Okay,' Jim continued, 'so I spoke to the chief detective who's assigned to the case. And they're not treating Leech's death as suspicious.'

Astrid hid her shock. 'Why's that?'

'They're still waiting for the full autopsy report. But at this stage there are no signs of any injuries. No bruises. No wounds. They say he must have fallen in the water somewhere and got dragged under because of his heavy backpack. It was full of leaflets about his latest campaign.'

'The cycle lane on the high street?'

'No idea. Is that important?'

'We'll see.' Astrid nodded sagely, but inside her mind was whirring. She knew she should really come clean to Jim. He was such a decent guy. But she couldn't resist squeezing a bit more information out of him.

'Right.' Jim carried on. 'The police say the leaflets in the backpack got waterlogged. That's what pulled him under. If more people had taken them from him, he might be here today.'

'It's a cruel world,' she said gravely.

Ahead of them, the driver had got out of the truck. He was a bodybuilder type. Bulging white T-shirt. His arms were so thick they couldn't hang down by his sides. Elbows sticking out, as if he were carrying two invisible rolled-up carpets. He wandered to the water's edge and leant on the tailgate of the truck.

Jim talked for another few minutes about the rest of his conversation with the chief detective. Which didn't give Astrid any more to go on. The police had no idea where Victor had gone in the water. And nobody had come forward to say they saw him on the evening he died. 'Between you and me,' he said, conspiratorially, 'I think the police are a bit out of their depth.'

'Why do you say that?'

'Don't get me wrong, they're a great bunch of lads. It's just...' He stopped himself. Backing away from saying something too harsh.

'Go on, Jim, you can tell me.' She nudged him in the ribs with her elbow. A little too hard, perhaps.

'Alright,' he said, shifting down the bench. 'Let's say if I was in charge, I'd do it differently. I'd start with a big local media appeal for information. Papers, TV, radio. Posters up on lamp posts. Make sure no stone was left unturned. But hey...' He crossed his legs and pinched the crease in his black trousers. 'As the chief detective was only too pleased to tell me, as they don't know if Victor fell into the harbour, it's not my jurisdiction.' He said these last three words slowly and deliberately, as it must have been a real quote.

'You ever think about joining the force yourself, Jim?'

'Woo, you just opened a can of worms there, Astrid. Long story, but I applied after I left the merchant navy and they turned me down.'

Astrid now realised why Jim was helping her. He had something to prove. A chip on his shoulder maybe, next to the gold stripes on his black jumper.

Static electricity played with a few stray strands of Astrid's fringe. The storm was getting closer. Out in the harbour, an inflatable was puttering towards the trailer on the slipway. Jim surveyed the valley. The rain was slanting down at the top of the river.

They probably only had a few minutes before it started to rain, thought Astrid. Best to get Jim's theories now. 'So, what do you think happened?'

He smacked his lips. 'I don't think he went over the side of the pier, or into the harbour.'

'Why not?'

'He'd have had to climb over the rail of the pier. Someone would have seen him from The George hotel. There's a beer garden on that side that's always busy. As for the harbour – there's over two hundred boats in there at the moment. A lot of people sitting out on decks. Again, someone would have heard or seen something.'

'Where did he go then?'

'I think he went in the Yar, further upstream. Bounced around on the riverbed until he reached the harbour. Then the ferry could have churned him out of the harbour mouth. It's in and out of there twenty times a day. Sets up a big undertow.'

Astrid shuddered. The thought of Victor getting churned around under the boats in the harbour, clunking dully against anchor chains... it wasn't worth lingering on. 'What about further down the shoreline?'

'Possible.' He nodded. 'East or west. There's cross tides down there.'

The inflatable was gliding up to the slipway. A young man, the bodybuilder's son maybe, cut the engine and hopped out. Between them they hauled the boat onto the trailer and lashed it down. When they'd both driven off, Astrid stood up. It was time to leave. Best not to push her luck any further, she thought.

'Thanks for asking around. It's good to hear what the police make of it.'

Jim raised himself to his feet. 'My pleasure. And I hope you don't mind me asking, but do you have any theories of your own?'

'It's early days, Jim, but let's just say I think your assessment is spot on.'

'That's good to know.' He nodded.

They walked the few yards to the gribble statue, where they went their separate ways. Astrid was about to cross the road when he caught up with her. 'Look, if anything comes up down at HMRC special investigations, you'll let me know, right?'

'Of course. We're always on the lookout for good agents.'

'Thanks, Astrid.' He beamed. 'Thank you so much.'

Astrid just made it back to the boat in time. As soon as she shut the cabin door and switched on the light, the rain began to beat on the metal roof. Like the light switch had turned on the rain as well.

The patter on the roof built up in seconds to a steady

thrrumm. Water overflowed the narrow guttering and washed down the windows, rippling the shape of the valley and hills. The wind picked up. The boat bumped against the mooring.

But Astrid wouldn't want to be anywhere else in a storm. Safe in a harbour. Cooking a meal – tonight it was tomato and garlic Bolognese. The steam from the boiling pan of pasta filled the cabin with a warm cloud. The rain on the roof harmonised with the classical music on the radio. Wagner – a roiling symphony.

She'd gone too far with Jim. Again. And this time she didn't have the excuse of too much wine. She should have come clean with him. But she'd been itching to hear if he knew anything about Victor Leech. It wasn't her finest moment, she thought. Especially as he'd admitted he was desperate to work as an agent, and she'd sort of – well definitely – told him she'd fix it. She could only hope the whole thing would blow over, and he'd never find out who she really was.

There was a rumble outside. Astrid turned up the radio. The drums rose to meet the thunder as it rolled down the valley. A whiplash of lightning cracked out over the marsh, the portholes flashing like lamps. She would sleep soundly tonight, in her bunk. Listening to a storm that could do her no harm.

Seventeen

The next day, the world felt brand new. Astrid rode up the valley on her bike and the air smelt pure and cleansed by the storm. She slalomed over the boardwalk, avoiding rafts of dried reeds that had been washed over from the river. The water had dropped back. The sun was out. Astrid felt as fresh as the minty blue sky.

Her guilt at leading Jim on hadn't receded much. It wasn't enough to stop her investigating the mystery of Victor Leech's death though. She still needed that distraction. And it still didn't add up.

Why was she so darn suspicious of everything? That's what a geography teacher at her boarding school had once said. 'You have a busy mind, Swift – but you use it too much to poke into other people's business.' He was later arrested for embezzling the money for field trips, so he might well have said that. But he had a point.

It would only take a couple more days to finish off her report on the art collection, so she would have plenty of time to look into the Leech affair. Although she didn't have much to go on at the moment. She swung round a corner of the boardwalk, the wheels clattering over the planks.

There was the yellowy-brown mud on his shoes. That might be something? From what she knew of Leech, he was a precious, fussy man. Not the sort of person to go romping about in muddy fields. And the more she thought about it, that mud was a very distinctive colour. She'd explored a lot of the countryside around Yarmouth and had yet to see anything like it.

There had been a text from Frank when she'd woken up. He'd suggested they all meet up earlier at the potting shed, around lunchtime, to catch up on their painting. Not that he'd put a brush to paper so far. That gave her the morning to explore the headland. Keep her eyes peeled for yellowy-brown mud.

By the time she'd reached the ridge of the headland, a scattering of puffy white clouds had appeared in the sky. '*Simpsons* clouds' – that's what she called them. Like the opening sequence in the TV show. This time she decided to cycle west. Up the gentle slope, towards The Needles.

On the other side of the slope was a high wire fence. Beyond it was a squat brick watchtower that wouldn't be out of place in post-war East Berlin. It was two storeys high with a triangular grey roof. Around it was a deep concrete wall. A small blue flag fluttered on a white pole.

She leant her bike against the fence and read the plaque attached to the wire. This was the 'Needles Coastguard Station'. There were some contact numbers underneath and an explanation that the watchtower was run by volunteers. To one side was a small metal box for donations. Astrid found her Chinese silk purse in her rucksack and rummaged around for some change. The only thing in there was a folded £20 note. She took it out to check if there were any coins deeper down.

'That is sooo generous,' came a deep voice to her side.

She turned to see a plump man in a white short-sleeved shirt and thin black tie. He was smiling at her.

'No, the thing is...' She waved the £20 note.

He stepped forward, eyes twinkling over pink cheeks set above a white goatee beard. 'So generous.' He plucked the £20 note from her fingers and posted it into the donations box. 'Thank you, dear. We are entirely dependent on donations.'

'My pleasure,' she said flatly. Was the grille big enough to get her hand in there later?

'Do you sail?'

Maybe she could get it out with chewing gum on a stick?
'Er... sorry?'

'Are you a sailor?'

'Yes I am.' Astrid zipped up her purse and shoved it back in the rucksack. 'I came over from Poole last week. I'm moored up at Yarmouth.'

'In which case, would you like to have a tour of the station? It's the least we can do for twenty quid.'

'Alright then,' she said, glancing at the bike. 'Is it okay if I lock my bike up on the fence?'

'Course it is.'

He opened a gate in the chain link fence and set off towards the watchtower. On the way, he went through the introductions. His name was Patrick Castle. His career as a chef in the navy was cut short after he slipped on a tin of luncheon meat in a storeroom. The injury forced him to retire five years early and left him with a nagging twinge below the patella that got worse in chilly weather. Not that it was slowing him down today. He nimbly took the stairs to the upper floor and swung open the door.

The room was glass on three sides, the widest section facing out to sea. At the front was a desk that ran from one side to the other. It was covered in charts, instruments, phones and short-wave radio sets. A woman with a honey-coloured bob with grey roots was peering at a computer screen through reading glasses. She had the same uniform on as Patrick.

'How it's going out there, Jane?' said Patrick.

'Had a kayaker overturn in Scratchell's Bay. But they managed to get upright again.' She sighed, barely hiding her disappointment. 'So, I didn't ring it in.'

'And that's pretty much what we do here in a nutshell, Astrid. We keep a lookout for anyone in trouble out there and call in the Coastguard if need be.'

'You've got a lot of equipment,' said Astrid, looking over Jane's shoulder. On the screen was a map of the coastline and sea below them. On the water were small red boat shapes with lines behind them showing the course they'd taken.

'We have indeed,' said Patrick. 'But this is the most important of them all...' he brought his finger to the corner of his eye '...Eyeball Mark One.'

Jane laughed. Although there was no doubt she'd heard this one many times before.

'I'm guessing summer is your busiest time,' said Astrid.

'Oh, yes.' He sucked in air through gritted teeth. 'All those fishing charters and weekend sailors. Then you throw in the jet skiers, the paddleboarders, even kids on lilos, and let's say, some days it's been very messy. Right, Jane?'

'It's been mayhem out there.' Jane didn't look up from the screen. 'Like a great big soup with idiot croutons.'

The pair were enjoying themselves. And so was Astrid. This was maybe even worth twenty quid, she thought.

She stepped forward and gazed down at the water far below them. She'd sailed through the same stretch to the north when she arrived. High above it now, it made sense. The Needles were the broken tail of a cliff that tapered sharply into deep water. Even from half a mile away you could see the currents funnelling between the three stacks of chalk. Beyond the lighthouse, seams of jade were broken up by creases of white. Rows of waves sprang up out of nowhere, then flattened back into green-grey swirls.

'There's a really complicated set of currents out there,' said Astrid.

'One of the most dangerous stretches to sail in the world.' Patrick joined her at the big window and pointed out across the water to the west. 'There are some huge tides running between the island and the mainland. East and west. And they're not always working together.' He held out his hands as if holding something large and heavy. 'Imagine you have a long oblong fish tank half filled with water, right?'

'Okay.'

He raised his left hand. 'You tip it up from one end, then before the wave reaches the other side—' he raised his right '—you tip that up and he water clashes with itself. That's what happens out there. Then you have to add the rocks and the dozens of wrecks.'

'Wrecks?'

'Yes, let me show you.' He went over to a pair of binoculars that were on a stand. After a bit of adjustment, he stepped back and invited Astrid to look through them. A dark grey shadow, the shape of a torpedo, shimmered under the surface of the water. Then a wave drew back and she could see a flash of rusty metal. The wave healed over it again. 'What is it?' she said, her eyes still trained on the water.

'That,' said Patrick, 'is the wreck of the SS *Varvassi*. It was a cargo ship that sunk in 1947. It was sailing from Algiers to Southhampton and got caught in a storm. Since then, it's sent dozens of other boats to the bottom.'

'Nasty.' Astrid stepped back from the binoculars. 'And just say you went overboard there, how long would you survive?'

Jane swivelled in her chair to face them. She breathed out a low whistle. 'Now, that is the million-dollar question.'

'You've done it now.' Patrick chuckled. 'It just so happens that drowning is Jane's specialist subject. Right, Jane?'

'Yeah, I'm a bit of an expert on drowning, if I don't mind flattering myself. It's a real science.'

'Okay,' Astrid said, 'let's say, if someone fell in this afternoon. How long would they have?'

Jane picked her pen up and wagged it at her. 'It's not as easy as that. You mind, Patrick?' She got up from her seat and Patrick replaced her at the screen. Then she went over to Astrid. 'Depends on a lot of factors.'

'Like what?'

'Okay then. The temperature at this time of year, high summer, is as warm as it gets – about sixteen degrees Celsius. But it's still cold water. If you fell in, you'd start losing heat quick. Thirty-two times faster than you would in the air. You know much about hypothermia?'

'Not much, sorry.'

'Don't apologise. Not many people do.' She put her pen in her top pocket. 'Body temperature is thirty-seven degrees. Now, when you get down to thirty-five degrees, that's when you start getting into trouble. Your muscles will become unresponsive. Your brain tissue gets cold, and you start to make bad decisions. You become confused. Begin losing consciousness.'

'Can you even give a rough idea?' asked Astrid.

'I'm afraid not,' Jane said firmly. 'It depends on so many things. Sea conditions. Fitness of the person. Whether they had a life jacket on.'

'Let's try this.' Astrid wasn't giving up. 'I'll give you an example. A woman falls in on a day like today. Calm seas. No life jacket.'

'Ah, problem is,' Jane interrupted, 'there's not many studies on women. Most of the research is for what they call a "standard man". Can you believe that?'

'Yes, I can. That's why it's "man overboard".'

'Damn right.' Jane laughed.

Patrick glanced up from his screen and muttered something like 'here we go again'. But Jane didn't notice it and ploughed on.

'Let's take you then, Astrid.'

'Okay then.' Astrid squared up to her.

'Right.' Jane stood back and looked Astrid up and down. 'Average height. Slim. Good BMI.'

'Does that matter?'

'It's one of the biggest factors that determines survival. Fatty tissue is a good insulator. Someone like Patrick could be happily bobbing up and down on the water for three times as long. No offence, Patrick.'

Patrick giggled. 'None taken, Jane.'

Jane studied Astrid one last time, from her shoes to the top of her head. 'One and a half to two hours maximum.'

'Then what?'

'You'd slip below the water. I'd say, looking at you, you could hold your breath for about thirty seconds. That's all – thirty seconds before you'd start to suck in so much salt water you'd never recover.' Jane rubbed her hands. 'That's why you can't underestimate the sea. It can catch anyone out.'

Astrid stared out to sea. A cloud drifted in towards land. Its shadow underneath slicked across the surface of the water. A thought came to her. 'Even Harlow Wade?'

Patrick sat upright. 'Did you know Harlow?' he said sombrely.

'No, I never met her.' The mood in the room had changed. Jane went over to the desk and started tidying a few things up. 'I mean...' Astrid considered showing them the HMRC letter. But it had got her in so much trouble before, she daren't risk it. 'I know her sister, Celeste.'

'I see.' Patrick relaxed. 'Listen, can I get you a cup of coffee?'

'Please.'

Jane studied the screen again while Patrick made the

coffee at a sink in the corner. He brought over a mug with an orange lifeboat on the side and pulled up a chair for each of them by the chart table.

Patrick took a long sip. 'Harlow Wade would never have had an accident at sea. She was too good a sailor.'

'Did you know her?' asked Astrid.

'I met her around the dock at Yarmouth now and then. She was a wonderful person, too. The town was so proud of her. She was bound to win the Fastnet the next day. No question about it.' He picked at his knuckles. Summoning up a story he'd tried to forget. 'You see, I was on shift that evening.'

'You saw her boat?'

'No. Which means she must have given The Needles a wide berth.'

'What about a distress call?'

'Nothing.'

They both watched a boat approach the seam of waves. Patrick stood up for a few seconds, a hand on the binoculars. But the boat hopped over the waves, the spray lashing the deck. Then it swung into the calmer water.

'What do you think happened then, Patrick?' asked Astrid.

'Her boat was never found, so it must have sunk somehow. Out of the blue, in fair weather. You know what my guess is?'

'Go on.'

'Shipping container.'

'A shipping container?'

'Yeah, sometimes shipping containers get swept off the decks of the big cargo ships. Most sink, but depending on what's inside them, they can float with only a bit above the water – like icebergs. They have sharp corners and if you hit them, they'll hole you. Unless you have a steel hull.'

'And Harlow's boat?'

'Her boat was reinforced carbon fibre. Strong, but no defence against a shipping container. That's what I reckon happened. It holed her boat below the waterline, and she started taking on water too fast to get a distress call out... but hey.' He shrugged. 'No point in speculating. It was a tragedy – that's all there is to it.'

Astrid asked a few more questions. Patrick answered them half-heartedly. An explanation was out there, but he'd given up trying to find it. When he'd finished his coffee, he went over to a bookshelf by the back wall and teased out a green cardboard folder. This was his 'cuttings file', and she was more than welcome to have it – if she wanted to read the whole story. 'I'm pleased to see the back of it,' he said, handing it over.

Astrid said goodbye to Jane, and Patrick escorted her out to the chain link fence. When they got there, he unlocked the gate. 'If you manage to work out what happened to that poor girl, please let me know.'

She shook his hand and promised him she would.

Eighteen

Astrid took a path down that clung to the side of a grassy slope. It was so steep there were concrete steps and a metal handrail. Next to it was a narrow white track, grass worn down by braver walkers. Astrid stuck to the steps, stopping after the first flight to take in the view.

On the end of the peninsula below her was a concrete platform. A square red-brick building was perched on the edge. She was down there in ten minutes, across a bridge over a crevasse in the rock past the gatehouse. The sign said *The Needles Old Battery*. It was another English Trust property. Good – it meant a tearoom and another strong coffee weren't far away.

The open area was scalloped by concrete bays. These, according to the information board, were Second World War gun placements. The cannons had gone, but the iron tracks they swivelled on were still there. Aimed out to sea at an enemy that never came.

Astrid carried on across the square towards the red-brick building. Sure enough, there was a café on the second floor. The walls on the way up were covered with old Second World War propaganda posters. The 'Dig for Victory' slogan over baskets of tubby vegetables. Churchill in profile, against a sky filled with Spitfires. Women in uniform, saluting. This was another place her father would adore. It was all so British and stirring. Not that she could think about him right now. There was the Harlow Wade file to go through.

Astrid ordered coffee and a blueberry muffin and took them over to a high seat in front of a window that looked down over The Needles. There were only a couple of other customers there.

She put the file down on the Formica ledge in front of her. It was full of articles cut out of newspapers, organised chronologically. All local papers at the start, then more national papers as the news reached the rest of the country.

First, she quickly scanned the headlines, feeling the story play out from dread – *Teenage sailing prodigy goes missing at sea* – to resignation – *Coastguards say Harlow Wade will never be found alive*. The hope evaporated as she went through the file. The facts, what few there were, giving way to speculation and grief.

She now had a much better idea of what had happened than after her quick internet search a couple of days ago. It was time to go deeper – to imprint the order of events in her mind. She went back to the start of the file and carefully read the articles under the headlines. The tragedy had unfolded like this.

At around 4.30 p.m., Harlow Wade had set sail on her boat *Whitecaps* from the private jetty at The Needles' Eye.

She told her father she was going to test out the boat for a couple of hours. Sail just past The Needles and come straight back. The Fastnet Race started the next day, so she wanted to make sure everything was running smoothly. That was the last time he spoke to her.

There had been no reason to worry. That afternoon, visibility was good. Winds were light – five to six knots from the south, so she could easily tack west, past Alum Bay and on to the The Needles.

The last time anyone saw her was 5.20 p.m. Thomas Davison, on board a mid-sized yacht called *The Aegean*, was on his way to moor up in Alum Bay for the night and saw Harlow at the helm of *Whitecaps*. She waved at him, and he waved back. Davison was thirty yards away, close enough to be sure of a couple of things.

One – Harlow was wearing a black baseball cap and a red sailing jacket, with no life jacket over it. This was her favourite red Musto jacket.

Two – Harlow wasn't clipped on at the rail. She'd turned to face Davison when she waved at him, and he could clearly see there was no line.

Given the weather and the tide, it was estimated that *Whitecaps* would have been level with The Needles by around 5.45 p.m. The sea conditions were gentle, so there was no reason for the Coastwatch to track boats coming through.

Over the next couple of days, the papers scrabbled for more details. Reporters spoke to dozens of friends of the Wade family. They all gave accounts of a young woman who loved sailing. A woman excited about life and about winning in her boat class at Cowes the next day.

Then forty-eight hours later they found her black baseball cap.

A dog walker was out early, around 7 a.m., on the shingle beach alongside Hurst Castle on the mainland. He'd seen the baseball cap washed up on the shoreline. He picked it up. Thought about keeping it for himself. But then he'd checked the size label, and seen the name written in pen on it – Harlow Wade.

By now, this was a big local news story, so he knew the name. He left the cap where it was and called the police, who came straight away. That's all that was found from aboard *Whitecaps*. A hat. Lying on wet, grey pebbles.

Astrid looked up from the file. She'd barely touched her coffee and it was now cold. She ordered another one, rolled a crick out of her lower neck and went back to the clippings.

In the next report there were a few quotes from Patrick. He'd told the reporter what he told Astrid up in the watchtower, except he didn't mention shipping containers. It was a mystery, he said. Harlow was a brilliant sailor. There was no reason for her not to get home safely. The journalist had pushed him hard, but he wouldn't budge. There was no point speculating. That wasn't going to stop other journalists trying.

Seventy-two hours after Harlow was reported missing by her father, the Coastguard called off the search. Now the theories started to emerge. Especially one. Astrid could feel the journalists nudging readers towards their preferred conclusion. That Harlow might have taken her own life.

They revisited Davison and asked him if, in that brief moment when he'd seen Harlow at the helm, he could tell her mood. He said he couldn't. They'd exchanged a 'friendly wave'. She'd smiled, then turned back to the wheel. That's all. He hadn't thought anything unusual about it at the time, and he still didn't.

The following Sunday, there were a few long articles about Harlow in the national papers. Astrid wondered if she'd even heard this story, but not engaged with it because it was about sailing. The Sunday papers portrayed Harlow as flawless. 'A sailing genius.' 'A model student' with excellent grades. Popular with other pupils and teachers at her private school on the island. 'The perfect sister.' There were pictures of Harlow and Celeste as young kids sailing together. It included the photo that must have been the inspiration for the sailing portrait Astrid had seen at The Needles' Eye.

There were photos of the Wade family – Harlow, Celeste and their father on a handful of different yachts. Some of Harlow in her early teens collecting trophies at ceremonies. She was about to become a champion sailor, about to make her father proud. Why would she take her own life? It was unthinkable. Whatever had happened to her, it was terrible. The poor kid, thought Astrid. It was such a waste.

Astrid finished her coffee and made her way up the path, the file under her arm. There was nothing in it that could get her closer to an answer. Nobody could. Thousands of people must have been over these same details in the file – that's all that was available – and come up with nothing. It was a tragic accident at sea – the result of a deadly shipping container maybe. Nobody knew. Three years later, four thousand tides... the truth was lost at sea.

She slipped the file into a recycling bin near the chain

link fence. It didn't weigh more than a couple of glossy magazines. But she felt much lighter when she left it behind. Then she unlocked her bike and set off down the path to Abbotsford Manor.

Nineteen

Astrid decided to take a tour of the gardens before she went to the potting shed. To see how the garden had coped with the storm. She needn't have worried. The flowerbeds were looking better than ever. Waves of colours – blue, yellow, red – tumbled across the grass paths. The hedges, refreshed by the rain, sparkled green. Stepping into the herb garden, she was struck by the scent of sage, rosemary and thyme.

If there was one thing she missed about living on the boat, it was growing pots of herbs. She'd had to leave the ones from the deck back on the jetty at Hanbury. Cobb had promised to water them, so they should be okay. Cobb – it was the first time she'd thought about him for days. And then it was about doing the watering. Perhaps it was time to admit that it really had been a summer thing.

Ahead of her was a tall, heavy-set man in a long waxed coat that only allowed a few inches of maroon cords to show themselves above his boots. He was about six foot tall, with grey stubble that matched his short, cropped hair. He was standing by a flowerbed, nipping off dead dahlia heads with secateurs and tossing them into a green plastic wheelbarrow to his side.

As she passed him, the man studied her for a moment. By the time she'd taken the path past the borders, he'd caught her up.

'Hullo, hullo,' he called after her.

Astrid stopped.

'You're… um.' He snapped his fingers, trying to spark the name. 'The art club were telling me all about you?'

'Astrid Swift.'

'That's it.' He pointed at her hair. 'The braids. They said to say hi if I saw you.'

'Oh, right. I keep forgetting I have them in.' She ran her fingers through her hair. Kath had done a good job with the braids. They'd been in all summer and hadn't frayed. 'And you must be Mr Rigby?'

'That's the one. Hugo Rigby – estate manager.'

'Pleased to meet you.'

He dropped the secateurs into the wheelbarrow. 'I don't normally do the gardening myself, but we're a bit short-staffed the moment. In fact, I can't find Silas, our new gardener. I don't suppose you've seen him? Thin chap, white hair?'

'No, sorry,' said Astrid.

'Not to worry.' Hugo wiped his hands on his coat. 'You heading towards the reception?'

'Yes – then on to the potting shed.'

'Smashing,' he said. 'I'll walk with you.'

They set off, ducking through an arch with a yellow rose trailing over the top. Astrid stopped and brought her nose up to a flower. It smelt of violets and lemons. A scent so divine it made her close her eyes. She opened them again and turned to Hugo. 'The gardens look marvellous. Well done.'

'Thank you.' He puffed out his chest. 'I'm very lucky to work here.'

'And the art club are very lucky to be allowed to paint here too.'

'No, no...' He waved her gratitude away. 'It's a pleasure to have you all here. That's what I want at Abbotsford. Visitors to turn a corner and see someone at their easel, a slave to their muse.'

'Yes, that's a lovely idea,' she said.

Hugo's shoulders relaxed. 'That's good to hear. You see, the top brass think I'm a stick-in-the-mud. A bit old-fashioned.'

'I'm sure they don't.'

'Oh, they do, Astrid. But some things are worth fighting for.' He marched over to a sign stuck in the corner of the flowerbed. 'Like this, for example.'

Astrid leant over and peered at the sign. There was a cartoon of a bee. Above were the words 'Why not waggle like a bee?' Astrid straightened up. 'Sorry, what am I looking at exactly?'

'Waggle like a bee.' He stressed the waggle.

'Okay?'

'They were foisted on me. There was a memo to all English Trust gardens to put up interactive signs for kids.'

'Oh, I see.'

Hugo picked up the sign out of the ground and held it up by its wooden stake, as if he were at the front of a protest march. 'Why not just look at the bloody bee? Let it do the waggling?'

'I guess.'

There was a bead of sweat on Hugo's brow. Astrid

wondered if he'd get more worked up if she agreed or disagreed with him.

'I agree.'

'Good.' His cheeks were pink now. 'They're all over the woods as well. "Hop like a squirrel." "Make a wigwam out of dead branches and sticks." But what if kids don't want to, Astrid?'

Astrid thought about telling him that it wasn't such a big deal. What was wrong with a few signs to get kids to have some fun? They didn't really ruin the gardens, did they? But Hugo seemed in no mood to compromise.

'It's the same with social media.' He hooked his fingers in the air when he said, 'social media', as if it wasn't a real thing. 'According to head office, I've got to establish a relationship with visitors. Tweet every day… or something.' He paused for breath. 'The only relationship I have is with Mrs Rigby and that's between me and her.'

'I guess most companies have to do this sort of thing?'

'But we're the English Trust. We're not like other companies, Astrid.' Then he shrugged. 'I know, I know… I'm a stick-in-the-mud. I need to…' His voice trailed off. It seemed for a moment that he was going to change his mind. As if he was gripping a rusty key in a lock, that was too hard to turn over. 'No, no…' He gave up trying. 'Tradition is everything. These gardens have been the same since Elizabethan times. And people love them. I know, because I take the visitors' book home every evening and read their comments. That's what warms me in bed at night.'

'That and Mrs Rigby.' Where did that come from? Nervousness, probably. Mr Rigby was very intense.

'Mmm… oh, yes,' Hugo said flatly, the joke doing little to lift his mood. He looked at the bee sign in his hand. 'Right, this is going in the office. I keep pulling them out and Silas keeps putting them back. He thinks they're wonderful,' he growled. 'He's only been here a couple of days and he's throwing his weight around.'

This seemed a good time to leave Hugo to it. She said 'goodbye' and he bowed in front of her. 'Good day, Astrid,' he said, earnestly. Then he marched off towards the reception, head held high.

She could see him fitting in here four and a half centuries ago. Sweeping through the gardens in a long fur-trimmed coat. Lord of the manor. 'Don't forget to put something in the visitors' book,' he shouted, waving over his shoulder as if tossing a chicken bone to some trailing hound.

Twenty

Kabir was the only person in the potting shed. He was standing by the sideboard, taking out his art materials from a drawer. 'Hey, Astrid,' he said, as she walked through the door, 'what about that storm?' He shook his head in disbelief.

'I know – it was incredible.'

'I was thinking about you.' There was concern in his voice. 'Were you okay on your boat?'

'Yes, thanks Kabir. Safe as houses.'

He picked up his drawing pad, flicking through it until he found his latest painting. She glanced over his shoulder. It was a rough sketch in pencil. An outline of the top of the house rising behind the hedge, the flower border curving off to the greenhouse in the vegetable patch.

'That's great, Kabir. You've really found a beautiful balance there,' she said.

'It's okay, I guess.' He smiled weakly. This was as close as he'd come to praising himself.

Astrid hooked her thumbs under the straps of her rucksack. 'You mind if I keep you company in the garden today?'

'Of course. I'd like that.'

Frank appeared at the door. Annabelle was a couple of steps behind him. He held it open for her and she gave a little flinch of shock.

Frank saw that Astrid had noticed the gesture and winked at her. 'You know me, Annabelle... always the gentleman.'

She looked at him distrustfully. 'Thank you, Frank.'

Astrid and Kabir waited for the other two to get their art materials together before heading out. The subject of last night's storm came up again. Annabelle had hardly noticed it. 'The house has lovely thick stone walls, so I didn't hear a thing,' she said.

Frank had been up to check on his chalet in the morning and found the satellite dish had been blown down, which would, he groaned, 'need the Sky man coming out'. And that eased the chat over to Annabelle and her new digital TV box, which had been a revelation.

'For the first few weeks I never ventured past BBC4,' she said. 'But then one night I accidentally sat on the controller and went into triple figures and—' she clutched her necklace '—it was another world.'

'What kind of world?' said Kabir.

'Oh, just...' She was briefly lost for words. 'A cultural desert. Documentaries about people with strange ailments. Orange people selling mops and hideous jewellery. Men laughing all the time and challenging each other. I think the channel was called Dave?'

'I like Dave,' said Frank.

'I'm sure you do,' Annabelle said, dropping some coloured ink pens into her bag. 'But why would you name a television channel Dave? I mean, why not Sid or Alan?'

They all kept quiet.

Annabelle was on a roll. 'And you know some of the channels have a "plus one", where it's an hour behind in case you missed it?'

They all nodded.

'Dave has one and it's called Dave Ja Vu.' She raised her hands as if this was the most ridiculous thing she'd ever heard.

'That's really funny,' snorted Frank. 'You see, it's like that thing when you think you've done something before.'

'No, I understand that, Frank,' said Annabelle tersely. 'My point is – if you can't be bothered to arrive on time, you shouldn't be given another bite at the cherry.'

'It's not a dinner party, Annabelle. It's the flippin' telly. The problem with you—'

'Tell you what,' interrupted Kabir, 'why don't we get out there in the sunshine?'

They all grabbed the last of their things – art materials, bags and fold-out chairs – and bundled to the door. Frank didn't hold the door open for Annabelle this time. It was going to take a bit longer for the cold war between them to thaw out, thought Astrid.

Astrid did know all those TV channels though. She'd spent many an evening on her own in the London flat, scouring the cultural deserts past the 150 mark. That's where she'd discovered *Dogs Need Homes*, which, she thought, would be well worth catching up with sometime.

Frank and Annabelle went their separate ways after they left the gravel drive. There was no sign of Wren, who'd said she might not make it. It depended on whether her father could give her a lift.

Astrid and Kabir weaved their way to the small lawn in the far south-east of the garden. They sat down on a bench and Astrid dug out her sketch pad and pencils from her rucksack. He agreed to let her sketch him and she waited for him to set up his easel before starting.

'Why did you want to take up art, Kabir?' asked Astrid.

'Is my art that bad?' He laughed.

'Not at all. I keep saying – you should stop putting yourself down. Confidence… that's the secret ingredient to painting.'

He put up the half-finished drawing on the easel. 'You know when you go to an art sale in a gallery, and the paintings that are sold have a little fluorescent dot on them?'

'A little sticker?'

'Yeah. That's what I want.'

'A sticker?'

'Very funny.' He laughed again. 'I want to have created a painting, hung it up for sale and someone has come along and thought – yes, I want to buy that. And then they put a little sticker on it.'

'Then you've made a sale?'

'There's a bit more to it.' He set his watercolour box on the ledge of the easel and lifted the lid open. 'If someone buys it from a gallery at a decent price, then I will know I've made a real piece of art.' He paused, nodding. 'That's what I've always wanted.'

'I'm sure it's going to happen.'

As Astrid started sketching, Kabir set the rest of his materials out on the ledge. A sable brush, a square of white cloth and a glass jar that was half full of water. He sat there for a minute, taking in the scene in front of them. Working out the flow of colours and shapes.

He reached out to pick up the jar, then pulled his hand back. His eyes fixed ahead of him. 'You see that, Astrid?' He pointed towards the far hedge.

Astrid stopped sketching and stood up. She'd seen it too. A faint thread of smoke was rising vertically into the sky. She'd have missed it if it wasn't highlighted by dark woods on the hill behind. When she turned to Kabir, he was on his feet.

'Are they having a bonfire?' he said.

'I guess.' Astrid sniffed the air. 'Something's burning.'

They both walked down to the gap in the hedge. Ahead of them was a greenhouse. It was set in the middle of a vegetable patch that gently sloped up to a big shed tucked under the branches of an oak tree. There was nobody around.

A wisp of smoke was curling from under the greenhouse door. Astrid took the lead, tiptoeing through a bed of pumpkins to get to the door. She peered through the glass. There was too much smoke inside to see anything.

Kabir tapped his fingers quickly on the metal handle of the door. It was just cool enough to grip. Standing back, he pulled the door open with a straight arm and smoke billowed out. They watched it rise and fold into the air until it was clear enough inside to go in.

Inside there was still a lot of smoke. Behind the acrid smell of smoke were other aromas. The earthy sweetness of leaves and compost. And something else. Tangy, sickly.

On either side were thigh-high shelves stacked with pots of seedlings. Tomato plants trailed up strings tied at the roof.

At the back of the greenhouse was a dark shape enveloped by the smoke. 'Hullo?' Astrid edged forward. She could feel her heartbeat in her chest.

Kabir opened a vent in the pitched roof and the last of the smoke funnelled out.

'Oh, no...' Astrid gasped in shock.

In front of them was a man seated in a metal chair, his hands gripping the armrests. He was staring lifelessly towards the door.

Kabir turned to Astrid. 'You alright?'

'Yeah, I'm fine... don't worry.' She stepped forward and studied the man from the ground up.

A pair of smart black slip-on shoes.

Then muddy work trousers.

Then a plain white T-shirt.

At the hem of the T-shirt was a black scorch that ran vertically for a couple of inches. As if someone had been trying to set light to the material but had only singed it.

Kabir leant over the man. 'I've got to check. But I think...' There was no point saying it. The man was dead.

Kabir brought two fingers to the neck of the man, just under the jawline. A few seconds later he drew his hand away, then used his thumbs to close both eyelids. The man looked peaceful now. His long thin face composed. Head upright, topped off with a thatch of hair as white as shaving foam.

On the ground to the side of the chair were the remains of a newspaper. Most of it had been burnt down to black wafers. The last triangle of print was smouldering. Astrid stamped on it until it was out. Then she reached up and opened another couple of vents. They waited until all the smoke had left the greenhouse.

'Do we know who this is?' said Kabir.

'I think it's a gardener called Silas. I bumped into Mr Rigby just now and he said he was looking for him. Said he was tall with white hair.'

'Okay.' Kabir checked his watch. 'It's 2.05. They'll want to ask questions… the police, I mean.'

'I'm sure they will,' said Astrid, as Kabir started backing out towards the door. 'Hang on a minute, Kabir. Let's take a closer look.'

Kabir stopped. 'Alright then. It can't do any harm.'

Astrid got near to the dead man. His face had a waxy sheen. There was some slight bruising, no more than a dark shadow, just under the hairline. Her phone was in her pocket, but it didn't seem right to take photos.

She stood to the side of the chair. There was no way round as the chair was up against the greenhouse frame. That's when she noticed the reddish marks on his skin, just above the neckline of his T-shirt. It was a delicate fern pattern that unfurled just under his right ear. Flat on his skin. As if someone had painted it there. Kabir was next to her, scrutinising the same marks.

'That's strange,' said Astrid.

Astrid found a pencil in her pocket. She worked the tip under the neckline of the T-shirt, drawing it out towards her. They both peered at the skin underneath. The fern mark ran down his neck and on to his chest. Astrid pulled the pencil away and did the same thing to the lower hem of the T-shirt.

The fern mark was there too. It must run all the way from his neck down to his hip.

'Okay,' she said. 'Let's see what else there is.'

Together they made a thorough examination of the rest of the greenhouse. They studied the glass panes, looking for marks or fingerprints. They turned the plant pots on the shelves. Knelt down and checked the earth floor. They worked quickly. Efficiently. Both sure of what they were doing. Getting the scene settled in their minds, so they could go over any details later. Looking for clues.

At 2.10 on Kabir's watch, they stopped. Their search of the greenhouse hadn't turned up anything usual. Nothing at all. They left, went down to the arch in the hedge and pulled a bench across so no visitors might wander up there.

Kabir rang the police. He explained that he was a retired doctor. That there was no need to call an ambulance – just send someone to record the scene and take the body away.

When he put the phone down, he leant back in the bench. 'Astrid?' he said. 'Are you sure you're an art restorer?'

She laughed. And instantly felt bad about her reaction. That poor gardener. It was probably nerves again, she thought. 'It's a long story, Kabir.'

'We've got time.'

She told him all about the investigation at Sherborne Hall. How she'd found DeVine's body in the icehouse. That she'd regretted not spending more time at what would later prove to be a crime scene. The police had dashed over the evidence too. Which meant the whole mess could have been solved sooner. This time, she was going to get it right. 'Just in case.'

'Just in case?'

'A single detail could make all the difference.'

'I'm impressed. You were very calm back there. I was going to leave, and we would have missed those marks on the body.'

Over by the entrance barn, a few cars were pulling into the car park. Families were getting out and trailing down to form a queue. Little did they know, on this glorious late summer day, the kids' interactive treasure hunt wouldn't be taking place in the vegetable patch.

'Those marks,' said Astrid, 'they were very odd, weren't they?'

'Yes – but I know what they are.'

'Really?'

'I've seen it once before. I know exactly what happened to the gardener.' He looked her in the eyes. 'He was struck by lightning.'

Twenty-one

Over the road from the gardens was a pretty stone church, hemmed in on the west by a graveyard of jumbled mossy stones. To the east was a village green with a stone cross and a handful of benches.

Astrid, Frank and Annabelle were squeezed up on the bench nearest to the road. Wren wasn't there. Her father had swung into the car park, seen the house had been closed to the public and driven off again. They all had a good view back to the house and the comings and goings at the vegetable patch. Which, so far, had been riveting.

First, a couple of police officers in uniform arrived. A young man and an older woman, who seemed to be in charge. Kabir greeted them at the gap in the hedge. He'd agreed with Astrid that it was best if only he told them what they'd found. He'd put in the emergency call, and there was no point them repeating themselves. So, Astrid had taken the others out to the churchyard and told them about their gruesome discovery, including Kabir's theory of the lightning strike, which now seemed the only explanation.

The older woman officer spoke to Kabir for a while. The young man stood next to them, writing down what they said in a notepad. Then Mr Rigby arrived and introduced himself, although every time he started talking, the young officer stopped writing in his notepad.

Ten minutes later, a man in a white coat showed up with a briefcase, a camera and a tripod. The two police officers escorted him to the path to the greenhouse. He put on a pair of surgical gloves and went inside. All you could see was his dark shape moving around behind the glass, bending over now and then.

Frank reached into his bag and brought out a block of tinfoil. 'Did you know that you're more likely to be killed by a shark than by lightning?'

'Is that true, Frank?' said Astrid.

'Sounds about right,' said Frank, peeling the tinfoil to reveal a stack of white bread and pink ham sandwiches. He peeled off a sandwich from the top of the pile and passed it to Astrid.

'Thanks, Frank.' She was really hungry as Mr Rigby had shut down the café straight away when he heard the news and sent all the staff home.

Annabelle gingerly took a sandwich and they all carried on watching.

Next, another man arrived with a black briefcase, and was ushered through the gap in the hedge. 'Ooh, here we go. Forensics has arrived,' she said authoritatively.

'Do you know how police crime scenes work, Annabelle?' asked Astrid.

'Only from those TV shows I watch. The one I really love has a sassy female coroner and a grumpy cop.'

'What are the chances,' said Astrid.

'I know,' said Annabelle. 'It's called *The Coroner*. It can be a bit gruesome, but I'm absolutely hooked.'

'Thing is…' Frank had been deep in thought. 'If you lived inland, there's no chance a shark could get you.'

'What are you talking about, Frank?' said Annabelle.

'Being more likely to be hit by lightning than eaten by a shark. Not if you're a Swiss farmer. Then you need to worry about the cows. So, the saying, really… mmm.' His voice trailed off. Then he said, 'Hey, I've got a joke about someone who was hit by lightning on a golf course, if you want to hear it.'

'Frank,' huffed Annabelle. 'It's a bit inappropriate. And we're on church ground.'

'There's a vicar in it. If that helps?'

Annabelle shook her head.

Frank looked to Astrid.

'Maybe later, Frank.'

Out in the garden, the two police officers were waiting by the door. The forensics expert was taking photos inside. Every so often, a flash of light lit up the greenhouse like a lantern.

'I wonder if they'll use one of those blue light thingies?' said Annabelle.

'It's actually called a black light. It's a short-wave UV light.'

'Ooh… tell me more,' cooed Annabelle.

'I use one to scan paintings – to see if they've been repaired recently. Or there's an earlier version of the painting underneath.'

'So how does it work?' Annabelle took her eyes off the

gardens for the first time since they'd sat down and looked at Astrid expectantly.

'Alright. This is how it works. Some things fluoresce under UV. Certain minerals in oil paints, for example – especially lead. Then there's everyday stuff – detergents, tonic water, antifreeze. They glow too. Of course, at a crime scene they'll be looking for other stuff.'

'You mean, blood and…' Annabelle brought her voice down to a whisper '…bodily fluids.'

Frank perked up. 'That's the thing with those forensic shows. They always go into the room. Any room. Kitchen, library… whatever. And when they turn on that blue light of theirs, it's all over the place. Up the walls. Over the wardrobe.'

'Frank… please,' protested Annabelle.

'It's like,' Frank continued, 'a waiter ran in and spilt a tray of soup.'

Annabelle shuddered. 'Thank you for that, Frank.'

Across the road, Kabir appeared at the entrance to the car park. He checked left and right, although there had been hardly any traffic since they'd been sitting there. Then he hurried over to the bench. The others budged up to let him sit down.

'Thanks for speaking to the police, Kabir,' said Astrid.

'No problem.'

'So, what did they say?'

'Not much. I told them I'd seen a fatality from lightning before. That's why I was sure this was what we were looking at. They took my details and told me they might be in touch.'

They all sat there, eyes front. Astrid knew it was a bit ghoulish, but she was hanging around to see the body brought out of the greenhouse. They all were. Frank passed a sandwich down the row to Kabir, who ate it quickly.

'Do you think they'll want to talk to me, Kabir?' asked Astrid.

'I gave them your name, but they didn't seem too bothered. They're treating this as a freak event. Which it probably is.'

'You think so?' said Astrid.

'Looks like it. The thunderstorm came over yesterday afternoon and Silas took shelter in the greenhouse. His metal chair was in contact with the metal frame. So, when the greenhouse was struck by lightning, he didn't stand a chance. He was in the wrong place at the wrong time.'

'What time do we think he was killed?' asked Annabelle. It was the first time she'd used the word 'we'. But it felt right. Sitting there on the bench, it did feel like they were a team.

'Okay,' said Astrid. 'Well, I was watching the lightning coming in over the headland from the boat. I remember looking at the radio clock and it was 4.15. Sometime around then.'

'I was in the Admiral's Arms in Yarmouth,' said Frank. 'It's about a mile away. Storm comes over at 4.30. Remember saying to Derrick the landlord it was going to do some damage; 4.15 sounds about right then.' He wolfed down the last sandwich and scrunched up the tinfoil into a ball. 'So, Kabir – what happens if you're struck by lightning then?'

'Oh…' Kabir stretched his legs out, trying to get the circulation going. It was an even tighter squeeze with four of them on the bench. 'It depends on luck, really. Everything from mild burns to, well, what happened to Silas. It's a charge of ten million volts. That can cause deep muscle burn, especially near the bone. That's the most resistant part of the body to electricity.'

'Fascinating,' drawled Annabelle.

Kabir continued, 'The strike can cause cardiac arrest. Or scramble the brain. Stop it from giving messages to the rest of the body.'

'What messages?' said Frank.

'Like remembering to breathe.'

The other three grimaced and inhaled almost in unison.

'And what makes the difference between mild injuries and a fatality?' said Astrid.

'Conduction, usually. If say, you're wearing rubber-soled shoes or wellingtons.'

Astrid replayed the scene inside the greenhouse in her mind. Her memory was crystal clear. Silas had been wearing smart black slip-on shoes. That was a bit odd. And the clean white T-shirt. Neither matched with his scruffy work trousers. There were no other items of clothing or footwear in the greenhouse. So, he must have changed before taking shelter.

An ambulance came down the road and turned into the car park. It didn't have its siren on. They all watched as two paramedics in green overalls took out a gurney from the back and manhandled it through the garden to the greenhouse. They pushed it in through the door, and when they came out again Silas was lying on top, under a blue plastic sheet.

The ambulance left a few minutes later, again with the light off. The two officers and the forensic expert wandered out to the car park. Mr Rigby bustled out of the reception to see them off, waving at their cars as if they were relatives leaving after a long and enjoyable stay, and they should come back soon. Although they all knew they wouldn't. There was no yellow-and-black crime scene tape across the path. No white square tent over the greenhouse. Their job was done.

'So that's it then?' said Frank. 'Case closed.' As if he'd read Astrid's mind.

'Maybe not.' Annabelle squeezed out and stood up. She turned to face the others. 'We should investigate.'

Astrid was expecting someone to protest. Frank might have said it was a bad idea, seeing he was back at odds with Annabelle. But they all sat there, nodding. Mulling the idea over. Knowing that this was too exciting to walk away. That's why those TV crime shows were so popular – because nobody ever gets a chance to poke around at the scene of a bizarre death.

Astrid remembered the UV light. She'd shown Celeste how it worked against the portrait of her and her sister. Instead of putting it back in her work case, she'd slipped it into her rucksack. She rummaged it out, holding it at arm's length in front of her.

'Is that what I think it is?' said Annabelle excitedly.

'It sure is,' said Astrid. 'A forensic detective's UV light.'

Twenty-two

The only vehicles left in the car park belonged to them. Frank's white panel van, Kabir's black Prius and the lemon-yellow Beetle that Annabelle described as her 'summer runabout'.

Mr Rigby had wandered the gardens, and when he was satisfied nobody was around, he locked up the entrance barn doors and rumbled off in his maroon Jag. He must have seen their cars were still parked up and assumed they'd gone off somewhere else. The beach maybe, which was down a path from the church. Before he left, he propped up the 'Gardens Closed' sign against a traffic cone at the entrance.

As soon as the Jag was out of sight, the four of them sprang up from the bench. They all knew the seriousness of what they were going to do next but didn't care. They were about to break into an English Trust property and investigate the scene of a death. It wasn't something you'd put in the visitors' book.

They decided to take the path up through the woods and sneak in on the other side of the valley. It was dry underfoot, and they made good progress. First, up a lane that plunged into a tunnel of overhanging beech trees. It was deep and rutted, about six feet lower than the ground on either side. Probably an ancient bridleway worn down over the centuries by horses' hooves and feet.

Then they turned off along a narrow path that wound over a carpet of last winter's leaves. Over a flattened-down wire fence. And on to a wider path that headed downhill. There was the acorn and leaf sign. They were back on the English Trust map.

When they were level with the vegetable garden, Astrid took the lead and turned to face them. 'I don't think we should worry about the greenhouse. We've had a thorough look around. Right, Kabir?'

He nodded.

'Let's investigate the shed though,' she said. 'The police didn't even bother.'

They agreed and Astrid pushed through the undergrowth, holding back the branches for the others. She caught them up by the shed door and swung it open.

Inside, they were hit by a musty smell of earth and old wood. There was a whiff of something sharp and chemical, probably from a shelf of cans of paints along the back wall. Propped against the other two walls were garden tools – spades, forks, clippers. A wooded crate filled with trowels and gardening gloves.

'What are we looking for exactly?' said Frank, closing the door.

'I'm not sure,' said Astrid, glancing round the room. There was still enough light filtering in from the single window to see clearly. There was a waxed jacket on a peg to the side of the door. 'I'll check the pockets.'

Astrid didn't need to worry about telling the others what they should do. They all got to work. Kabir went over to the shelves and began moving the cans of paint. Frank checked the walls and floors. Annabelle examined the garden tools, running her thumb along the edge of the spades to check their sharpness – or deadliness, as she was clearly thinking.

Between them, they discovered nothing of interest. Astrid took the grubby packets of seeds she'd found in the jacket and pushed them back into the pocket.

'Let's get the UV light out then,' said Annabelle eagerly.

Astrid took the waxed jacket down from the peg and hung it over the window. It was almost complete darkness apart from a sliver of light creeping under the door. Kabir found an old potato sack and tucked it across the gap, so the room was now pitch-black.

'Excellent,' said Astrid, bringing out the UV lamp from her pocket. She clicked it on and held it up, casting a faint blue light, as soft as mist, over the shed. Then swivelled very slowly round, stopping on Annabelle. Her necklace was glowing bright blue.

'Oh, look at that,' said Annabelle, turning the stones on the necklace in her fingers.

'It's amber, isn't it? Amber is one of the minerals that fluoresces.'

'It is amber, yes. My husband bought it for me when he was on business in Prague. The stones are—'

'Nobody cares, Annabelle,' came a voice in the dark.

'I heard that, Frank,' said Annabelle.

'Okay, guys. Let's concentrate,' said Astrid, going over to the shelves. A few of the labels on the paint cans glowed white. She swung the lamp close to each of the walls. Near the floor. High up at the roof. But there was nothing. No shining specks or stains. Nothing suspicious. 'Sorry, guys, I don't think we'll find anything,' she said, her hand dropping by her side.

'Wait,' whispered Kabir. 'There was something in the corner, near the door.'

They all looked to the corner. It took a few seconds to see it. There was a faint glow behind a pile of sacking. Astrid stalked over and, pushing the sacking aside, gripped a pair of boots and held them up. The two glowing white objects were sports socks, one in each boot. She switched off her UV light. 'Frank, can you take the jacket from the window?'

They blinked as the light flooded into the shed. Astrid had a closer look at the pair of boots. 'Yes, it's just socks. They add fluorescent dyes to some washing powders.'

'Nice little pub quiz fact there,' said Frank.

Astrid put one of the boots down and turned the other upside down. Inside the gap of the heel and sole was a wedge of dried yellowy-brown mud. There was a ridge of the same dirt between the sole and the upper. She ran a nail under the heel and broke off a lump. She ground the dirt between her fingers. A shiver of excitement passed through her. This was a huge breakthrough, she thought. The first clue that there was a connection between the deaths of Victor and Silas.

'What is it?' asked Kabir. He'd noticed Astrid was smiling to herself.

'This mud looks exactly like the mud that I found on Victor Leech's shoes. The ones he wore the day he died.'

Astrid then told them how she'd visited Victor's widow up at the cul-de-sac. Offering to take his clothes to the charity shop. Going through the bag. She skated through this part, not sure if they'd approve of tricking a recent widow. She didn't need to worry. They all said they would have done the same thing.

'So where does this new information take us, Astrid?' asked Annabelle.

'Okay. It means Victor and Silas visited the same place.'

'Continue...' Annabelle made a circular motion with her hand. As if teasing out a conclusion from Astrid she'd already reached.

'And then within forty-eight hours, they're both dead.'

'Which means?'

'Okay, well—'

'Which means...' Annabelle stepped into the middle of the room '...we're now looking at a double homicide.' She put her hands up. As if she was a champion gymnast who'd just made a perfect landing. Waiting for full marks from the judges.

'Hang on... hang on.' Kabir damped Annabelle's celebration. 'We're forgetting something, aren't we?'

'We are.' Astrid knew what was coming.

Kabir continued. 'Silas was struck by lightning. That's how he died. I'm sorry, Annabelle, you'd have to be God to arrange that.'

'I guess.' Annabelle slunk back to the shelving and idly picked up a red bottle of tomato feed.

Astrid got her Chinese silk purse from her rucksack and took out another receipt. 'Even so, this is a big development.

And we need to know where that mud came from.' She dropped a few crumbs of dirt in the middle of the receipt and folded it up.

Annabelle put down the tomato feed and came over. 'Good thinking,' she said, watching Astrid tuck the square of paper back in her purse. 'It should be a clear ziplock bag, of course. But we'll make do.'

They carried on discussing the yellowy-brown mud. Where it might have come from. Frank had done a lot of building on the island and said he'd never hit clay this colour. Kabir said he'd rambled across the whole island and never seen anything like it. There was a rare seam of clay out there. But where?

As they talked, Frank took some measurements of the shed with a tape measure he said he always kept in his pocket. The measurements had nothing to do with the case, he explained. He needed a new shed and liked the proportions of this one.

They shuffled out into the sunshine and swung the door shut.

'Right then – phones out.' Annabelle dipped into her Orla Kiely shoulder bag and brought out a pink smartphone. 'You know what we have to do?'

They all looked blank.

'We need to set up a WhatsApp group.' She paused. 'And let's call it The Art of Murder Club.'

Twenty-three

Astrid got up at first light and took the bike up to the headland. She hadn't slept much the night before – the same thoughts on loop. The lightning. Impossible to arrange? The mud. Too much of a coincidence to ignore?

If she was being honest with herself, up until now, she'd wanted Victor's death to be suspicious. So she'd have something to distract her from her own unhappy thoughts. But now – there was no doubt. Something sinister was going on.

As usual, she pushed her bike up the last steep hundred yards of track. The trail was studded with sharp limestone. No mud though. Where was that yellowy-brown mud? That a healthy man had stepped in. Then drowned where nobody saw.

Where a gardener stood. Then met their death by ten million volts of electricity.

The mud would unlock it all. The mud was the key.

She got to the brow of the hill and the whole of the Isle of Wight appeared before her. This had become her favourite view on the island. You could see all four points of the compass.

South – sheer cliffs and the slate-grey English Channel.

West – the headland rising then tapering sharply down to The Needles.

East – the meadow sweeping down a flank of white cliffs broken by Freshwater Bay. As if a line of washing had been pulled down and pegged into the ground.

North – the Solent, hazy in the morning mist. Pushing into the scalloped bays of Totland, Yarmouth and Alum. There was something she hadn't noticed before. Above Alum Bay was a car park and a cluster of white buildings. A chairlift projected out over the cliff and dropped to the sea. It must be some kind of theme park.

Astrid got back on the bike, pointed it east down the grassy path and started freewheeling. The air was heavy with the scent of white clover and the vanilla of gorse bushes.

Swifts dashed across her path, skimming inches above the grass to pick off the flies above the cow pats. They flew out over the cliff, stabbed a wing down and turned back sharply. Swallows spend most of their life in the air. That's what she'd read in one of Uncle Henry's books. They travel back and forth from Africa, feeding and sleeping on the wing. Earlier this summer, she'd found a young swallow in a field above Hanbury. It had been knocked out of the air somehow and couldn't raise itself off the ground. She'd placed it on a stone wall and waited until it found its strength and flew off. Maybe it was here. Chasing ahead of her as she flew down the hill.

At the Tennyson Monument, she put the brakes on. Then she veered off to the north down a track through gorse bushes, bouncing down rutted tracks past farms and wheat fields, until she hit the muddy River Yar and was back at the boat by seven.

★ ★ ★

She ate breakfast – a bowl of wheat biscuits that were the size and texture of scouring pads, but with a splash of milk and chopped bananas, were quite tasty. Then she finished the quick sketch of Kabir that she'd barely started the day before. As it was still early, she had time to have a Google around on the laptop and check Frank's theory that sharks were more dangerous than lightning. Turns out it wasn't true. Close, though.

On average, lighting kills roughly 2000 people each year around the world. Sharks claim about a half-a-dozen lives. Surprisingly, cows are five times more dangerous than sharks. Maybe that's why Swiss farmers put cowbells on their necks, thought Astrid. So they can hear them creeping up on them.

It was definitely time to leave for work.

She made a flask of coffee and went to the high street to buy her usual working lunch for later – a 'meal deal' from the mystery supermarket. It was £3 for a sandwich, snack and drink chosen from a chiller cabinet at the back. Which of course threw down a challenge – to get what would be the most expensive combination without the 'deal'. Why bother with £1 egg and cress sandwich, when a 'cheese triple' was worth twice as much? Then load up with a jumbo-size bag of tortilla chips, washed down with the highest priced energy drink. A natural one. Not the ones that make you want to go snowboarding or shout in the street.

So far, she'd peaked at a total worth £6.27 – all for £3. It was the kind of small triumph that gave her a spring in her step as she left the shop. Kath would be proud. Since Astrid had been on the island, she'd sent her a postcard and exchanged a bunch of texts. Although she hadn't explained the latest mystery she'd been thrown into. They could catch up later. There had still been no reply from her own father though.

By four o'clock, a straight seven hours of working with a half-hour break for lunch, the last of the paintings were photographed and tested. She stood back from the long table and cracked her knuckles. Now all she had to do was write up a report for Andy Marriot.

What happened next was up to Celeste – the only heir to the Wade estate. She could pay off what HMRC reckoned they were owed then sell off the collection, along with the house. Astrid took the dust sheet from the table, folded it up and packed it in her work case. Then she walked to the door. Under the sealskin canoe, and the pennants hanging down from the beams. Past the figureheads either side of the door and down the two flights of stairs.

On the ground floor, she stopped. Held by the sense that she was leaving too early. When she'd first looked around the house, there were two rooms that were locked. Maybe she should check them again.

The first door was still locked. She instinctively ran her hand along the top of the frame. Sure enough, she felt a small cold key. She put it in the lock and it turned. The door creaked open and she fumbled for the light switch. It was a deep room, with blue velvet curtains drawn across the view to the rear gardens.

There was a bed by the far wall. No bedspread. The only sheets were draped over an armchair and a wardrobe. As if someone had changed their mind about covering things up, and just walked out. It was a teenager's room. She could tell straight away. There were schoolbooks on the desk among mascots and fluffy pens. And there were posters everywhere. Of sailing boats carving through waves the height of a house. Tacking down jade seas. A map of the world with red pins. A calendar on the wall, turned to August 2018.

There wasn't a sound. The house was asleep – waiting to be woken up. Flattered by new paint. Windows cleaned to let the sunlight in. A new family to come and write a new story for it.

Waiting. Perfectly still. Just bricks and glass and wallpaper. Lifeless, because everything had stopped in this room. Harlow Wade's old room.

The town was busy and noisy and she was glad of it. She left the house after she found Harlow's room, and didn't look back.

Halfway along the high street, she saw Wren coming out of a shop on the other side of the road. She was heading to the square. Astrid crossed over and caught up with her.

'Hi there.'

Wren looked up and smiled. 'Hey, Astrid. How you doing?'

'Yeah, good thanks. What you up to?'

'Just getting some art supplies.' She patted a large black folder that was tucked down by her side. 'Needed a new portfolio for my drawings.'

Astrid checked her watch. It was 4.30 p.m. 'You fancy getting a drink? Something to eat?'

They settled into a table at The Chatterbox. There was only

half an hour before closing, and the place was clearing out. Coffee and cake – that was the order. Astrid said she was going to pay – 'my treat – no arguing' – as she'd saved so much from a week of meal deals. She explained her tactics as Wren listened politely then said, 'I've been maxing out the meal deal for ages.'

'Oh, is that right?' said Astrid, more deflated than she was expecting. 'You beat £6.27?'

'Yup – £6.59 if you get the ham and cheese triple.'

'Mmm… smart move.'

They both burst out laughing. Melody drifted over to the table to take their order – two coffees, and two slices of red velvet cake, as recommended by Melody. It was the end of the day, so she was cutting big slices now, because she was 'beyond caring'.

When Melody went back inside the café, Astrid asked to see Wren's artwork in the portfolio. She passed it slowly across the table. Astrid went through it as Wren sat silently, fiddling with the silver rings on her fingers. Avoiding eye contact.

There were hundreds of drawings and paintings, from snippets of views and details of trees and plants to full-size compositions. Warrior queens posing against night skies filled with pale moons. Dragons trapping goblins between their claws. These must be based on video games she'd never heard of, Astrid thought. As she got deeper into the file, the work got better and better, the technique more assured. There was nothing that Wren couldn't do.

'You know you're a brilliant artist, Wren?'

'Aww… thanks,' Wren said, without looking up.

'No, you really are,' Astrid said firmly. 'And I need to know that you believe that.'

Wren swept the hair from her face and looked at her. 'Okay, I do.'

'And you can handle so many mediums. Watercolours, oils, pen and ink. And everything you do has your own style to it.' She began slipping the artwork back into the portfolio. 'What are you going to do with this talent of yours, Wren?'

Wren shrugged.

'Do you go to art college at the moment?'

'I have a place at the Royal College of Art in London at the end of summer.'

'Woo,' Astrid whistled. 'That's one of the top colleges for art in Britain.'

Wren took the file from the table and tucked it back down beside her. She let her hair slip over her eyes. 'I don't think I'm going to go.'

'What?'

'It's complicated.' Wren angled her body away from the table and gazed out to sea.

'Wren, listen. It's not my business, but I have to say this – you must take that course. You have such an incredible talent and you can't waste it.'

Melody approached with a tray held out in front of her. Wren said quietly, 'We'll see.' A hitch in her voice. Then she drew herself up to the edge of the table and rubbed her hands. 'This looks fab,' she said as Melody laid out the drinks and plates of cake. The discussion about art college was clearly over.

They ate in silence for a minute or so, each mouthful bringing Wren back to her usual enthusiastic self.

'Good, huh?' said Astrid.

'Delish.'

Their phones beeped at the exactly the same time. They both raised an eyebrow. Astrid reached into her bag for her phone. Wren retrieved hers from a pocket down by the armrest. They read the message, then Astrid said, 'Annabelle wasn't joking about setting up that WhatsApp group.'

Wren read the message out loud, even though Astrid could see the same thing. 'Welcome to The Art of Murder Club. This will be the hub for all information, clues and theories on the deaths of Victor Leech and Silas the gardener.'

'The death of the gardener...' said Wren, slack-jawed.

Astrid put her phone down. 'I was just about to tell you. The gardens were closed for a reason yesterday. Something very strange happened.'

For the next five minutes, Astrid laid out the story. Starting with how she and Kabir had found Silas's electrified body in the greenhouse. Ending with the discovery of the unusual mud on Silas's boots, the same mud that was stuck to Victor Leech's shoes.

Wren wolfed down the last of her red velvet cake. She ran her finger round the plate and licked it. 'This is going to be great – between us we can solve this.'

Astrid lined up her fork on the plate and crossed her hands. 'I'm not sure if that's such a good idea.'

Beep

They each picked up their phones. 'Here we go,' said Wren. 'Frank's in.'

Frank
Happy to take charge of this, Annabelle.

Beep

Annabelle
Thanks, but I'll lead the investigation.

'This could get out of hand,' said Astrid. 'I've already told a whopping lie to the harbour master – don't ask – and I don't want to draw any more attention to it.'
Beep

Frank

A small video appeared on the screen. Three seconds of a buck-toothed toddler shaking their head, a perplexed expression on their face.
Beep

Annabelle
Let's not use GIFs on this group, Frank.

Beep

Frank
Landed a big one yesterday!!!! 37 lbs on sweetcorn and Spam. Size 16 hook.

Beep

Annabelle
What?

Beep

Frank
Sorry. That was meant for my carp fishing group.

'That's exactly what I'm talking about,' said Astrid. 'This could go seriously wrong. And I could get in a lot of trouble.'

'Come on, Astrid.' Wren made praying hands. 'It'll be wicked.'

'I'm not sure, um…'

Melody came over and collected up the plates and empty cups. She told them the café was now closing but they could hang on for as long as they wanted. As she spoke, a volley of beeps came in on their phones. Astrid paid the bill, leaving a nice tip.

Wren thanked her and was straight back to the phone. 'Kabir is keen.'

Kabir
I might be able to get hold of both coroner's reports. I have a few contacts.

Annabelle
That would be marvellous – are you sure?

Kabir
What's the worst that can happen? I get struck off?

Frank
Do it!

'You see, Astrid… there's a lot of skills in this group.' Wren's eyes glittered with excitement. It was nice to see she was well clear of her gloomy patch earlier. 'We could crack it together.'

Beep Beep Beep

Annabelle
What about you two – Astrid and Wren?

Kabir
Come on. We need you both.

Frank

Another GIF. This time an animation of a ginger cat with huge eyes and a downturned face. The word 'Pleeease' underneath.

Astrid turned her palms up in resignation. 'Alright.'

'Yussss!' Wren started typing a message to the WhatsApp group, reading aloud as she thumbed in the words.

Astrid is with me now and we are deffo in. Long live The Art of Murder Club.

Then she pushed her fist out to bump with Astrid's. As she did, she noticed the time on her digital watch. 'Hey, I better split.'

'Your dad picking you up?'

'No, no. He doesn't know I'm here. I'm getting the bus.'

'Okay, well, I'll see you later.'

Wren backed out and navigated her way down the pavement towards the bus stop. A green double-decker with Southern Vectis written on the back eased into the kerb. The driver came out and helped her aboard. Astrid's phone beeped a few times. The news that the group was complete had obviously gone down well.

Astrid had to admit that, between them, they did bring a lot to the table. Her art forensic skills, Frank and Wren's local knowledge, Annabelle... well, there might be a few tips Annabelle had picked up from those TV shows that could come in handy. If she relaxed a bit. And tried to get on with Frank. Then maybe working as a team wasn't such a bad idea.

Twenty-four

Astrid sat at the table, content that she had nowhere else to go. She took out her sketch book and dashed off a quick drawing of Wren from memory. Then she sat back and stretched her legs out, facing the last golden rays of the evening. She eyed the rail of the pier. It was almost chest height. Could Cynthia really have thrown her husband over it? She was strong enough to lift two metal garden chairs without blinking, but a grown man? That was another kettle of fish.

A family of five shuffled up to a spare table. They scraped the metal chairs back and sat down, the father lifting a white plastic bag and plonking it down in the middle of the table. He dished out a parcel of fish and chips. Astrid watched them tear open the paper wrappers and dig in with their fingers.

Ten minutes later, Melody emerged from the side door of the café. She locked up, then crossed the entrance of the pier and walked on past a row of parked cars. When she reached a stone slipway down to the waterline, she stopped and checked over her shoulder. Then she tiptoed down to the shore.

Strange, thought Astrid. The double-checking that she wasn't being followed bit. Which was a good enough reason to follow her. Astrid gathered her things and walked through the entrance of the pier.

She leant over the right-hand rail. There was no sign of Melody on the sliver of shoreline below. It was only twenty yards long. After that, the water came all the way up to the sea wall. So there was no way Melody could have gone that way. She must have turned back and carried on under the pier.

On the other side of the pier was another short stretch of shingle beach at the bottom of the beer garden of The George hotel. No sign of Melody there. So, she must be under the pier.

The gaps between the big wooden planks were too thin to see down there. All she could hear was the waves lapping up against the rocks. Astrid left the pier and followed Melody's route past the parked cars and down the slipway.

There was a jumble of rocks before you got under the pier. Astrid clambered over them and blinked in the shade. Melody was sitting in a shallow bowl of dry sand, her back against a sloping flat rock. She exhaled a cloud of grey smoke. Astrid caught the whiff of marijuana.

'You mind if I join you?'

Melody kept her eyes straight ahead on the low waves forming around the pier. 'Sure…' she said sleepily. 'I'll budge up.' She shuffled sideways a few feet, and Astrid sat next to her. Five yards ahead of them, gentle waves rushed at the sand, the sound echoing off the planks above them.

'This is a good spot,' said Astrid. 'I'd have loved this as a teenager.'

'It's my favourite place to get my buzz on.' Melody took

a long drag on her joint, the tip glowing orange. Then she blew the smoke out of her nose. 'Need to come down after my shift to decompress.'

A family walked above them on the boards. They could hear perfectly an argument they were having about some chocolate the kid wanted.

'The acoustics are weird down here,' said Astrid.

'Yeah, it's great. You can hear what people are saying... if you wanna tune in.' She pushed her heels into the sand. 'You ever been a waitress?'

'A couple of summers at uni. It's not bad money. But the customers...'

'Tell me about it.'

'Most were pretty good. But some couples...'

'The ones on dates, right?'

'Definitely the worst.' Astrid leant back against the rock. 'Especially the man. They'd always want to taste the wine, then make a big deal of pretending it was no good and send it back. You just give them the same thing and they love it.'

Melody chuckled. 'You want a drag?' She held out her joint.

'I'm good, thanks. Not my thing.'

'Sure, sure.'

'And there's all that finger-snapping,' Astrid carried on. She deepened her voice. '"Can I get the cheque?"' She laughed. 'As if they're trapped in some nineties' American rom-com.'

'Tell me about it,' Melody said again. 'And it's all about the allergies now.'

'Is it?'

'Yeah – we're red hot on allergies in the café. We have

to be. Nuts. Milk. Wheat. Right? Then you get one you've never heard of. Like today. Some posh lady... sailing type. Should have stayed in Cowes. She says she'll die if she eats a caper.'

'A caper?'

'Yeah. Whatever that is. I say I've never heard of them. She says, "Well, I'm not sitting here playing Russian roulette with your salad niçoise if you don't mind." Gets up and storms out.' Melody threw her head back and roared with laughter. Then she abruptly stopped laughing and stared at the planks above her, as if unsure why she wasn't looking at the sky at night. She turned to Astrid. 'Sorry – do I know you?'

'Oh, you served us about ten minutes ago.'

'My bad. Busy day.'

'And I was here a few days back. When they discovered that body in the water. Remember?'

'Remember?' Melody sat up straight. Eyes wide. 'Nothing happens on the island and then that. Unbelievable. All those crabs. You ever seen *Deadliest Catch*?'

Astrid shook her head.

'Deep-sea fishing TV show. They pull up these big cages from the sea and they're like... like, full of crabs. Full. It was like that... but a face. Awesome.' She pinched the joint between her thumb and forefinger. The end glowed orange, burning close to her skin. 'It is.' She flicked the butt out into a wave, which gobbled it up back into the sea.

'So, Melody.'

'Yup?'

'The man who got dragged out of the water – did you ever see him hanging around the pier?'

Melody wiggled her nose. She said she couldn't remember. That there were so many customers every day and she tried her best to forget all of them. Plus, she confided, most of the time she was 'baked'.

The tide had retreated almost as far as it would go. You couldn't tell just by looking at it. Astrid had thought about going for a sail that afternoon and checked the charts. Low tide was 5.26 p.m. But then she'd bumped into Wren, and then Melody, and was now under a pier.

Melody got up, brushed some crumbs of weed from her sweatshirt and said goodbye. Then she double-checked that Astrid wasn't 'the Feds'. Which Astrid said she wasn't, assuming that meant the police. Melody said goodbye again, then went into a monologue about her job and her co-workers, most of whom she liked. Then she raised her hand, palm facing forward, and made a circular motion that seemed to surprise her as much as Astrid. 'Bye.'

'Bye, Melody.'

Astrid watched her retrace her steps over the sand, then sank back against the rock. It was a good spot. You could see all the way up the coast. Along the sea wall to The Needles' Eye. Beyond to the private jetty that jutted out from the gardens on the peninsula.

The sea had retreated enough to leave a few feet of dry land at the base of the sea wall. You could now walk all the way to the pier of The Needles' Eye, if you wanted to. Anyone could leave the high street and get access to the gardens. Victor could have.

Astrid picked her way through the rocks at the base of the sea wall. She made good progress and was at the private jetty and up the ladder about five minutes later. Standing for a moment, she thought about what Victor might have done next if he'd gone this way. Where would his nosiness take him? The pier was in good sight of the house. So, unless he was feeling bold, he'd probably want to quickly get to the cover of the bank of rhododendrons ahead of her.

The bushes were over ten feet high, with tightly packed leaves. She closed her eyes, put her hand over her face and pushed in, her work case snagging on twigs. Once through, she ducked down. There was a lot of space under the canopy of leaves. Twisted ropes of branches spun out from a central trunk. Some had sunk down to the bare earth, resting on their elbows then rising up again. She stepped over the branches and shouldered her way out into the light again.

On the other side was a meadow. It was the shape of a broad thumb pushing out into the sea. A few yards away was a faint path beaten down by the tread of feet. It appeared from a gap in the bushes – which was probably the easiest way through. She joined it and walked out into the meadow. The grass either side was knee-high. Then it opened out into a mown square the size of half a tennis court. You wouldn't see it unless you were upon it.

And there in the middle was an oblong of freshly dug earth. It was about three feet by seven. The size of a grave. Her heart skipped a beat. To the side of the oblong were some lumps of earth that had been dug out and not put back. Some of the lumps were yellowy-brown – exactly the same colour as the mud on Victor's and Silas's boots.

★★★

It took her another twenty minutes to get back to the boat. She just managed to get to the beach by the pier before the water reached the sea wall. Back at the boat, she put her work case on the table and opened it, her hand trembling slightly. It was a shame that none of the others were here. Everyone, especially Annabelle, would have loved to be in on this. In a few minutes she would know whether there was a connection between the deaths of the two men and the mysterious trenches that she'd just found.

She took out the following items:

- A bottle of clear Gamsol solvent
- A small glass pipette
- A magnifying glass
- A pair of scissors
- Three acrylic paint brushes – size 4, medium
- Three glass phials
- Three small square sheets of white watercolour paper

When she'd arranged them neatly on the table, each phial and a brush alongside a fresh sheet of paper, she searched in her purse for the three samples that were folded into receipts. She took the first one – *Victor's boots*, as she'd written in pen – and gently unwrapped it, tapping the earth into the hinge of the receipt. Then she held it over the lip of one of the phials and nudged the crumbs down with the tip of the brush. She went through the same process with the other two samples, making sure she had the same amount of earth for each phial.

Next was the solvent. Two drops for each phial. Screw

on the lid and give it a vigorous shake. Already she could see that the colour of the liquids was the same – a rich oily umber. Her heart gave another flutter. But there was still one more thing to do before she was sure.

On each piece of watercolour paper, she painted a square from the samples. Each time she used a different brush, working the colour up to the edge of the paper. After a minute, they were dry. She lined them up alongside each other, so their edges touched.

Taking the magnifying glass, she studied the colour from one sheet to the next. And back. There was no discernible difference between the colours of each sample. Only a mass spectrometer could tell with one hundred per cent certainty. This was good enough though. She sat back to steady herself.

There it was. Victor and Silas had stood on that freshly dug earth, out by the meadow. Hidden from the house by the bank of bushes. Then forty-eight hours later, they were both dead. Only she, Astrid Swift, had noticed. Just in time. Before the evidence faded and history healed over the truth. The trenches were still there. But what, or whom, was in them?

Twenty-five

Annabelle
A grave!!!

Kabir
Grave?

Wren
Grrrave? Holy F!

Frank
You sure, Astrid?

Astrid hurriedly punched in a response. She could see that Annabelle was typing and didn't want her to get out of sync with the conversation. Or have Annabelle take control – this was her investigation.

It is exactly the size of a grave. There was some earth to the side that had been dug out but not put back in.

Wren sent a black-and-white GIF of a pale vampire rising

stiffly from its coffin, which Astrid knew was from *Nosferatu* –
the original version. Then Annabelle's contribution popped up.

> The way I see it is we have to investigate this grave. If
> the earth there is exactly the same as on Victor's and
> Silas's shoes it's our strongest lead yet. The police aren't
> interested so it's up to us.

Annabelle's next message appeared almost instantly.

> Sorry, Wren, we agreed not to use GIFs in the group.

> *Frank*
> (With a GIF of Homer Simpson shaking his head and the
> subtitle 'No Way'.)
> No, we didn't. You be you, Wren.

Annabelle didn't respond for a while as Astrid and the
others, in a torrent of messages, formed a plan. They were
going to dig up the grave (everyone agreed that's what it was).
And it had to be tonight before the evidence 'deteriorated',
as Kabir said. Which was a chilling thought that needed little
more explanation.

Frank had some tools he could bring – spades, flashlights,
ropes. Kabir said he'd be on time, but had to think of an
excuse to get out to the house. It was best, he said, that he
'kept his wife in the dark'. Which prompted Frank to make
a joke about mushrooms that sort of free floated in its own
loneliness on the message thread, while everyone wondered if
that was the first time Kabir had mentioned he was married.

Then Wren said she'd sneak out and get a bus into town. They could all meet at the gates of The Needles' Eye. Various meeting times bounced back and forth before the four of them agreed on 9 p.m., just after dark. They waited for Annabelle, who eventually got over her huff and said this:

Right. I'll be there at 9pm. Probably a bit earlier. I have a nice Canon DSL camera, which I can use to take some photos of evidence. I'll also buy some plastic gloves and ziplock bags. But let's hope we don't have to use them.

Everyone knew she didn't mean the last bit. She was itching to find something gruesome and pop it in a ziplock bag.

Around two hours later, Astrid turned the corner into the alley alongside The Needles' Eye. Annabelle was already there, standing in the shadows. She pulled up the collar of her overcoat and stepped out into the light of a streetlamp, as if she were in a black-and-white detective movie. 'Are you alright, Annabelle?'

'Couldn't be better, Astrid. This whole thing is just so...' She grinned inanely. Astrid had thought *she* was excited to be doing some late-night excavating, but Annabelle was in another league. 'I can't believe we're here. Investigating a crime.'

Astrid leant against the gates. 'Maybe a murder?'

'I know – even better,' gushed Annabelle. 'The thing is. Do we even have any suspects for either of these deaths?'

Astrid leant against the gates. 'For Victor, there's always Cynthia.'

'His widow?'

Astrid told her how Cynthia had seemed almost relieved that her husband had died. It was understandable, she said. Now Cynthia could emerge from the shadow of her overbearing husband and be the centre of attention for once. Was that enough of a reason to kill him? Annabelle was sure it was.

'She's our chief suspect then,' she said, rubbing her hands together. 'Now, who's in the frame for Silas?'

'Mr Rigby.'

'Okay. Let's hear it,' she said matter-of-factly.

'I met Rigby in the garden and he was complaining about the new signs. The ones for the kids. You know – waggle like a bee. That kind of thing.'

'Oh, I quite like them.'

'Yes, and so did Silas. Mr Rigby has been pulling them out and Silas has been sticking them back in again. Which really annoyed him.' When she said it aloud, Astrid realised how absurd that would be. To kill someone over signs. Again, Annabelle had no doubts.

'It's a motive. Let's not rule it out.' She smiled. 'And well done.'

This was the first time Astrid had spoken to Annabelle alone. One on one, she was much friendlier.

Footsteps were getting louder from around the corner. Astrid rubbed the goose bumps on her arms. It had got much chillier now the sun had gone down. She reached into her bag and brought out a long-sleeved fleece top – a new purchase from the charity shop.

Frank and Wren rounded the corner. Frank had an old-fashioned canvas duffel bag slung over his shoulder. There were some wooden handles poking out the top. Wren had a basket on her lap with torches and camping lamps in it. Astrid finished putting on her fleece as they came up to them.

'Lovely night for it,' said Frank, throwing the duffel bag to the ground with a clank. He pointed at it. 'Brought some spades. Pickaxe. Some rope.'

'Rope?' said Astrid.

Frank rubbed his hands. 'We don't know what's down there. Could be heavy?'

The thought hung between them. Something heavy could be down there, and between them, they might have to haul it out with ropes. It was a slightly less irresistible idea now, so they were glad when Kabir appeared round the corner to puncture the mood.

He was wearing tennis gear – pressed white trousers and a white shirt under a cream V-neck jumper. In one hand he had a black sports bag. In the other, a tennis racket, which he waved cheerily at them. They stood in silence, staring at him.

'You lot okay?' he said anxiously.

'It's the, um…' Annabelle looked him up and down. 'The outfit.'

'Oh, right. Yes.' He pinched at his jumper. 'Sorry, sometimes you forget you're wearing clothes.'

'But why are you wearing those clothes, Kabir?' asked Wren.

'Well, I've actually told Jean, that's my wife, that I'm going to my regular tennis session at the sports centre tonight. Which I feel is acceptable. All marriages need secrets. Right?' He gave them a thumbs up, but no time to reply. 'Anyway,

I'm quite pleased to get out of tennis. I'm terrible at it. My second serve is shocking, and I have no backhand to speak of.' He paused for breath. 'Sorry, I'm rambling because it's so exhilarating to be here. Isn't it?'

'It sure is,' said Wren, flipping on a torch from her basket and pointing it under her chin. 'It's almost too delishushly exciting,' she moaned.

'Sorry, Wren,' snapped Annabelle, 'we need to concentrate.' The bossy Annabelle was back.

Wren switched off the torch. 'Soz.'

'Right. Now, do we all know the plan?' said Astrid, keen to take the organising role before Annabelle did.

They all nodded.

'Then... let's do this,' she said, fishing her key out of her pocket.

'Hang on,' said Frank. 'We need to synchronise our watches.'

'Er... why?' said Annabelle. 'We're not splitting up, are we?'

'No, we're not,' said Astrid.

'Okay,' mumbled Frank. 'Seemed like the sort of thing we should do.'

'Right then – let's crack on.' Astrid checked back down the alley then opened the iron gate. They all filed through and waited for her to lock it again.

Ahead of them, the house sat in the dark, the ridge of the roof almost fused with the inky black sky. The only light was the faint glow of the mainland to the north. They made their way round the gravel path to the back of the garden. It was pitch-black. Completely silent – except for the crunch of the gravel and the rattle of Frank's duffel bag.

A light went on in an upstairs window. Wren whispered. 'There's someone there?'

'No, no,' said Astrid, 'there's a few lamps on timers in the window. It's to make the house seem occupied.'

'So, it's okay to turn the torches on now?' said Annabelle.

'Yeah – that's fine.' said Astrid. 'We're well away from the gate now.'

Wren switched her torch on. She rooted in her basket and handed out torches to the others. Astrid led the way, fanning the light on the path. Annabelle, Wren then Frank followed, with Kabir at the back. He swung his torch beam out into the garden, throwing a silver glow over the tops of the trees. High in the branches, something clattered through the twigs, sending a fall of leaves.

'Jeez.' Kabir's voice cracked. 'What was that?'

'Something that lives in a tree?' said Frank. 'Just a wild guess though.'

'Ignore him, Doctor,' said Annabelle.

'Please, call me Kabir.'

'Listen, guys.' Astrid stopped and turned to them. 'There's nothing to worry about. So, try and stay calm.' It felt like she was trying to convince herself though. Now they were here – in the pitch-darkness – it was all a bit creepy.

She wasn't the only one who was nervous. Annabelle kept checking over her shoulder at every noise. Or stopping to stare up at the light in the window, as if the house might wink at her. Wren and Kabir didn't say a word. Only Frank seemed to be relaxed. He whistled to himself, the duffel bag swaying at his shoulder. As if he was a sailor on shore leave.

They stopped when the path reached the gap in the

rhododendrons. It was overgrown, the branches on either side meshing together. Astrid stepped through, pushing her back against the cold leaves so there was room for the others to squeeze past.

On the other side, they lined up in front of the meadow. Astrid scanned the meadow and found the path out to the broken earth. There was a dampness in the air now that hung low to the ground. Each step felt like pushing softly through a cold current. 'Here it is,' said Astrid, pointing out the oblong of broken ground with her torch.

Frank propped the duffel bag on the grass and worked at the string around the neck. When it was loose, he tipped out the contents – two pointed spades, a pickaxe and a coil of thick rope. He held up one of the spades. 'Who fancies it?'

Kabir picked a leaf out of his jumper. 'Sorry, I better be careful. Or Jean will be asking why I went to play tennis and came back covered in mud.'

'Sorry,' said Annabelle. 'I'd rather not get too grubby if you don't mind. I was in a rush and could only find my new Superga pumps.'

'No problem,' said Astrid. 'You can all point the torch beams on the ground as me and Frank dig.' She put the torch in her pocket, took the spade from Frank and went over to the trench.

'Before you get started,' said Wren, 'are we sure this is a grave?'

'Okay, look at this.' Astrid took the torch out and slowly scanned the edge of the broken earth. 'It's exactly the same dimensions as a grave, isn't it?' The others muttered in agreement. Astrid pointed at the jumble of earth. Here and there were clods of dirt that were cut square on one side. 'There, see? It's been dug out by hand, with a sharp spade. You agree, Frank?'

'Definitely.'

'And look at this.' Astrid cast the torch beam to the side of the earth. The grass was flattened down and muddy. 'You can see that the dirt was set aside over there. Then something was maybe put down the hole.'

'Probably,' interrupted Frank.

'Probably put down the hole,' said Astrid. 'And we have to find out what it is.' She laid the torch down next to the side of the broken ground. The beam pointed low over the water. She picked up the spade and stuck it into the soil. The others gathered round in a semicircle, like herons round a goldfish pond.

'One more thing,' said Kabir.

'Go on,' said Frank, his spade held in both hands.

Kabir continued. 'Are we, absolutely, and I mean one hundred per cent, sure this is a good idea?'

Astrid ran her hand over the back of her neck, which was cold from the damp air. Or just the fear of what they might find. 'I'm sure it is. And it has to be done tonight,' she said, raising her boot and forcing the spade deeper into the earth.

Wren handed out a couple of camping lamps that she said she'd found in her father's garage. Kabir set them out at either end of the dug earth. They cast a soft yellow light over the ground, enough light not to bother with the torches. The other three started idly switching their torches on and off. Or pointing them up in the branches or out at the pier.

Astrid had done some digging with her uncle in his garden

when she was younger. Planting flowers and shrubs. It was even easier now she was older. Frank also knew what he was doing. He explained that he used to have an allotment, until he got thrown off for burning a car tyre. Plus, he'd done a fair bit of digging on building sites, so it was 'child's play'.

The two of them worked steadily, throwing the soil well away from the hole so it didn't drain back in. The earth was damp and heavy after the storm. The first six inches at least. Then it became drier and easier to dig out. In only half an hour Astrid and Frank had the trench dug out to knee level.

Astrid took a breather, sitting back on the lip of the hole. Frank prodded the ground with the spade to check if they were going to hit something. A slight breeze had picked up and small waves were breaking on the sea wall.

'I heard something,' hissed Annabelle, aiming her torch at the waves. The beam dissolved before it got there.

'For crying out loud, Annabelle – chill out,' said Frank. 'I thought you liked all this CSI stuff.'

'It's a little different to when you're watching it on TV, Frank.'

'You were alright in the shed at Abbotsford,' he added.

'Big difference. We're now standing around in the dark digging up...' she shuddered '...something.'

'*Someone*, you mean,' replied Frank.

'Good point,' said Wren, narrowing the beam of her torch on Frank's boots. 'So what do we do when we find the body?'

'Let's make that decision when we get to it,' said Astrid, dropping back in the hole.

A few minutes later, the work got harder. They hit a heavier layer of clay, which kept sticking to the spade. Astrid ran her thumb over the edge. She got Wren to shine the torch on her hand, rubbing the smear of clay between her fingers. 'You see,' she said, 'yellowy-brown. Just like the clay that was on Silas's and Victor's boots. I think we're getting closer.' Astrid heaved out another couple of spade loads, then a torch beam flashed over her eyes.

'Careful, guys,' she said, blinking quickly.

Wren and Annabelle had their torches pointed out to sea. A boat was juddering in from the bay. Their torches weren't powerful enough to make it out.

'Astrid?' murmured Annabelle. 'This isn't good.'

'Frank... Can you switch off your lamp,' said Astrid.

Frank dropped his spade, hopped out of the hole and killed the light. They listened to the boat's engine getting louder. Then it cut, as it floated up towards the private jetty. Wren, Kabir and Annabelle angled their torches out at the jetty, pasting the boat with a ghostly haze. It was an inflatable of some sort. That's all they could see. A dark figure stepped up to the stern and threw a rope onto the jetty.

'Switch your torches off,' whispered Astrid.

They were plunged into darkness. Blinking to get their night vision back. They still couldn't see a thing, only hear steps climbing the ladder up onto the jetty.

There was a dry rasp of rope on wood – someone was tying up the boat. Heavy boots marched towards them over the broken planks. Moving fast in a direct line towards them.

'We should go,' Annabelle whispered.

'It's too late.' Astrid gripped the spade in both hands, feet wide. Frank stepped next to her and took up the same stance. The others lined up behind them. A second defence.

Kabir took his tennis racket from his case and held it up, two hands on the grip.

The boots went quiet, dampened by the grass. They were on the meadow path now. Twenty feet away.

Annabelle murmured 'No, no…' Her voice almost hysterical. In front of them, the dark shape loomed nearer. They were about six foot tall. Broad-shouldered.

There was something hanging from their right hand, which swung by their side. They crossed into the mown section. Still on a direct course towards them.

The five of them huddled up, breathing hard. Saying nothing.

Then the figure stopped, a few feet away. They could hear them breathing heavily… slowly raising the object in their hand. There was a *click*.

And a bright light flooded over them.

Then a booming voice. 'What the heck are you playing at?'

Astrid put her hand up to shield her eyes from the torchlight. Which then dropped to the ground.

'Jim… is that you?'

Twenty-six

Astrid sat in front of the desk in Jim's office. He was on the other side. Silent. He hadn't said anything since she walked in two minutes ago and waved at her to take a seat. And she hadn't said anything either.

Once, she'd read a magazine article explaining that humans have a part of their thinking called the 'chimp brain'. It's the impulsive part. When we're challenged for being in the wrong, the chimp in us rushes out and starts arguing back. After a while, another more reasonable part of the brain kicks in. It calms the chimp down and apologises. Astrid knew the chimp in her brain was bigger than most. She got defensive quickly. Had to make big apologies later.

But right now, as Jim straightened his tie and fixed her with another sour stare, she realised the chimp was cowering away in the corner of her mind. Which was the best place for it. Right now, she was in big trouble, and was going to have to take what was coming.

Eventually, Jim put his palms on the table and drew a long breath through his nose. 'Astrid, do you know what you and your friends could have done?' he said, not expecting an answer. 'Waving lamps and torches on a shipping headland. Do you know how dangerous that is?'

'I don't, sorry.'

'A boat in the channel could have mistaken your lights for a marker. They could have run onto the rocks. People could have drowned.' He clamped his hands on the side of his head and went, 'aargh…'

Astrid kept quiet. *Best let him get it out of his system*, she thought.

Jim got up and paced the room. 'It's my duty as harbour master to enforce shipping rules within tidal range of this harbour. I…' He paused, wagging a finger at her. 'I could arrest you, Astrid. You know that?'

She let her eyes drop to the desk. There were three things on it. A large black stapler. A wire in-tray heaped with paperwork. A silver framed photo of his family – he was in the centre with his arms gathering in two tall teenage boys. A petite blonde woman was leaning in from his right.

'But seeing as you are working on the authority of HMRC, I will let this slide.'

'Thank you… that's, um, very kind,' she said, dampening her surprise. She might not be in so much trouble as she thought.

'Who were those other people with you, Astrid?'

'Other people?'

'Yes, the four people with you.'

'Whistle-blowers.'

'Whistle-blowers?'

'Yes, you see…' Her mouth was dry. 'Some local contacts who gave me information in relation to the case.'

'Including Pete Sampras?'

'That's Kabir. He's a local doctor – a very useful source. I wish I could tell you more about it, Jim. But unfortunately, I can't.' There was a crack in her voice. Just a quaver of doubt, but he picked up on it instantly.

'Is that right?' He stared at her suspiciously.

She shifted in her seat. 'Well, it's getting late. I should probably get back to the boat.'

'Hand over that letter.'

'Uh?'

'That letter you showed me when we first met.'

Astrid slowly pulled out the sheet from her pocket and slid it across the table. He picked it up and started reading. Slowly, he brought his hand up and pinched the gap between his eyebrows, as if to release some growing pressure that was building there.

This reminded Astrid of the time the headmistress had dropped into the art class and seen a sketch she'd done of her, which wasn't too flattering. Warts and all, literally. She'd looked at it with the same expression as Jim's – so Astrid knew what was going to happen next. Except there wasn't going to be the annoying Katie Warburton laughing at the back.

He slapped the note down hard on the table, so the photo frame fell over. Astrid reached out to prop it back up. 'I'll get that—'

'No, just... no...' he spluttered. 'Leave it.'

Astrid slunk back in her seat.

'Right... this note says HMRC give you the authority to carry out your work as an art conservator at The Needles'

Eye. That's it. That's the limit of your powers.' He folded the paper in half. Ran his thumb over the crease again and again, his face getting redder, then pushed it back to her. 'It doesn't say anything in here about playing silly buggers with your friends in the dark. Does it, Astrid?'

'No, it doesn't,' she said quietly. At least it was only her getting the grilling. Jim had let the others go their separate ways when they reached the gate. Then he'd summoned her to his office. 'But the thing is...'

'What now?' He sounded more exhausted than angry.

'The thing is.' Now that Jim had got his anger out of his system, she might as well explain her theory. 'Jim...'

'What?'

'Can I tell you why we were there tonight.?'

'Oh, go on then. It's only ten o'clock at night,' he said flatly.

Astrid told him everything she knew. Every connection, from seeing Victor Leech's body being pulled from the water to finding the rare mud out on the meadow at The Needles' Eye. The same mud that was on Leech's shoes and on the boots of Silas, a gardener who'd taken a job at the English Trust after leaving The Needles' Eye. Now both of them were dead – most likely murdered. She knew the mud was the key. So tonight she'd come back with some friends, to find out what was down there.

He listened, stony-faced.

'I have reason to believe there's something very significant about that trench.' She paused for dramatic effect. 'Or should I say grave?'

'No, let's say trench.'

'Okay. Trench... grave, you're right. We don't know at this stage.'

'And do you know who might be behind these two deadly murders?' he said, with a twinge of sarcasm.

'I'm not sure yet.'

'What about the English Trust? Are they wrapped up in this web of lies and murder?'

'Not this time.'

'Not this time!' He roared with laughter. 'Right then. I think I've heard enough.' He got up and strode to the door. He pulled it open flamboyantly, stepping aside. 'And awaaay you go.'

Astrid got up and took a couple of steps towards him. 'You're not going to arrest me then?'

'No.' He planted his hands in his pockets. 'It's late. And I've got an early start.'

'Thanks, Jim,' she said, hurrying past him and into the cold air.

He didn't say anything for a moment. He just stood there. Then he gave a tired sigh. 'If you want my advice – I'd just get on with the art restoration. There's nothing to investigate, Astrid. Nobody to blame – except the weather. Someone drowned. Someone was hit by lightning.'

Astrid shrugged. 'Maybe.'

'No, no. You don't get it.' His face flushed, the anger rushing back. 'It's the Dunning-Kruger effect and you're on the peak of Mount Stupid right now.'

'Dunning who?'

'Don't worry... look it up sometime.' He gripped the door

handle. 'Let's call it a night, eh?' And he shut the door hard behind him.

It had not gone well. She would be the first to admit that. She lay in bed cradling her second glass of red, thinking over the evening. No, it had gone very badly. But what would have been a good result? Finding a body in the trench? She should probably give up on digging around in that patch. They'd got down deep enough to hit untouched clay, so there wasn't going to be anything else down there.

She'd left one of the portholes open, and the cool salty air from the marsh slowly poured in. It was good to clear her head. Lovely to feel toasty in the sleeping bag, but have her ears tingle from the cold. She took another sip of the wine; it was warm and oaky. Checked her phone.

Everyone from The Art of Murder Club had been in touch on WhatsApp to see if she was okay and that Jim hadn't thrown her out of the harbour. She thanked them for checking in. Told them Jim was furious but wasn't going to take it further – they were all in the clear. They agreed to meet up the next afternoon to discuss the case. As if there was any chance of talking about anything else. Astrid was about to switch off her phone when she thought about what Jim had said last. The Dunning whatsit theory?

A quick poke around on the internet, and even with half the spelling, she got there soon enough. The 'Dunning-Kruger' effect was a psychological theory that says people overestimate how competent they are at something. Knowing a little about a subject makes them feel they're experts. And it's only when they learn a bit more that their confidence plummets because they realise how much more they need to know. There was a graph to show it. That early surge of confidence is known as 'Mount Stupid'. According to Jim, that's where she was.

'Oh, yeah?' Astrid huffed. Her inner chimp, which for the entire dressing-down from Jim had sat politely in the corner, was now hopping about. 'Peak of Mount Stupid,' she muttered. That was too harsh. She knew an awful lot about art and chemistry. If she said it herself, she had a sharp, deductive mind. Stubborn, maybe. Nosy, certainly. But she would make a very good police investigator. That's why, whatever Jim said, she wasn't stopping now. She'd just have to keep out of his way, that's all.

With a twist of her wrist, she drained the last of the wine. Propped the empty glass on the ledge by the bookcase and wriggled down further in the sleeping bag.

Twenty-seven

Michael Bublé? She'd had a dream about Michael Bublé, and it wasn't even Christmas. Must have been the red wine and the cold air. Bublé had been gliding around on stage in a shiny grey suit. Crooning into a stand-up microphone. Winking at the audience. At one point, he brought two fingers to his mouth and blew a kiss directly to her. She took a glug of her coffee and shivered. Very odd.

There was a tap on the porthole behind her. Frank's face was at the window.

When she got up there, he was standing on the deck. Hands on hips. Whistling in appreciation. 'Very nice, very nice indeed.'

'Morning, Frank,' she said vaguely.

'You okay, Astrid?'

'Yeah, yeah, just trying to forget a dream I had about Michael Bublé.'

'Okay.'

'Thankfully, it finished before George Clooney turned up and they started fighting over me.'

He stood there for a few seconds in confusion. Then clapped his hands. 'Right then. Let's have a look around.'

When he'd given the cabin a good inspection – running the sink tap, knocking on the side of the wood panels with his knuckles, flicking the light on and off – he sat down by the table and spread his arms across the back of the bench. 'Very, nice indeed, Astrid.'

'Thanks.' Astrid went over to the kettle to make the coffee he ordered. White. Two heaped sugars.

'You know what I say about sailing?' said Frank.

'Go on.'

'It's like caravanning, but with more vomit. But this…' He scanned the cabin. 'It's luxury. You've done it up lovely.'

'I can't really take much credit. I inherited it from my uncle, and he'd already spent a lot of time renovating it.'

'Well, he did a fantastic job. I used to a have a little boat, you see. Nothing much. Twenty-footer. Just to muck around in. Sold it and got the chalet instead.' He patted the bench. 'Happier on dry land.'

She brought Frank's coffee over to the table and sat down opposite him. They went over the night before. Frank admitted he was a bit disappointed to be let off by Jim. If he'd been arrested he'd have got out of jury service, which he didn't want to do.

They both agreed they should carry on with The Art of Murder Club. They would run it past the others this afternoon, but Frank was sure everyone would agree. He said that after they'd left Astrid at the gates, Kabir and Wren were still keen. Only Annabelle was a bit worried – she didn't want a criminal record in case Etsy had rules about that sort of thing. But she was still prepared to risk it.

When he'd finished his coffee, Frank said, 'You know, I

was thinking about that patch we were digging last night. I don't think it's a grave.'

'Really?' Astrid sat upright. 'Then what is it?'

'A foundation test trench?'

'A what?'

'Right – the thing is, when you're constructing a building, you have to dig out a trench to test the soil. I've been on a few building sites, so I know what I'm talking about. You see…'

Frank kept talking, but Astrid wasn't taking much of it in. She kept looping back to the same word he'd said: 'building'. She held up her hand. 'Frank, go back a bit. What building?'

'Um, what? Yeah – you dig out a test trench to see the conditions for foundations. Before deciding to put in a planning application.'

'Whoa, whoa…' Astrid waved her hand again, in the motion of a teacher wiping down a blackboard with a duster. 'Planning permission?'

'Listen, Astrid,' snorted Frank. 'Are you going to let me explain, or are you just going to keep flapping your hands about?'

'I'm going to let you explain,' she said. Sitting back, tight-lipped.

'Right, soo… as I was saying. If you're doing any construction, especially on the coast, you're going to have to test the ground. Make sure it's stable enough to take a foundation for a building. The dug-over earth we saw last night. It's not a grave, Astrid. It's a construction trench.'

'That makes sense.' Astrid didn't know anything about

construction. But she could imagine how much that land would be worth for a developer. A wide, flat area of ground. High and safe above the waterline.

They had another coffee and bounced the idea between them until it curdled into a fact. The 'grave' was a construction test trench. The peninsula was a prime location. One any developer would 'give their right nut for' – Frank's expression. Three acres, right by the sea. It would go for a fortune. If the planning permission went through.

'That's what you need to check,' he said. 'Get yerself down to the planning department in Newport. See if an application has been put in for that site.'

'That's your best idea so far, Frank.' Astrid slapped a hand on the table. 'And you know why?'

Frank shrugged. 'Tell me.'

'Because, according to his widow, Victor Leech paid them a visit every week.'

'Victor Leech?'

'Yes, that's what she said. He was always down there checking out the latest planning application that had come in. Maybe he discovered something?'

'Maybe he did.' He drained his second coffee. 'When do you want to go then?'

She reached for her phone. Took out her HMRC letter from her pocket. It was getting a bit battered now. It still looked official, though. 'I'll see if I can get a meeting straight away.' She held up the letter. 'Part of HMRC's urgent investigation.'

'Great. I've got the Mondeo in the car park. I'll drive you down there.'

Twenty-eight

There are, on average, one thousand nine hundred and twenty-three hours of sunshine every year on the Isle of Wight. That's what Jim had said the first time she'd met him.

Sitting in the office of the Yarmouth planning department – Room 317, third floor, by the lift – it was clear that few of those hours of sunshine made it through the single window in front of her. It was mid-afternoon. A cloudless day. Yet only a sliver of light angled into the room, slicing the corner of the desk in front of her and creeping out to a withered pot plant in the corner.

The problem was, a tall red-brick building had been constructed only ten yards away. It blotted out the light, creating a gloomy space that served as the car park. Which was where Frank was, listening to the car radio. *How the heck did that building get planning permission?* thought Astrid.

If she hadn't got so many other questions, she might ask Beckett. That's how he'd introduced himself when he'd greeted her at the reception. Without explaining whether it was his first or last name.

He was standing on a low stool by a wall entirely taken

up with shelving. The top of his head was bald and shiny. It poked out of a band of woolly grey hair, as if a large bird had laid an egg in a smaller bird's nest. 'The files are alphabetical. And all this…' he pointed to the left corner of the top shelf '…from here to here…' his finger angled across three shelves '…are planning applications that were contested by Victor Leech.' He levered out a box file and stepped down from the stool.

'Listen. Thank you for doing this so promptly,' said Astrid.

'Honestly.' He batted away her comment. 'All part of the service.' He put the box file down on his desk and slid into the chair opposite. 'Did you know Mr Leech?'

'Not at all.'

'Lucky you. The man was a royal pain in the arse.' A hesitant smile creased his pale face. As if he had just realised that he could finally say this, now that Victor wasn't here. 'He objected to everything we tried to do. Everything. You couldn't change a light bulb in a streetlamp without him firing off half a dozen official objections.'

'You ever think about employing him on the council?'

'Better to have him inside the tent pissing out than outside the tent… That kind of thing?'

'I guess.'

'No, he wanted to be an independent voice. Holding the council to account. Making sure that "local democracy was working". That's what he said.' Beckett stretched out in his chair. 'Of course, it wasn't about local democracy, was it?'

'Wasn't it?'

'No – it was all about power and attention. The fame.' He put his hands up in front of him and spread them apart, as if they were framing the sign above a cinema entrance. 'The Victor Leech show. The Isle of Wight's longest-running production.'

'Yes, you might be right. I was up on the estate where he lives and he's a bit of a local hero up there.'

'That's his demographic. The "twirlies", as they're known.'

'Twirlies?'

Beckett explained that anyone on the island over the age of seventy got a free bus pass. But you weren't allowed to use it until after 9.30 a.m. 'So, a lot of the pass-holders get on the buses in the morning and ask the driver, "Am I too early?",' said Beckett, rolling the syllables together so it sounded like 'Am I "twirlie?"'

'Right,' said Astrid, 'bit of local jargon there. Thank you.'

'My pleasure.' Beckett rubbed his angular chin. 'Now then… let's see what Victor's last complaint was.' He flipped open the lid on the box file then snapped it shut again. There was a lot more to get off his chest. Victor Leech had clearly kept him in this gloomy room longer than he wanted. Week in, week out. Now he was free. Well, free at least to concentrate on the applications for loft extensions and drop-down kerbs, or whatever else was in the other box files on the shelf. 'You know… shall I tell you how he did it?'

'Please do.'

'Okay. Victor comes down here every week. Usually, four thirty on a Friday afternoon. He demands to see the latest planning applications. Then he goes away and starts spreading misinformation to his neighbours. About how awful a new zebra crossing or cycle lane or what-have-you is going to be. It's scaremongering and it works.'

'But why would it?'

'Ah, yes. Here's the thing. He targets the...' Beckett searched carefully for the right description, 'let's say, more impressionable residents.'

She knew exactly who he was talking about. The elderly residents in the cul-de-sacs and quiet roads up on the hill. 'They're not stupid though.'

'Not saying they are, Astrid,' he said. 'They're just more... fearful of change. So, he gets them feeling angry and anxious. Then he tells them the best thing for them to do is bombard the council with emails saying how they feel.' He paused for breath, then surged on. 'Next thing he does is organise a petition. Goes door to door, collecting signatures. Now he can hold it up and say, look: the council needs to listen to the...' he hooked his fingers in the air '..."will of the people".' A rare flush of colour had come to his cheeks.

'That's fascinating. Thanks for—'

'No, no. I've not finished.' Beckett took a deep breath. 'You see, Victor then contacts the local papers and they get involved. But the papers don't report the facts – that, say, the zebra crossing is actually a good idea. Or a cycle lane makes people healthier. No, they just report the "controversy".' More hooked fingers. 'They run a series of stories whipping up the outrage. Even though they know it's fake news. The truth is already getting left behind.'

'That's what they say, don't they?' said Astrid. 'A lie can travel halfway round the world before the truth can get its boots on.'

'Exactly right.' He bounced his chair closer to the desk. 'So now it's a political hot potato. Residents' feelings are being "trampled on by the council". That kind of thing. Of course, the councillors themselves don't believe a word of it. But they're worried they'll lose their seats in the next local election if they don't do something. So they demand the plans are thrown out, for an easy life. And ta-da... old Victor comes up smelling of roses.' Beckett swept his hand across the table, as if he'd just revealed a card trick.

'What you're saying, then—' Astrid leant in '—is that Victor Leech was gaslighting a whole town just for the attention?'

'That is exactly what I'm saying.' He clapped his hands together. 'But hey, he's dead now.'

His rant out of the way, Beckett had perked up. He'd been waiting to tell his theory to someone, anyone, for a long time. Now he turned his attention to the box file. He hummed happily as he took out a beige folder and rifled through the sheets of paper inside.

These were, he said, official planning application forms. There was another copy on computer, but they were legally obliged to keep a paper version. The folder in his hand was Victor Leech's last battleground. Beckett speed-read the pieces of paper, mumbling under his breath. 'Access permission requests. Dated 26 June. Uh, huh... for a waterside development complex. On the peninsula at The Needles' Eye.'

'The Needles' Eye?' Astrid sat bolt upright.

'Yes – down on the waterline near Yarmouth Harbour.' He unclipped a document from a handwritten letter and pushed it across the desk.

Astrid picked it up and studied it, a tingle running through her fingers. There it was – The Needles' Eye. Below the brief description Beckett had read was a map of the peninsula with a red dot in the middle. Exactly where the trench was in the meadow.

'What is the development exactly?'

Beckett took the document back and read it again. Slowly this time. 'Ah, yes. It's a bit vague. You see, this is a preliminary application. At the start, you just pay the council to discuss the potential issues. The likelihood of getting it through. It's so you don't waste money on architect and surveyor fees.'

'And Victor had seen this document?'

'Yes.' He picked up the handwritten letter. 'This is his first complaint. The first of many, no doubt.' Beckett scanned the letter, picking out choice phrases. 'An eyesore. A blight on the coastline. The council should be ashamed of themselves.' He folded up the letter. 'The usual stuff, really.' He was about to put the letter back in the box file. Then he stopped. 'Silly me. I don't have to keep this, do I?' He balled the paper up and lobbed it into a wastepaper bin by his feet. A grin on his face.

'And who is behind the application?' asked Astrid as calmly as she could. She knew she was getting close to another big clue.

Beckett checked all the forms in the box file, but drew a blank. He said he'd check the payment on the computer to see if the name was on there.

He prised open a laptop on his desk and waited for it to load up. The sliver of sunlight had swung away from the window and the only light in the room was the glow of the screen. Beckett dabbed at the keyboard with a thin forefinger. Eventually – 'Okay… got it. Here's the company that paid the application fee. You want to hear it?'

'That's why I'm here.'

'Okay.' He cracked his knuckles. 'It's called Mistral Industries.'

Twenty-nine

It was hot inside the Mondeo. The air trickling out of the vent on the dashboard was warm, with a bitter oily smell. Astrid closed the vent and wound down the windows as Frank yanked the gearstick down to second to get over a hill, the cogs biting on metal somewhere in the steering well.

Her theory of what had happened was at least running smoothly. Astrid laid out the facts one by one. Frank listened, eyes on the road.

Fact – Victor Leech had seen the planning application for a development on the grounds of The Needles' Eye.

Fact – He had gone to investigate the test trench the day before he'd died.

Fact – The next day, he was found dead. Drowned under the pier.

Crrrunk. Crrrunk.

Frank cleared the hill and cranked up through the gears. The speedometer nudged fifty miles an hour. Enough to set up a tinny vibration on the side pocket of his door. 'Then we have the Mistral Industries connection,' said Astrid. 'We have to—' Fifty-five miles an hour – the humming got louder.

'Hang on.' Frank reached down by the door panel. He lifted

out an empty Lilt can, crushed it in his hand, then tucked it snugly in the door panel next to some old newspapers. The humming disappeared. It was quickly replaced by a rattle from inside the glove compartment. 'That'll be the travel sweets.' Frank leant over, one hand on the wheel, and opened the catch. He pulled out a round tin of boiled sweets. The rattling stopped. 'Want one?'

'Go on.' Astrid helped herself to a sweet. She handed one to Frank. Further down in the glove compartment was a copy of Gabriel Tranter's book, *Get What You Want*. It was the copy that Tranter had signed at the Cowes opening party. She pulled it out of the glove compartment and looked at his profile photo on the back.

Frank was already ahead of her. 'I know what you're thinking, Astrid, but no way. Tranter would never be involved in this.'

'Based on what, Frank?'

He slowed the car. 'Okay… well, he's massively rich already. A local hero. He's just not going to do anything dodgy at this stage in his career. He has everything he wants.'

'But Mistral Industries was on the application form.'

'Huge company, Astrid. There's no way he'll know what everyone in his organisation is up to.'

'Alright, Frank. Let's see what the others think.'

Annabelle stood by the sideboard in the potting shed, steam rising from a mug in her hand. 'I've never even heard of Gabriel Tranter.' She pinched the end of the string attached to a teabag and flipped it into the swing bin. 'I mean, who is he?'

Frank ground his fingernails into the armrests of the leather armchair. He picked up Tranter's autobiography, which he'd brought in from the car, and held it out towards Annabelle, the cover facing her. '*This* is Gabriel Tranter,' he said firmly.

Annabelle squinted at the cover. 'No idea.'

Frank rolled his eyes. 'You should read it, Annabelle. In fact...' he slipped the book onto the sideboard '...everyone should read it.'

'He's like the Isle of Wight's Jeff Bezos.' Kabir was sitting behind his easel, gouging a spoon into the corner of a Thai Curry Pot Noodle – Astrid's recommendation – which added a hint of lemongrass to the room.

'Who's Jeff Bezos?' said Annabelle.

'Amazon,' said Astrid.

'The bald guy,' said Frank.

Annabelle shook her head.

'He wants us to travel into space,' said Kabir.

'Let's just say I don't know either of them,' said Annabelle. 'Save ourselves a bit of time.'

'The thing is—' Kabir tapped his spoon on his lower lip '—would someone that powerful and rich, with so much to lose, be involved in murder?'

'That's what I told Astrid in the car,' said Frank.

'Tranter has a lot of companies,' Kabir continued. 'He probably doesn't know everything that's going on.'

'Again,' said Frank. 'That's what I said in the car. He might not even know about this planning permission?'

'He sounds clueless,' said Annabelle.

Frank shook his head in disgust. 'Clueless... hah.' Then

he didn't say anything for a full minute, which was a sign he was sulking.

Since arriving at the potting shed, Astrid and Frank had brought everyone up to speed with developments. Except Wren, who had yet to turn up. The others were delighted that things were moving again with the case. After the abortive trip to The Needles' Eye and the dressing-down from Jim, all had seemed lost. Now there were new clues and connections – the strongest link to Mistral Industries. And they were about to get even more excited.

'You know when I bumped into Gabriel Tranter at the opening party, he invited me to go sailing with him.'

'Shut up!' Frank sat up. 'You didn't mention that.'

'Sorry,' said Astrid sheepishly.

'And you're going to go, right?'

Three pairs of eyes were trained on her.

There was a crunch of heavy feet on the gravel. Kabir, who was nearest the door, peered out. 'Look lively, everyone – it's Rigby.'

They all hurried into position. Kabir and Annabelle picked up brushes and pulled their chairs up to their easels. Astrid dug out her sketch pad from her bag. Frank riffled in a drawer and found an A4 pad and a biro. He jumped into his chair just as Mr Rigby poked his head round the door.

'Ah... now, that's what I like to see – my wonderful artists, lost in their work.'

'Oh, Mr Rigby.' Annabelle pretended to be startled. 'There you are.'

'Sorry, I'm not staying.' He stepped into the room, blinking in the half-light. 'You know, it's a lovely day – are you sure you wouldn't prefer to be outside? Painting "en plein air", as they say in France.'

'Nope, we're fine here, mate,' said Frank, doodling intently on the pad. The others were fixed on their canvases. Heads down. Itching for Mr Rigby to leave.

'Right, well, don't let me interrupt the creative flow.' He stepped back, then held out his arms on the door frame and stepped back in.

Kabir groaned, then artfully segued into a cough.

'Terrible business with the gardener, don't you think?'

Nobody replied. Their heads down over their work. Astrid had started sketching Annabelle. Then Frank broke the silence. 'I guess these things happen.'

'To be fair, not that often,' said Mr Rigby. 'I mean, I've never heard of anyone being hit by lightning before.'

'You're more likely to be killed by a shark,' said Frank. 'That's what...' The others darted stares towards him. 'Ignore that.' He continued scribbling on his pad.

'Right then.' Mr Ribgy clapped his hands. 'I'll leave you to it.'

When he was a few strides down the gravel drive, Kabir shut the door and turned to Astrid. 'You have to go sailing with Tranter.'

'Yes, Astrid,' chimed in Annabelle. 'Carpe diem.'

'Carpe diem?' Frank looked confused. 'Fish of the day?'

'No, Frank,' replied Annabelle. 'Seize the day.' She turned to Astrid, her hands in a praying position. 'You have to go.'

Astrid took in their eager faces. 'I guess I should. But he's so ridiculous.'

Frank muttered something like, 'You could do a lot worse, love.'

Astrid ignored him. 'I'm not sure I could even pretend I like him.'

'Thing is,' said Kabir, 'we need to find out why the name Mistral Industries is on that planning application.'

Astrid sighed. She knew it was true.

'You could wear a wire, Astrid,' said Annabelle.

'A wire? Where would we get one of those?' said Frank.

'No idea,' said Annabelle.

'Okay, I'll go sailing with Tranter,' said Astrid. 'You all happy?'

They were. Very happy. Especially Frank, who'd asked if he could come along. She politely told him it wasn't a good idea. Frank made one last plea – he'd be 'as good as gold'. Just sit in a corner somewhere, not saying a word. But Astrid was strict. It would be easier to get some information out of Tranter if they were alone together.

For the next ten minutes they discussed Astrid's line of questioning. She had to be discreet; Annabelle and Kabir were clear on that. Frank didn't say anything. He sat despondently in his chair avoiding eye contact. This was the second time he'd narrowly missed meeting his business idol.

Astrid finished her sketch and said goodbye to the others. She was going to spend the rest of the day getting on with the report on the art at The Needles' Eye. Out in the garden, she sat down on an empty bench and fished out her phone.

She found the text from Tranter that she'd ignored, selected the number and waited for it to ring through, her eyes drifting up over the hedge to the manor house. All she could see was the chimney, the lightning conductor glinting in the sun. It was another bright day. A week of them lined up after the storm. Maybe it would be more fun sailing on his yacht than she thought.

Her call clicked through to a pre-recorded message. 'It's Gabriel. I'm sooo sorry I can't take your call.' His voice so syrupy it was making her ear feel sticky. 'Leave a message and I'll get right back to you.'

Astrid reminded him how they'd met at the party. She apologised for not replying to his message. But, she told him, she was still keen to go out sailing on his yacht if the offer was still there. A quick 'cheers'. That should do it. There weren't many days of the Cowes Festival left. Hopefully he still had some time.

She slipped her phone away in her rucksack and weaved her way out through the garden to the car park. As she was unlocking her bike from the railings, Wren glided over. 'Hey, Astrid – you going?' she said, disappointment in her voice.

'Yes, got to dash. Sorry. But hey…' She tapped the side of her nose. 'There's been a development in our little murder mystery. The others will tell you all about it.'

'Ooo… delish,' purred Wren, setting off in the direction of the potting shed.

Out of the corner of her eye she saw Wren's father's minivan. He was staring at her. She wheeled her bike towards the exit and when she was halfway across the car park, he unclipped his seat belt and got out.

There was no doubt this was her father. He had the same heart-shaped face. Long dark hair that was centre parted and swept back in a silver clip. He walked straight towards her with quick strides, his mouth set in a determined slash.

She stopped. Waited until he was a few yards away and said breezily, 'Hi, I'm Astrid.'

'I know who you are,' he said. The accent was the same as Wren's, although there was a tautness to the words. 'I know exactly who...' He paused, trying not to let his anger run away with him. 'Wren has told me all about you. How you've been giving her advice about her art.'

'That's right. She's got a real talent. Don't you think?'

She saw his knuckles whitening above a line of silver snake rings. He shoved his hands in his pockets, as if it was best for both of them if they stayed there. 'Yes, she's gifted. And I should know, because I live with her.' He shuffled his feet in the gravel. 'You don't.'

'No, I don't. But I know that it would be a shame to waste that talent.'

'You mean, not going to art college in London. Right?'

'Yes, that's right.'

He bared his teeth slightly. There were still people drifting out of the gardens. She was glad they weren't alone. 'She's not going to art college.'

'Why not?'

'Listen.' He shook his head. 'I don't have to explain it to you. I'm her father and I know what's best for her.'

'Do you though?'

'No, no...' He backed away a few steps, jabbing his finger at her. 'You should mind your own business.' Then he spun on his heels and marched back to the van. She noticed it had a square plate on the back, with the words Hackney Carriage along the top. He must be a taxi driver.

Beep

It was a text from Tranter.

Hey Astrid – yeah, let's sail tomorrow. 5 o'clock best for conditions. Any good?

She replied:

Sounds great. Where do you want me?

The yacht is up at Cowes. Will send a driver to Yarmouth for you at 4.30pm.

Okay. 4.30pm at the…

Best avoid Jim, thought Astrid. Keep well away from his office.

…Ferrylink booking office. What do I need to bring?

Just yourself, Astrid. Everything is on the boat. No phone – let's have a digital detox! Enjoy the sailing.

She signed off with a thumbs-up emoji. Put the phone down. A minute later, Tranter sent another text.

Why did it take you so long to decide?

Astrid paused. What could she tell him? That his company, or one of them, had been digging around on some land that didn't belong to them. And she needed to know if he knew.

She typed...

I was thinking – it's not every day you get a chance to sail on a yacht at Cowes Week.

His reply bounced back.

You won't forget it. See you tomorrow.

That was sailing with Tranter sorted then. She got on her bike and headed home.

Thirty

Astrid put her sketch pad down on the table in the cabin and opened it up on a new page. It was nine in the morning. Time for a 'to-do' list.

This was something she used to do, but had given up because she never finished all the tasks she wrote down. Not even close. Usually, she'd added some easy things to the list at the end of the day so she at least had something to tick off. Things like – put socks in drawer. Have wine. Blink.

Today, it felt like she had the energy to get everything on a list done. On the table was a fresh thermos flask of coffee – which would save time getting up to turn the kettle on. A new pack of Co-op 'own brand' shortbread fingers. The portholes were open. The breeze was setting up a wave on the river that made a soothing *slufffing* noise against the hull of the boat. It was going to be a very productive day.

She wrote down a list of about a dozen things and set about sorting them out straight away.

First – *Deal with the toad of an ex-husband Simon*. His email about the apartment had been getting too comfortable in her inbox. Thinking about it, it did make financial sense to hang on to the flat. If it was true, as he'd said, the place was earning more money than she was.

She opened his email on her phone and reread the message. The formal 'Dear Astrid'. The patronising I-know-what's-best-for-you attitude. It was pure Simon. He was always like this in emails when he wanted her to do something.

Then there was the evening 'business networking', followed by the hurried laundering of his clothes when he got in. How hadn't she noticed his affair? There were 'more red flags than a Chinese parade' – that's what Kath had once said to her.

Astrid now wasn't in the mood to reply to him. He could wait for her answer, and she could move on to the next item on the list – *Kath*. She composed a jolly email with a bit of news. The painting collection. Her observations of the island. Sailors! Nothing on the murder mystery though. There weren't enough answers yet.

Number three – *Cobb* – a friendly postcard. Just saying hi. And a couple of lines of 'Crossing the Bar', the poem at the base of the Tennyson Monument on the headland.

And may there be no moaning at the bar,
When I put out to sea.

The poem was written by Tennyson late in his life. It was a plea to God to allow him into heaven. So not perfect – but it felt appropriate enough. She had missed Cobb – just not enough to see a future for them both. And she was sure he'd know that now too.

Then she blasted through the rest of the list. Pay the

harbour mooring fees. Two more bills – phone and boat insurance. Cancel some subscriptions. Renew membership of the English Trust – the least she could do, seeing as she was spending so much time there.

There was one more thing on her list.

Wren.

She circled her name with her pen. Wren's father had been blunt. She should mind her own business. But then, how could he hold his daughter back? Okay, she didn't have kids. But that made her opinion even more useful. Didn't it? The independent outsider, who could see the obvious. Wren should go to art college. Or she'd regret it for the rest of her life.

Her pen hovered over *Wren*. She added another couple of circles round the name, then slapped the pen down. This was something that needed to be dealt with. In person.

Wordsworth Close was in a knot of residential roads shaped roughly like a pretzel. They were all named after poets. Although it was hard, Astrid thought, to see what delicate prose might spring to mind wandering lonely as a cloud through these streets. The houses were nice enough. Small, narrow-shouldered. The proportions of the tiny houses you get in the Monopoly board game. Made from a sheeny red brick, with white-framed windows. Starter homes for families that end up being final homes because of soaring house prices.

Astrid squeezed past a silver panel van that was parked half on, half off the pavement. She kept an eye out for house numbers. Ninety-seven, to be exact. She was pleased with how she'd got the address. Wren had logged her surname on WhatsApp – it was Peterson. Her father was a cab driver. A quick search at Companies House, on GOV.uk, and she had his registered address.

Astrid carried on past a Volvo estate with ladders on the roof. Then a line of three panel vans with business names on the side – *Auto Parts 24/7*, *Patio Steam Cleaning*, *Woof Woof Dog Walking*. This would be Annabelle's nightmare. It was 'all soo trade'. She was putting words in Annabelle's mouth, but was sure she wouldn't mind them being there. And, to be fair, six months ago she might have been just as sniffy. That was the old Astrid though.

Okay, the houses could do with a lick of paint. The front lawns hadn't seen a mower for a while. But then people here had busy working lives. Young families. Not like the bungalow residents up on Merrivale Road, who had the whole day to potter in the garden.

Eventually, Astrid found number 97. Wren's father's minivan was sitting in the middle of a tarmacked drive. There was a gently sloping ramp up to the front door.

Astrid rang the bell. Nobody came. She stepped back from the door. The minivan was parked up close to the bay window so its rear end wouldn't stick out into the pavement. She squeezed between the front bumper and the window ledge, brought her hand up to her forehead to stop the glare on the glass and peered in. The lights were off. It was hard to make out anything other than the rough shape of a sofa.

On the other side of the minivan was a wooden door. It swung open easily, revealing an alleyway down the side of the house. At the end was a small garden. Not much more than a patchy lawn hemmed in by an eight-foot-high panel fence that smelt of creosote. Attached to the back of the house was a wooden pergola that shaded a concrete patio. The only outdoor furniture on it was a white plastic table with matching chairs.

Astrid was about to turn round when she saw Wren's dad appearing from the door of a shed at the bottom of the garden. He noticed her, shook his head, then turned his back on her to lock the shed door. Astrid sat down on one of the plastic chairs and waited for him to cross the lawn.

'Make yourself at home,' he said sharply.

'I rang the bell.'

In his hand were loose loops of green cable, dotted with coloured fairy lights. He began to unravel them, laying them out on the patio. 'It's Wren's birthday next week. I'm having a surprise party for her. Few friends. A barbecue.'

'That's nice.'

'Did you know it was her birthday?'

Astrid shook her head. It felt like a trap.

'And that's because you don't know anything about my daughter. Do you?' The trap was sprung.

'I know that she has an amazing talent for art. And the Royal College of Art is one of the best places in Britain to nurture that talent.'

'Yeah, you said that yesterday.' He started threading the fairy lights up one of the pergola posts. When he reached the top, he balled up the lights and swung them over the beams. They hung down in shallow 'U' shapes. 'And I haven't changed my mind. It's not a good idea.'

She noted he used 'I' when he talked about decisions to do with Wren. Not 'we'. Did he let her make any decisions? Astrid looked round the garden. There were a couple of touches she would say were down to Wren. A Green Man pottery face on the wall. A tall toadstool sculpture in the flowerbeds. If she was asked, she'd say only the two of them lived here. And had done for a while.

'What does Wren's mother think?' Astrid instantly regretted asking the question.

He levelled his eyes at her. 'Who?'

'Wren's mother.'

'It's just the two of us. Something else you didn't know.' He got up on one of the white plastic chairs and started winding the rest of the lights down the end post.

'What will Wren do if she doesn't take this offer?'

'She'll be fine. There's a lot of work on the island. Especially in the summer. She can still do her art as a hobby.'

'A hobby. I think…'

'No, no.' He stepped down from the chair. 'Do you know why you're doing this?' His voice tightened.

'Go on. I'm intrigued,' she said, crossing her arms over her chest.

'You know, interfering in other people's lives. Without knowing what's best for them.' He carried on winding the lights, not even looking at her. 'I'm Wren's father. I know what's best for her – and it's here. Her home. There's no point getting her hopes up about going to some college in London.'

'Then you're trapping her.'

He let the lights fall from his hand. 'But you don't know

Wren's limitations.' His voice was a notch from shouting. 'How is she going to deal with living in a big city?'

Astrid got up. She knew she only had one more thing to say. And she wanted to leave it hanging there, even though he wouldn't agree with it. 'I don't know your name.'

'Michael.'

'Okay, Michael.' She took a deep breath. 'I think you're hiding behind her disability. Because you don't want her to leave. I can understand that. She's amazing and you want her to be around all the time. But you'll stop her being who she wants to be, and you'll regret that one day.'

He was calm. Because he hadn't let her words get close to him. 'You have kids, Astrid?'

'No, I don't.'

'Then you don't know what you're talking about.'

'I can imagine it's the same for all parents though. The fear of letting their kids go out in the world.'

'You know the best thing you could do, Astrid?'

'Go on.'

'Try and sort yourself out. You know, fill whatever sad hole you have in your life. Face up to your own problems, before you try and solve other people's. And do it in a way that doesn't involve my family. Do you understand?'

Then he went to an outdoor socket and plugged in the lights. They worked. 'Oh, yeah…' He stood back and admired them. 'Yeah, Wren's going to like that. Don't you think?' he asked breezily, as if they hadn't discussed anything else.

'I think she will.' She put her rucksack on and went back down the alley.

★ ★ ★

At the end of the road was a signpost that said *Yarmouth Harbour 3/4 mile*. It pointed down a narrow alley. On one side was a high wood-panelled fence that ran down the back of the houses. On the other, wheat fields stretched out to the horizon. Astrid pushed her bike ahead of her until she got past the houses. There was a bench looking out over the fields. She sat down, closed her eyes and inhaled the fresh air. Bearing the sadness as it came.

In the middle of the field was an oak tree. The farmer had sown the wheat around it, so it stood in an eye of green grass. She stared at the tree. Watched the breeze ripple through its leaves. Like a shiver of feathers on a bird's wing.

It had hurt. The things he'd said. Because it was true. She'd already admitted it to herself. Instead of dealing with her loneliness, she'd interfered in other people's lives. Trying to change Frank, so he'd get on with Annabelle. The whole investigation into Victor Leech's death. It was easier. Encouraging Wren to go to art college. No, she thought – she was right about that. And she wasn't backing down.

Thirty-one

It took less than fifteen minutes to get back to the boat. Once inside the cabin, she switched off her phone and stuck it in the drawer by the sink. To avoid temptation. She wanted to concentrate on the report on the art collection. Forget all about the case, and what Wren's father had said.

She worked steadily. Uploading the photos. Describing what was needed to bring each piece of art to market in the best condition. The time, materials and cost involved, and how much that might add to the sale price. Just as Andy Marriot had asked.

It was nearly four by the time she looked up from the laptop. Almost half the paintings were logged. She crooked a knot out of her neck. Then rustled up a very late lunch of cheese on toast and changed into her sailing gear. It was time to meet Tranter and find out what he knew.

Cowes was a town that was serious about sailing. The car that was sent to pick her up was a big fancy Range Rover, with black-tinted windows. But crawling along the seafront, packed with visitors, few people stepped aside. Nobody gave the car much attention. This was a boat town. Hundreds of gleaming yachts were moored out in the bay or jammed in the marinas that ran in a broad curve up to where the sea narrowed to a wide river.

On the other side of the road, away from the water, were the hotels, apartment blocks and yacht clubs. The yacht clubs stood out. They were three- and four-storey town houses with black metal balconies where the guests sat out, binoculars trained out to sea. Ahead, as the car slowed, was the grandest of them all.

It was like a French chateau had been plonked on the headland. The same circular towers with a conical roof and ivy trailing up the brickwork. It was guarded from the boulevard by a high stone wall that curled round the headland. Out front was a mast on which fluttered sailing ensigns, and a big blue-and-white striped awning that shaded a terrace. Astrid was about to check her phone to see which sailing club this was, then she remembered she'd agreed to leave it at the boat.

The driver hadn't spoken more than a handful of words since he'd picked her up at the Ferrylink booking office. A nod and a 'madam' as he opened the passenger door. A single-word reply to a couple of her questions. So she'd left it. Happy to look at the window as the countryside washed by.

He pulled the car in to the verge, got out and opened her door. When she stepped out, she asked him about the chateau building. '*That* is the British Yacht Society,' he said, surprised she wouldn't know.

He escorted her down a jetty where another man in a

black polo shirt with 'Mistral' on the lapel took her to a speedboat. He made the chauffeur look chatty – silently standing at the back with the outboards, eyes over Astrid's shoulder.

Five hundred yards from the shore, he slowed the engines. Tranter's yacht was floating in front of them – all sixty feet of it, from stern to prow. It was pure white, except for a dark-blue band along the hull that was broken by three square tinted windows. A towering grey mast was set just ahead of a domed cabin mostly made of glass. The wash of the speedboat fanned in, and Tranter's yacht nodded gently at its anchor. As if it had woken, smelt the salt in its nostrils and was eager to get going.

The speedboat swung round to the stern. A platform had been lowered just above the waterline to reveal a head-height storage area. Inside was a smaller inflatable tender, and to one side was a steel ladder that angled up to the deck. The boatman lined up alongside the platform and Astrid stepped out and climbed the ladder. The speedboat slewed round and roared back to the harbour.

Tranter was waiting for her at the top of the ladder. He was wearing a black waterproof jacket and matching trousers. 'Welcome aboard.'

She gazed around the boat. 'Okay, you win. This is amazing.' Which she really didn't want to say, because she didn't want him to think she was impressed by him. She wasn't – not by him... the boat, though. It was magnificent.

The decks were made of teak. Laser cut and spotless. The boards slinked down both sides and poured seamlessly into the cockpit well, then into the cabin. The lights from the cabin shone up through the doorway. The way, in pirate movies, a treasure chest full of gold coins shines. 'Is this the boat you'll be competing in the Fastnet Race?'

'No, no. That's *Mistral 2*. She's a pure ocean racing boat.'

'Where's that boat then?'

'We have her in dry dock at East Cowes at the moment. We're running some flow tests on the new rudder. This though...' He set off towards the cabin. She followed. 'This is one of the finest sailboats in the world. The Hallberg-Rassy 64.' He patted the steel rail. 'It's built for a bit more comfort. But it still handles well in any weathers. Yup... she's a fantastic boat.' He stepped down into the cockpit, which was about three feet deep. 'You ready?'

'As I'll ever be,' she said, stepping down next to him.

Before them was a huge helm with six spokes. It was covered in beige suede around the rim. In front of it was a control panel in the shape of a 'T'. On the top was a flat computer screen. To the left, radios and GPS panels. To the right, the silver engine thruster and a series of red and green buttons as big as tangerines. He pressed a button and the platform behind slowly hinged up, closing the compartment. 'Glass of wine?'

'Er... maybe not.'

'You sure?'

'Go on then. White, if you have it.'

'There's a cellar on board, so yes.'

'Of course there is.' She laughed. 'In which case, I'll have a glass of white Burgundy.'

'I think there's a nice Puligny-Montrachet you might like.'

'Yes, that'll do.'

It was his turn to laugh. 'You didn't think I knew what a white Burgundy was. Did you?'

'Maybe.'

'And will there be any more tests this evening, Astrid?'

'We'll have to see.' Which felt sickly, having to say it. But it was better to make him think she was flirting with him, rather than poking around for information.

He whistled down to the cabin door. Almost immediately, the boxer guy appeared at the bottom of the steps. Tranter raised two fingers. 'Two glasses of white Burgundy. Thanks, Cristo.'

'I thought that...' Astrid hoped she didn't sound too shocked. There was something deeply creepy about that guy. 'I thought it was just the two of us?'

'Mmm, yeah. Sorry. We sort of need a crew of three for a boat this size. That okay?'

'Sure, no problem.'

'Cristo and I go back a long way. It's an amazing story.'

She doubted it was. 'I'd love to hear it.' Best to get him chatting. Loosen him up before she eased into the planning application.

Tranter looked wistfully down at the cabin door. 'He came to one of my seminars. Paid for it with the last money he had in the world. He placed his faith in me – so I took him under my wing. That's what I'm all about.'

'Good for you.'

Tranter reached through one of the gaps in the helm and hit a button. At the prow of the boat was a metallic rattling as the anchor raised. Tranter continued with the story. 'His business had gone bust – the dotcom bubble burst on him.

So, I offered him a job in one of my tech companies, and he's worked his way up into the inner circle.'

'Lucky him.'

'I know. But he deserves it. He has two engineering degrees. And he's incredibly creative.'

The boat had shifted a good twenty yards sideways, even though there was little wind. Astrid glanced over the side and saw a clump of seaweed drifting towards them, twisting and turning before slipping under the hull. 'There must be a strong tide in the bay,' she said.

'There is. We better go.' Tranter pressed the ignition button and eased the silver engine throttle towards him. The boat set off, humming smoothly like a deep whale song.

'You not going to switch on the computer navigation?' asked Astrid.

'Not today.' He turned the helm through his hands. 'We're going to do some real sailing. Just get out there. Read the waves. Feel the wind.'

'But there's a lot of reefs and wrecks out there?'

'Seriously – relax, Astrid. There's too much tech in this game. Too many people using the iSailGPS app on their phones. What happened to just sailing? Do you agree, Astrid?'

'You know, I do. I've not been sailing long, but I really love watching the weather and checking charts.'

'That's exactly what I'm talking about.' Then he snapped his fingers. 'Hey… did you leave your phone behind?'

'I did.'

'Fantastic – digital detox. Feels great, doesn't it?'

'Yeah – I guess it does.'

'Course it does. Out here…' he took a hand off the helm

and raised it to the horizon '…you're free. Nobody can get in touch with you.'

A few minutes later, Cristo brought the two tumblers of wine and handed one to each of them without saying a word. They clinked glasses. Cristo set his glass down on the edge of the cockpit. Astrid kept hold of hers. The boat motored onwards, the jumble of battlements of Hurst Castle appearing out on the mainland. Astrid had to admit, it was all rather perfect. Chilled burgundy. Balmy weather. At the wheel of a yacht that was worth as much as her London flat. You could see why people dreamt of this. Worked hard or cheated to get this. She needed to stay focused though. This was her only chance to find out what he knew about the land at The Needles' Eye.

'It's good that you can get so much time off work,' she said. 'I mean, a company as big as yours. Do they not need you in charge all the time?'

'No. I'm lucky, Astrid. I have a lot of people around me I can trust. That's another of my business secrets.'

'I know – get good people around you and take them with you on the journey.' This was one of the few quotes that she remembered from skipping through his book.

'Hey.' He swivelled round to face her. 'You read the book?'

'Couldn't help myself.'

He spun the helm slightly, checking a small flag on the mast that was being nipped at by the breeze. 'I'm glad. Which bits did you like?'

'The stuff about you building your business empire. It's huge – media, software, hedge funds. But no property development, which surprised me.' She studied him carefully. But he didn't react.

'Why's that?' he said calmly.

'Mistral could have ridden a couple of property booms there.' She was getting closer. Stalking up on him for an answer. 'You hit every other business trend.'

'Hang on.' He stopped staring at the small flag. 'The breeze is probably good enough to get the sails up. South-westerly. We can take a port tack out past The Needles.'

'Sounds good.'

Tranter pulled back the throttle and the engine died. He dabbed at a green button. There was a whirring from low inside the mast and a small triangle of grey mesh sail rose from the notch between the mast and the boom. The triangle expanded, slicing out the sky, until it went taut and bowed out with the breeze. The boat hung over a few degrees. Tranter spun the helm a quarter turn and the boat nosed into the waves.

'Impressive.' Astrid gazed at the sails.

'All push-button activated,' he said. 'It's cutting-edge stuff.'

There were no other yachts on the water. Not enough wind to bother with, thought Astrid, unless you had a yacht with a sail as big as a tennis court. To the south, the orange scar of cliff above Alum Bay bled into the white headland, which slowly tapered away to The Needles. Not far off the red-and-white lighthouse, a bank of grey cloud was moving in.

'So Mistral and property development. Why do you ask?'

'Oh, I heard a rumour, that's all,' she said casually.

'What rumour?'

'That Mistral were investing in land on the island.'

'Where did you hear that?'

'You know. Small island.' Astrid finished her drink and put the glass down next to his. He still hadn't taken a sip.

He rolled his shoulders and sighed. 'Alright, Astrid. I'll be honest with you. You know that's my whole deal, right? Being honest.' He stared at her. 'What exactly do you want to know?'

'Uh… sorry.' Astrid was distracted. Cristo had come up from the cabin and was making his way towards the prow. In his hand was an orange life jacket.

'I don't mind telling you,' Tranter said wearily. 'I'm planning to build on the headland site at The Needles' Eye.'

'Oh, right,' said Astrid casually, hiding her excitement. 'What are you trying to build?'

'A yacht club.' He paused. 'Well, it's going to be more than that. It's going to be cool. State-of-the-art facilities. The most luxurious club on the island.'

Ahead of her, Astrid could see Cristo fiddling with something in the pocket of the life jacket. A green light blinked from inside it.

'Sounds a good idea. To take on the yacht clubs of Cowes, right?' Astrid glanced aimlessly out over the water. As if she wasn't that interested. But she was. He was admitting everything.

'Exactly. I'd never be a member of those stuffy clubs.'

'And Celeste Wade?'

'What about her?'

'She's inherited the estate. Are you working together?'

'Sort of,' he said flatly. 'She thinks it's going to be some eco education centre or something. But we'll cross that bridge when we come to it.'

'Cross that bridge?'

'Plans change, don't they? She might not be around.' He fixed her with a stare. Reading her expression. Searching for a sign that betrayed her.

He raised his hand towards Cristo, who was standing by the rail holding the life jacket over the water. He nodded and Cristo threw the jacket out in the water. It bobbed through the waves, running diagonally away from the boat towards the mainland, the little green light staining the water.

'Why did he throw that over?' asked Astrid.

'Because it's your life jacket.'

'I don't understand,' she stammered.

'Okay, let me explain,' he said, his hands apart, as if he were presenting a speech. 'The life jacket has a personal locator beacon. It's switched on now so the rescue services will be alerted to a MOB.'

'A man overboard signal?'

'Yes.' He paused. 'Or woman overboard.'

She stepped out of the cockpit to the side rail. The orange jacket was a dot now. Winking as it dropped between the waves. 'Gabriel. I won't say anything.'

'Just a sec,' he said, spinning the helm so the boat carved round out against the breeze. 'Let's set a new course. Put it on auto.' He pressed a button and took his hands off the helm. Astrid could feel the panic rising, burning off the alcohol.

'I promise, Gabriel,' she pleaded. 'Nobody else knows.'

'It's too late, Astrid. Sorry. In five minutes, you're going overboard. But hey—' he put his finger on his chin '—air-sea

rescue will be searching for you in the opposite direction.'
He checked over the side. The boat bounced over a set of
peaked waves. 'The tide changes beyond here. It heads out to
sea. I know these waters better than most people.'

She knew them too, from the charts. And he was right.

'You'll be floating out towards the Atlantic. Never to be
seen again.' He held out both his hands, gathering in what
would have been applause in a seminar.

'Wait... Gabriel.'

'Yes.' He pointed at her, as if picking her out of an
audience. 'Go on.'

'You're prepared to kill for this?'

'Yes,' he said, as if any other answer was absurd. 'Because
I always get what I want.' He turned from her, checked his
watch, then waved over to Cristo, who was sitting patiently
on the corner of the cabin. 'Cristo!' Gabriel held up five
fingers. 'Five minutes.' Cristo nodded and checked his watch.
'Okay, I've got stuff to do.' He stepped round the helm.

'Couple more questions... please.'

He stopped. Smiled. As if the seminar was overrunning
– but hey, he was Gabriel Tranter and an audience was an
audience. 'Alright. Couple more. Then I better get on.'

'Okay.' Astrid came closer, glancing down out of the corner
of her eye. There was a panel flush with the cockpit. A storage
locker. Maybe there was something in there she could defend
herself with. 'So, Victor Leech? Why did you kill him?'

'Leech?' he said, confused.

'The local campaigner. Drowned under the pier.'

'Oh, yeah.' He ran his fingers through his hair. 'The
NIMBY guy. I was told he'd been nosing around at the

planning department. He was going to start a campaign to block the permission for the new club.'

'Did you kill him yourself?'

'Course not.' He laughed. 'As I said – surround yourself with people you can rely on.'

'Cristo?'

'Yes – Cristo. He followed Leech. Found him snooping around the gardens at The Needles' Eye. He'd discovered the test trench we'd commissioned.'

Another quick glance. The storage door had a silver handle, no lock. Just flip it round. Pull. That should do it. Hopefully.

'We were just going to warn him off,' Tranter carried on. 'But he said that you can't silence democracy. Some pompous crap or other. Cristo struggled with him on the jetty in the gardens and he fell in. Tide must have carried him out under the town pier.'

'And Silas, the gardener?'

Cristo checked his watch. 'Three minutes,' he muttered.

Three minutes for Astrid to finalise a plan. Keep Tranter talking in the meantime. 'You got rid of him as well?'

'We had to,' said Gabriel. 'He'd come back to pick up some tools and he noticed Cristo heading to the jetty. He followed him and saw Cristo and Leech struggling on the jetty. When Leech's body turned up, the chances were he'd go to the police. We had to make sure that didn't happen.'

Gabriel went over what happened in a series of bullet points. How he and Cristo had both gone up to Abbotsford Manor and waited for Silas to finish his shift. They'd sat in the car and seen the lightning storm coming in on a direct line to the manor house. They had a live weather app on their phone.

Astrid checked the weather herself. To the port, five hundred yards away, the bank of clouds was staying put. The breeze was dying out.

Back to the story, which Tranter was relishing. Cristo, he said, had gone off to the shed to deal with Silas. He'd hidden behind the shelves, waiting to strangle him with a reel of extender cable he'd found. But Silas rushed in and changed his boots quickly, because the storm was coming. On his way back to the car park it started to rain heavily. So, he took shelter in the greenhouse.

Astrid kept egging him on, keeping an eye on the panel of buttons. Trying to remember the order he'd pressed them in. She had one minute. No more than that.

Tranter began to wrap the story up. He said that Cristo saw a flash of lightning at the back of the house. That's when he had the idea to make it look like an accident. He used some pliers and cut the extender cable to reveal the wire. Rushed out and hooked it up to the base of the lightning conductor on the house. Then he unwound it round the back of the hedge and clipped it on to the metal greenhouse frame. 'The storm sweeps in, bang on line…' said Tranter, clapping his hands, 'and zap! Guy didn't stand a chance.'

'Cristo gets the employee of the month, right?'

'Told you. Smart guy. Extremely creative.' Further down the boat, Cristo was getting to his feet. He rolled his neck like a boxer just before the starting bell.

'Wait. Please – one more question,' she begged.

Tranter waved a hand at Cristo, who stood still. 'Make it quick.'

'What about me? You've planned all this in advance.' He nodded. 'So how did you know I'd found out about the development?'

'My contact at the planning office.'

'Beckett?'

'Dunno… never asked his name.' He shifted impatiently. 'Listen, Astrid, don't take this personally. It's just, you know…'

'Yes, I know. You always get what you want.'

He gave a smug smile. 'Yeah…' Then he picked up both glasses – his was still full – stepped round the helm and took the stairs down into the cabin. When he was inside the door frame, he pressed a button on the wall and a wooden slatted door hushed up, sealing him in.

Astrid took in a deep breath through her nostrils. The air was salty – electrical. It charged her. Right then, she made a decision. She was going to survive. She had a plan and she was going to put it into action. It was as simple as that.

The storage panel.

Duck down.

Turn the handle… click.

Swing it open.

Over her shoulder, she saw Cristo approaching. He was halfway down the side of the boat.

Inside the locker was a spare blue fender, a coil of white rope and yellow rescue flare the size of a roll of tinfoil. She took it out and placed it to one side. Then she searched the floor of the locker. There were some tools there. Pliers. Paintbrush. Yes – a silver spanner, about ten inches. Perfect.

She picked it up and hurried to the closed door of the cabin. Slid the spanner in the lowest slat and twisted it until it was firmly jammed in place.

Cristo was standing by the edge of the cockpit, watching her. 'Don't make this any harder than it has to be.' This was the first time she'd heard him speak. It surprised her. His voice was soft, well spoken. Almost apologetic.

'You don't have to do this, Cristo.'

'I work for Gabriel,' he said blankly, stepping into the well.

'Then you're going to have to catch me, you weirdo.' She scrambled out onto the starboard side and backed away down the side of the boat. Around the dome of the cabin were long glass skylights. Astrid could see Tranter down in the cabin. He was seated on a cream sofa, staring at a laptop on the table. He looked up at her, annoyed. That was the emotion. Annoyed – that she was still alive.

Astrid stepped slowly backwards towards the stern. Cristo followed her, staying ten feet away. He was calm. Because they both knew it. There was nowhere to run. Around them was miles and miles of cold sea, waiting to chill the life out of her. Nobody to hear her scream. She might as well be floating in space.

Part two – get him where she wanted him.

One backwards step at a time. Feet wide – trip now and it would all be over. She edged back until she was level with the mast. Then put her right hand on it, and ducked round to the other side of the boat.

He couldn't see her now because she was behind the sail. She ran, as fast as she could, back to the helm. When he appeared round the mast, he was surprised to see her there. He balled his fists at his sides – angry at being fooled. That's where she wanted him. Angry – that's when he'd make the mistake.

She stood up on the lip of the cockpit, stared straight at him and slapped the top of the cabin. 'Come on, Cristo. You can do better than that.' She slapped again. And again. Drumming him forward. One step at a time to the side of the cabin.

She glanced up at the sail. There wasn't much breeze But it was steady, and there was just enough of it. 'You ready, Cristo?' she said under her breath.

She put both hands on the cabin roof and made a fast shimmy. Left. Right. That quick movement did it – like a cat reacting to the tug of a ball of wool, Cristo jumped up on to the cabin roof and strode towards her.

Astrid dropped back down into the cockpit and banged on the button to switch off the auto-sail. There was a jarring inside the mast and the helm shifted in her hands. The boat was alive again.

Cristo stood there. Confusion flashed across his face.

Then Astrid cranked the helm down. Anticlockwise. The boat lunged to the port side. The sail fluttered, went taut like the muscles of a horse about to take a high fence, and the metal boom scythed through the air.

Cristo didn't have time to react. He barely collected the idea of what was going to happen before it was knocked out of his head. The boom caught him a few inches above his temple, knocking his head sideways with a dull *thunk*.

He spun round almost 360 degrees then fell backwards. He lay sprawled on the edge of the deck. An arm across the rail. Half conscious.

The cabin door rattled and whined, the motor straining to lift it up. But the spanner held it in place. She could hear Tranter shouting something at her. Slapping the woodwork with the flat of his hand.

Astrid looked up and saw that Cristo was now sitting up and rubbing the side of his head. He took his hand away and his palm was dark red. He stared at it, as if it didn't make sense. About three inches above his ear was a pink triangle of scalp. A rivulet of blood ran down from the point, down his neck and on to the collar of his shirt.

Astrid picked up the yellow rescue flare at her feet and stepped out of the cockpit. On the way, she hit the button for the platform. The hydraulics hissed and the panel slowly dropped away to the water level.

Cristo was still clutching his hand to his head. Behind him, the cloud bank filled the sky like a grey curtain. Only a hundred yards away and slowly getting nearer.

She jumped the last couple of steps of the ladder down to the platform. Ducked down into the space in the hull and tossed the rescue flare into the back of the inflatable. Now for the third part of the plan.

Get the hell out of there.

Back into the big current taking her inland.

Use the flare to get rescued.

There was a grey plastic handle on the prow of the inflatable. She gripped it and hauled the boat out onto the platform. Then she pushed it into the water, which was now glassy calm. With one hand on the side to bring it into the platform, she jumped aboard.

The cloud bank had swallowed up the boat, the grey mist

swirling and folding around her so she couldn't even see the name *Mistral* on the stern. What a boat. Tranter could tell his cellmates all about it. That's where he was heading.

Across the middle of the inflatable was a simple wooden plank. She sat down on it and found the oars tucked down the side. They clipped easily into the rowlocks. With her back to the prow, she dug the oars into the water and the inflatable slowly moved out from the platform. A few more strokes and she was free. A few hundred more and she would be back in the current taking her to safety.

Then the inflatable stopped, as if it had hit a wall.

It was such a jolt that Astrid almost slipped off the seat. She caught herself with a straight arm and settled back up on the plank. Another couple of hard strokes of the oars and she realised what the problem was. At the stern of the inflatable was a rope leading to the platform. It must have snagged there. She scrabbled over to it and began working at the knot. Twisting and tugging with her fingers. It wouldn't budge it.

'Come on…' she hissed.

The rope was tight. The engine was silent. Had the yacht hit another current and started drifting away from her? No – there was another slow tug on the rope. Someone was drawing her back to the boat. Cristo must have got his strength back.

Astrid's fingers worked at the knot. It wasn't getting looser. And now she had to pull in the rope with one hand to give her some slack. Then she felt it in her hand. Cristo was reeling her in. She jumped to the prow of the inflatable and grabbed the rescue flare.

Holding it in both hands, she tried to read the instructions on the side. The writing was too small. All that made sense was a red arrow pointing to the white plastic cap on the end. Which must be the bit to aim. Must be. On the other end was a short red cord.

Another tug on the rope Another yard closer. She could hear his voice in the mist. Goading her. 'Astrid. You be good now.' He almost sang the words.

'Come on, Cristo.' She called back. 'You can do better than that.'

The rope snapped straight, water spraying from it. The boat surged forward... and she stumbled back, felt a sharp stab of pain as her head hit the wooden seat of the dinghy, and she rolled over the side.

The coldness clamped around her.

Swim.

Her limbs didn't respond.

Swim.

Please.

Swim...

The weight of her clothes was pulling her down. One last breath. Drag in as much air as she could.

Then the water sealed around her. She was on her back, looking up at the surface. A hazy glow through the fog. The dinghy to her right. How long did she have?

Thirty seconds.

Someone her age. Her fitness. That's what Jane had said. Then the air in her lungs would rush out. The saltwater rush in. Suffocating her.

Twenty-five.

Was this it? Here?

Your life was supposed to flash before your eyes. All those

moments that mattered crushed into a hyper-speed video. But there was only sadness, as burning as the cold water.

Twenty.

For the whole of her life, she'd only truly loved one person. And they'd loved her. Not her husband. Or boyfriends. Or friends. It was her father – just her father.

She saw him now. A single image. Was that what you were given?

He was holding her hand. The first day at primary school. She walked ahead to the classroom door, then turned and ran back to him. His arms folded around her. He kissed her forehead – told her it was going to be alright. He'd always be there.

Now she'd never see him again.

Ten.

The pain gripped her chest.

Her head pounded.

The dinghy drifted over the light.

Swim. NOW!

Her legs jerked. Then kicked. Arms swept down by her sides. Working together. Finally… climbing up through the water. Her head about to explode.

One

last

surge…

And she broke the surface. Ssssucked in air like an inward scream. Gasped. Again and again, until her lungs stopped hurting.

Treading water, she slowly spun round. The fog was still hanging over the water. She could only see ten feet ahead of her. The dinghy was now to her left. She made a few slow, strong kicks towards it. The Isle of Wight was less than a mile away, somewhere out there in the mist. Too far to swim.

She'd have to get back onto the yacht... and deal with both of them there.

It wasn't too hard to get back into the inflatable. Once she got an arm hooked over the side, desperation took over. She clambered aboard, the adrenaline keeping the cold at bay, for now.

The flare was still in the bottom of the boat. She picked it up again. At the stern, the line hung limply in the water. Cristo must have heard her fall overboard and let the dinghy float out.

She called to him through the fog. 'Hey, Cristo. I'm still here.'

It was like waiting for a shark to take a bait. A few seconds later and the rope twitched, then went straight. It pulled the inflatable towards the yacht. Smoother this time. Hand over hand.

Astrid knelt behind the plank, took the white cap off the end of the flare and pointed it in front of her. One hand on the cord. Getting steady.

One flare.

One shot.

'It's over, Astrid.' His voice was only a few feet away.

The stern of the inflatable nudged up against the back of the platform. A shape stepped forward, the mist falling from his shoulders like a cape. Cristo was sneering at her. He was holding a boat hook in both hands. He pushed it out and snagged the side of the boat, swinging it into the platform.

Astrid leant back on the stern. Levelled the rescue flare and pulled the cord. The flare crackled then… *frrruzzz*.

An orange ball of flame shot from the end. Straight as a laser. Right into Cristo's chest in a bloom of bright gold and orange light. Cristo moaned and stumbled backwards into the space in the hull, brushing the sparks from his shirt. They fell to the platform and danced at his feet.

Astrid jumped from the inflatable and swerved past him to the ladder. She threw the flare towards him, the orange smoke pouring from it, mixing with the fog to make a roiling orange cloud. She was up on the deck before he could find the first rung of the ladder. Straight to the control panel. Hit the button, and the platform rose from the waterline. Snapping Cristo in there like a Venus fly trap.

She could hear him coughing below her feet. Stamping at the flare. Tranter was still banging on the slatted door, but he was still stuck. What was it with these alpha males? They always had to make so much noise when they didn't get their way.

She waited until they'd both calmed down. Accepted they'd lost. Then she checked the digital chart, started the engine and swung the boat round on a course back to the harbour.

Thirty-two

Astrid stood in the shower for a good twenty minutes, the hot water drawing the deep cold from her body. Eventually, she stopped shivering. Then she retraced what had happened. And she shuddered again.

Tranter had tried to kill her – as if she was nothing. A speck of mud on his suit to be dry-cleaned away. He'd got Cristo to do the dirty work and got on with his day. Because he was sure she wouldn't fight back. It was insulting.

Astrid leant her head against the shower wall, letting the hot water trail down her back. The shower was filled with steam. It felt calming. To be surrounded by water. Her feet planted on dry land this time. She whispered. 'You did good, Astrid.'

She had. She'd trapped Tranter. Taken Cristo out with one blast of the rescue flare. Then she'd motored the yacht back to Yarmouth Harbour, calling the police on the way.

There was a launch waiting at the harbour entrance for her when she arrived. On board were three uniformed police officers, two men, one woman. They told her to drop anchor. Which she did. There was no way she could steer a yacht that size into the small harbour.

Then the woman police officer climbed on board and helped her into the launch. Astrid had found a spare sailing jacket in a locker in the cockpit, which she'd put on over her wet clothes. It had stopped the wind, but she was still feeling chilled to the core. The men stayed on the yacht to deal with Tranter and Cristo.

Once she sat down, the female officer unpacked a silver reflective blanket and gave it to her. It was the kind they hand out to exhausted runners at the end of marathons. She slipped the blanket over her shoulders and drew it tight over her chest. Arms tucked underneath. The female officer asked if she was okay. Astrid nodded, and the officer swung round on the engine bench and raced the launch back to the slipway.

There was an ambulance parked up by the water, its rear doors open. Two paramedics in green boiler suits with lots of pockets stepped out and helped her into the back. They were both women. Matching blonde ponytails, maybe sisters. And they had kind voices. They checked her over. Pulse. A stethoscope to her chest. With each check, their worried expressions melted away. They asked her questions.

'Did you swallow any water?'

'No.'

'You sure?'

'Yeah. Sure.'

They were pleased. The older of the women explained about secondary drowning. Seawater on the lungs is bad news. It inflames the air passages. You think everything is okay, then an hour later, on dry land, you start to suffocate.

Then they checked her pupils with a penlight. The younger paramedic put gloves on and ran her fingers over the bump on Astrid's head where she'd hit it on the plank of the inflatable. She parted the hair. Peered at the bump. That's all it was, she said – 'a bit of a bump'. Now they were joking and laughing. 'The full MOT,' said the older paramedic. 'Free on the NHS.'

Astrid looked around the ambulance at all the tubes, defibrillators, clear Perspex boxes full of needles and bandages. She'd had a lucky escape. The paramedics agreed – 'a very lucky escape'. She could now go back to the boat, or if she was up to it, give her statement to the female police officer who was waiting outside.

She decided to give her statement. Get it out of the way. The police officer took her over to one of the benches and wrote it all down in her notebook. She hardly interrupted, only to offer sympathy. Or to make sure she'd heard correctly, shaking her head at how awful the experience had been. After half an hour, it was done. The female officer closed her notepad and told Astrid she should take it easy for the rest of the day. Have a hot shower. Try and relax.

The shower juddered. Astrid turned up the heat a notch for one last blast. She was feeling back to normal now. Her body, at least. Her mind – there was a hairline crack there now. She'd been so close to death – seconds from the end. And it hadn't been peaceful. No meadows and sunlit uplands. No hands sweeping through ears of corn.

It had been… she held back a tear. It had been – so damn sad.

She got out of the shower. Then dressed and made some

strong coffee. She'd seen her father as he was when she was a young girl, because that was the last time she truly knew him. Life had drifted. His problems had got in the way, and now he was out of touch. Hundreds of miles away. Her sister and mother were distant figures too. One thing at a time though.

She took her phone and rang his landline. The call didn't connect. Maybe he had a new number. She sent a text to her sister, Clare.

Bit worried about Dad. You heard from him?

It was time to get some fresh air. She took the trail upstream. When the path met the boardwalk, she remembered the person who had followed her that first night. The figure that had slunk back into the reeds. It must have been someone working for Tranter. They probably saw her working at The Needles' Eye and had been spying on her since then. That's how he knew to send the car to pick her up at Yarmouth Harbour. She'd never told him that piece of information. She should really have spotted that.

At the fork of the path, instead of taking the right fork out to Abbotsford Manor, she peeled off left. The path zigzagged up through the woods, emerging on a lower shelf of the headland. She sat on the grass, facing out to sea. Trying to empty her mind, of Tranter, the whole case, her father. So she was just in this moment – the burning edge of the present. Feeling lucky to be alive.

Half an hour later, at around eight thirty, she made it back to the harbour. She crossed the car park towards town. She wasn't ready to turn in for the night. Then she saw something in the marina that stopped her in her tracks. Among the thicket of white masts was one that stood a few metres taller than the others. Tranter's boat was still there, moored on the end of a jetty. Nobody was on board. The police would probably tow it off later, she thought. Maybe sell it off, now his business empire was about to collapse. Which was all down to her.

She was so busy congratulating herself that she didn't see Jim coming out of the harbour master's office. He called for her to come over and retreated into the building.

The door of his office was open. She went in and shut it behind her.

'Hey, Astrid. Take a seat,' he said, without making eye contact. He seemed distracted, fussing around with a few things on his desk and, for the first few minutes, making small talk about Cowes Week and the weather.

No wonder he was on edge, thought Astrid. This was a big criminal case for him. He didn't want to make any mistakes. After years of sorting out insurance claims for dented hulls, he was dealing with two murders and an attempted murder.

Eventually, he brought out a fresh notepad from the top drawer and plucked a biro from a pen pot on his desk. 'Okay, so the police have shared your statement with me. I've had some time to read it and would like to go over it with you. Just to make sure.'

'Sure?'

'Yes – to see if there are any new details you've remembered? Or if there's anything you want to change?'

'No, my statement covers it.'

'Sometimes, on reflection, events may seem different.'

'Different?' She folded her arms. 'No. I'm not changing anything.'

He nodded, then brought out a thin green cardboard file from his drawer. 'Alright – let me refresh my memory then.' He took out the two or three pages of handwritten notes. The ones the female police officer had made. He skimmed over them, curling his lip.

'When do you think the court case will be?'

He waited to finish the page. 'Court case?'

'Gabriel and Cristo… when will they go on trial?'

He went to the window and opened it. A draught sucked into the room. He stood there, leaning against the window ledge. 'Astrid…' He shook his head. 'There's a lot of what you told the police that doesn't add up.'

'Doesn't add up?' She could feel the heat burning on her cheeks. 'Are you saying I'm lying?'

'You say that like you never do.'

'What, seriously…?' she stumbled.

'You told me you were working as an undercover agent for HMRC. Remember?'

'Sure, but I made a mistake. I had too much to drink.'

'Is that right?' he said knowingly.

Behind him, Astrid noticed a black Range Rover pull into the car park and glide to a halt just out of view. Jim came back to the desk and sat down. Then he ran his finger down the page and stopped on a line. 'You say here you had one glass of wine on Gabriel's yacht. Was it just one glass?'

The air in the room felt stale, even with the window open. 'Jim…' She kept the anger down in her voice. Trying to sound rational. 'Jim. I had one drink. Then Gabriel explained I knew too much about his development, and he had to get rid of me. That's when Cristo came after me.'

Jim checked the clock on the wall above the door. He had one last glance at the file, then closed it. There were footsteps in the reception outside.

'One drink. I promise,' she pleaded. 'Everything I told you is true.'

Jim wasn't listening. He got up from behind his desk and brushed the front of his jumper.

There was a sharp rap on the door.

Then Jim said 'enter', or something.

Then Gabriel Tranter walked in.

And Astrid felt like she was drowning again.

She got out of her seat and backed away to the window. The ledge was waist height. She could scramble out, if she needed to. Then she saw the black Range Rover about twenty yards away. Cristo was standing against the driver's door. He was picking idly at his hand, which was wrapped in a white bandage. He'd see her and she'd be trapped. The road on one side. The harbour wall on the other.

When she turned back to Jim, he was shaking Tranter's hand and muttering apologetically. Tranter took the other seat by the desk and didn't say anything.

'It's fine, Astrid,' said Jim. 'We're just going to have a friendly chat.'

Tranter smiled at her with a look of pity.

Astrid leant against the window ledge, which pressed into the small of her back. She pointed at Tranter. 'Why is *he* here?'

'Here's the thing, Astrid.' Jim went and stood by Tranter. 'Gabriel has kindly agreed to drop all charges against you.'

'Charges against me?' she snorted.

'For damaging his boat. The flare.'

'You're both insane.'

Jim sighed and turned to Tranter. 'I'm sorry about this, Gabriel. I know you have better places to be.'

'Like jail,' shouted Astrid.

Tranter put his hand up. 'Okay, I'm not going to take this further, and neither is Cristo. But you have to admit what really happened on the boat, Astrid.'

Astrid composed herself. 'I know exactly what happened. You tried to kill me.'

'I tried to kill you?' Tranter laughed.

'The last time I heard a laugh that smug, it came from my ex-husband. He tried to make out I was a liar too. It's not happening again. I know what happened on the boat. It was all friendly to start with – just showing me your big yacht.' She was talking fast and she knew he was waiting for her to slip up. 'We had one drink.'

'A few drinks.'

'One drink.'

'I showed the police the empty bottle of wine. They know I'm teetotal. Cristo is too.'

'One drink.' She ploughed on. The heat returning to her cheeks. 'Then I started to ask you about why Mistral Industries were involved in the planning permission for the development. And the death of Victor Leech. That's when you admitted it all.'

'Admitted what?'

'How you got rid of him. Covered your tracks. Same with Silas, because he saw Cristo kill Victor Leech and you were worried he'd go to the police.'

Tranter said, 'I thought you might realise how silly you've been. Once you'd got over your hangover. As usual. Jim told me you like a drink.'

During their sparring Jim had watched them with his hands in his pockets. Not saying anything. Now he interrupted. 'You do like a drink, don't you, Astrid?'

'So what?'

Tranter turned to Jim. 'Don't worry. I've seen it before. Many times. Women who, let's say, don't know how to hold their drink.'

Astrid was close to swearing. Loudly. But she managed to hold it together. 'Listen, Jim, I wasn't drunk on the boat. He must have poured the wine away.'

'Astrid, please. That's enough.' Jim went round the desk and took out another green file from the drawer. 'Gabriel has given me his version of events. As the allegations were made when you came into harbour, I will be guiding the Hampshire Police on which version has more credibility.'

'No, wait. You have to listen.' She stepped forwards. 'What about the life jacket? The one Cristo threw over the side before we got over the main current.'

'What about it?' said Jim.

'They turned on the locator beacon and threw it into the current heading inland. So that's where rescue would look for me.' They were both watching her closely. Listening for a fault to prise open her story. 'Then when the current had switched direction, they were going to throw me in.'

Jim held up her green file. 'I know, I've read what you said. And it all sounds so... far-fetched.'

'It's the truth.'

'And here's another thing that doesn't add up.' Jim checked the file. 'When you thought you were in mortal danger, you didn't call the police?'

'I didn't have my phone.'

'Is that right?'

'Yes. He told me to leave it on shore. We were having a digital detox, or some crap. It was all part of the plan.'

Tranter interrupted. 'Come on, Astrid. You had your phone. You kept asking for selfies. It was embarrassing.'

'No, I didn't,' Astrid howled.

'Okay, okay...' Jim slapped the file on the table. 'You've had your say, Astrid. Now let's hear how Mr Tranter saw the events of last night.' Jim smiled, then said in an oily voice, 'Gabriel... if you'd be so kind.'

Tranter crossed his legs. Then he sat back and spoke slowly. 'As you know, I'm a very high-profile, very successful man. I don't want to flatter myself...'

'Pfuuh!' Astrid laughed. 'That's all you want to do.'

'Astrid,' barked Jim. 'Let Mr Tranter have his say.'

'Thank you.' Gabriel put both hands on his knee and continued. 'As you can imagine, I get a lot of attention from the opposite sex. So, when Astrid asked if she could come sailing with me, I was cautious.'

Astrid pushed her back against the ledge, so the pain would distract her from shouting out.

'She said she was a keen sailor,' Tranter continued, 'so I agreed. I thought she would be good company. We got on okay to start with. But then the wine started to kick in. I'd opened a bottle for her and noticed that she'd finished it before we'd even got out into the main current.'

He kept up the lies as Jim listened attentively, shaking his head in disapproval now and then. Tranter denied all the accusations against him, blaming everything on her. It was Astrid who'd taken off her life jacket and accidentally dropped it in the sea. She'd become aggressive when he'd repulsed her advances. She'd had to dig her nails into her palm for that one.

Tranter then claimed that when he'd gone down below to make her a coffee to sober her up, she'd jammed a spanner in the door, trapping him inside. Cristo had tried to get her away from the helm and she'd got into the inflatable dinghy and stumbled over the side. When she got back in, she'd fired a flare at Cristo as he was trying to help her out.

It was all lies, designed to make him look like the injured party, and Astrid unhinged and vengeful. And Jim believed every word. 'But as I say—' Tranter uncrossed his legs and stared at Astrid '—I'm a patient guy and I'm prepared to move on. Forgive and forget, Astrid. What do you say?'

'Never,' she shouted. 'You tried to kill me, and I'm going to see that you get locked up.'

Tranter turned to Jim. 'I tried…'

'I know you did,' sympathised Jim. 'You did your best.'

Astrid knew there was no point arguing. Jim had heard Tranter's story already, and taken it hook, line and sinker then. She walked away from the window ledge, taking a wide arc past both of them to the door. She stood there, one hand on the door handle, the other pointing at Tranter. 'Just keep away from me. You and that psychopathic henchman of yours. Do you understand?'

'Don't worry, I'm going nowhere near you. I'm staying in Cowes for another couple of nights, then I have the Fastnet Race and I'm gone. And if you try stalking me anymore, I will press charges.'

'Hah.' Astrid balled her fists. 'I'm going nowhere near you.'

'Well, just to make sure, Astrid—' Jim had put the files away and was standing over his desk, hands planted on it '—I think you should leave the harbour. What shall we say, let's have you gone by first light?'

'Don't worry. I'm going.' She hurried out of the door, leaving it open behind her. Then she took another corridor away from the car park and out into the light. She found a bench by the river and sat down. Put her head in her hands and let the anger and hurt drain slowly through her fingers.

Thirty-three

Astrid knew she had to get out of the harbour. But she wasn't leaving the island – not until she'd brought down Tranter. Frank had mentioned that he'd managed to avoid paying the harbour fees by mooring up in a bend further up the river. His secret spot. Well, it was a shared secret now.

She unplugged the charging cable on the gangplank. The boat's batteries only needed a bit of a top-up. Same with the water tanks. There was enough food – tins, milk, pasta and fresh vegetables – to last a couple of weeks. Then she unwound the ropes at the stern and prow of the boat. The name, *Curlew's Rest*, shone in the last rays of the sunset. Her Uncle Henry had left her a boat and a mystery to solve.

Now she was on to her second. And she was going to crack this one too. Tranter might have tried to brush her off, dry-clean her away. But he'd never met someone like her. She would never give in. Never crumble. Right, Astrid? 'You know it,' she said to herself, throwing the rope onto the deck and climbing over the rail.

The light of the day was fading fast. The headlights of cars bounced over the big arched bridge. The marker lights blinked red, green, white out beyond the harbour. She left her own lights off on the boat. There could be someone out in the reeds watching her now. One of Tranter's spies. She was pretty sure he wouldn't sully his hands with this anymore. He'd be back in Cowes tomorrow, getting ready for the Fastnet Race. That's not to say he wouldn't get someone else to sort her out.

Astrid peered out through the glass window of the control cabin, taking a line on the river ahead. The water glinted silver against the dark thickets of reeds. Narrowing as it turned, left then right. At one point she could hear the keel scraping over the silt. It was high tide and falling. There was no getting back to the harbour now. Not that she wanted to.

In a hundred yards, the river widened slightly. She heard the engine find a lower note as it passed over deeper water. Then the river formed a wide shoulder that pushed into a copse of trees on the far bank. Astrid slowed the boat down to a couple of knots, the wash barely breaking on the mudflats.

In the near dark, she could make out a jetty ahead. It was a simple wooden pier, about four feet wide, that jutted just beyond the reeds. She cut the engine and nudged the boat alongside. There were no lights in any direction. The hills and trees were blackboard dark, against a grey sky dusted with stars.

The current pinned the boat to the jetty. Anchor down. Prow line tied up on the worn post. She locked up, her tiredness ambushing her. Then she went down below and slid into her sleeping bag, asleep before she'd zipped it up.

Thirty-four

Standing on the deck in early morning light, Astrid realised just how perfect the mooring was. The boat fitted snugly into the slight curve of the old jetty. Its prow formed a 'V' into a bank of high bulrushes. Its stern was shaded by another of clump of reeds that pushed out in the river. It was as if *Curlew's Rest* had chosen this mooring herself, nestled in and rubbed her flanks against the posts to settle an itch.

She did a full circle on the deck. There was no way anyone could see her. Even on the far bank, the boardwalk was hidden by bulrushes. The jetty was falling apart. There were missing planks – two, three spaces here and there. It felt safe, and that's what she wanted after the mess of yesterday. Nobody should find her here. Even at high tide, there was barely enough depth to sail in. They could come for her through the woods, maybe. But the jetty would sort them out. Stepping out into the dark, they'd fall through the gaps.

She made two slices of toast and strawberry jam, layered thick for a sugar rush. That should wake her up – and the coffee, stronger than usual. At the cabin table, she went through her phone. First, she blocked Tranter's number.

Just in case. Then she scrolled through The Art of Murder WhatsApp group.

There had been a flurry of messages last night. Everyone wanted to know how her sailing trip with Tranter had gone. When she didn't reply, the messages had tailed off. Nobody was too worried. Why should they be? She'd gone out yachting with one of the island's most respectable figures. Who would think he'd try to kill anyone, in broad daylight? That's why it was so galling. Tranter knew nobody would believe her. His word against hers. Jim had proven that yesterday in his office.

She sent a message to the group. At least they'd trust her.

Hey – I can't explain here. But I have most of the answers. Victor Leech. Silas. The digging at The Needles' Eye. Can we meet after lunch 2pm? I'll explain everything then.

All four of them replied straight away and said they could make it. They'd obviously been waiting by their phones for her news.

Astrid used the rest of the morning to finish off her report for HMRC. It was done by noon, then she made herself lunch. The best cheese on toast – strong Cheddar shaved over thick brown bread, with a dash of Tabasco sauce. Might as well use up the cheese and bread while it was fresh. She wouldn't be going back into town for who knew how long. Until she'd sorted out Tranter, one way or another.

At half past twelve, she put on her hiking gear. Then she locked the boat and clambered up onto the jetty. One hand on the post, she stepped carefully forward, testing each plank with her lead foot, to see if it cracked before taking her full weight. With the wider gaps she had to jump, breathing a sigh of relief when it took her weight at the other side. At the end of the jetty was a big willow tree, its branches draped down to the water. She parted the curtain of leaves and squeezed through.

Nothing grew in the shade. The ground was covered in a black mat of dead leaves from last winter. She pushed on, stepping over the knuckles of tree roots. Inhaling the cool air that smelt of damp earth. It was like walking through the breath of some moss-covered giant who lingered in the shadows.

Eventually she found a faint path that was pocked with deer hoof prints. The deer probably took this route down to the water to drink under the willow tree, she thought. They would find their way out to clear ground, further south. She followed the path and it became drier as she climbed away from the river, until it burst out into the sunlight, the headland looming before her. Ahead was the path that cut through the next woods to Abbotsford Manor. She was there ten minutes later.

Everyone was in the potting shed. They were seated in a semicircle facing the door. There was no sign of any art being done.

'Well?' said Annabelle as soon as Astrid crossed the threshold.

Astrid stood in front of them and told the whole story. How Tranter had admitted he'd got his assistant Cristo to bump off Victor and Silas. And how she was due to be next, but she'd fought them off on the boat and sailed it back to harbour. Only to find that Jim, the harbour master, was taking Tranter's side. They listened in shocked silence until she'd finished talking.

Then Kabir spoke. 'That sounds quite an ordeal. I'm very glad you're okay, Astrid.'

They all agreed. Annabelle came over and gave her a hug, which was welcome, if unexpected. Frank dragged over a chair and Astrid slumped into it. When she'd finished the story, it felt complete. Of course it did. How could it go any further, she thought? Tranter was rich and powerful. There was no proof and nobody would believe her. He'd won – and that wasn't fair.

Kabir read her mind. 'Sorry, Astrid. I can't see how we can beat him.'

Frank reached over to the drawer and brought out Tranter's autobiography. He gripped it in both hands, shaking his head. 'I'm gutted. I looked up to this guy.'

Astrid asked him to hand over the book, and he passed it to her. 'Keep it,' he said.

She stared at the title. 'Get What You Want,' she mouthed, then placed the book on her lap. 'So, listen.' She sat up. 'Let's go round the room. What do we all want?'

'Er… why?' said Annabelle.

'Just bear with me here,' said Astrid. 'I mean, deep down. What's that one thing each of us wants?'

'This is going to make sense, isn't it?' asked Kabir.

'I hope so. Maybe you could start, Kabir.'

Kabir didn't hesitate. He repeated what he'd told Astrid earlier. About seeing one of his paintings hanging on the wall with a little "sold" sticker in the corner. 'Then I'd know I was a real artist,' he said. The others muttered their approval.

'That's a great start,' said Astrid. 'Now, who's next? Wren?'

'To go to art college,' said Wren. 'But you know that, Astrid, don't you?'

Astrid nodded. Then turned to Annabelle, who was looking at her feet.

'Can we go to Frank?' said Annabelle.

'Of course... Frank.'

Frank sucked air over his lower lip. 'Hot tub.'

'That it?' said Annabelle.

'Yup, a big hot tub for the chalet. Then I'm golden.'

They all looked at Annabelle, who was shifting in her chair. They could see there was something she wanted to say. They all stared her down until she cracked.

'Okay, you win.' She brought her hands up to the side of her face, made a slight aargh sound and said, 'Nothing. That's it. Nothing.'

'Nothing?' said Kabir.

'Well, no. I have everything I want. That's why I'm a snob.' Frank raised an eyebrow, which Annabelle noticed. 'Yes, Frank, I am aware that I'm a snob. But I enjoy it, so that's fine.' She went over to the kettle and switched it on. Then started fussing with the cups. 'Ghastly mugs. Should be bone china.' She grimaced. 'You see, I can't help myself. But the thing is... I know I'm lucky. Because I've got this.' She looked to each of them. 'I really love this group. Including you, Frank. I just don't like to admit it.'

'Aww, cheers, Annabelle.' Frank winked at her.

'Well, that was revealing,' said Wren. 'Like when Cruella de Vil says she only kills puppies because she's lonely.'

Annabelle laughed. 'Bit harsh.'

Astrid took the book again and held it up. 'Here's my theory, then. I don't think that Tranter has got what he wants.' She rifled through the pages. 'Here's a man who seems to have everything. Fame. Boats. Houses. But that's not enough, is it? He can't stop. Because deep down, there's something he can't have. He's just distracting himself from the fact he hasn't got this thing he really wants.'

'That's very good, Astrid.' Kabir gave her a small round of applause. 'He's so driven, isn't he? If he was truly content, he'd stop having to prove himself.'

Wren said, 'But knowing that, how does it help us bring him down? Which is what we want to do, right?'

'Damn right,' said Astrid. 'There might be something in the book somewhere. His weakness. A weapon, I dunno. We've got nothing else at this stage.' She held out the book to Frank. 'You want to go through it?'

'No need,' he said. 'I know it like the back of my hand.'

'Okay, what do you reckon?' said Astrid.

Frank started on a potted history of Gabriel Marcus Tranter. His early life in London. His family and his father, who taught him to sail. The business success. They listened intently as the story drifted past. Hoping to hear something to get a hook into.

'Tell me more about his father,' said Kabir.

'It's always the father, isn't it?' said Astrid.

'Usually is,' said Kabir. 'It sounds like Tranter was very loyal to his.'

'Oh yeah,' said Frank, 'he put him on a pedestal. In fact...'

'Go on,' said Astrid.

'Okay, I remember he mentioned in his book his father wasn't allowed in the British Yacht Society in Cowes. He got blackballed for some reason and that stuck in Tranter's craw.'

'Really? He told me he had no time for those stuffy clubs.' Astrid flipped through the book to find the photos.

Wren held up a finger. 'What's the British—'

'The BYS,' interrupted Annabelle, 'is the most prestigious sailing club in Britain. If not the world.'

'Sounds swanky,' said Wren.

'It is,' continued Annabelle. 'Members are royalty, business barons, admirals. It's the pinnacle of sailing high society.'

'Which means,' said Kabir, 'you can't exactly walk in there.'

'Well, no,' said Annabelle, 'and you're going to have to trust me with this one, as I know all about social climbing. These are people who believe in etiquette and rules so much that they can't believe anyone would break them. Which is exactly why we are going to walk in there.' She picked out her car keys from her bag and jiggled them at Astrid. 'Right, Astrid – I'll drive.'

Thirty-five

Annabelle parked her car outside her 'summer pad' in Cowes. It was a pink two-storey terraced house on a side street running up from the waterfront.

Inside, it was neat and tastefully decorated. The hand of an interior designer wherever Astrid looked. Annabelle ushered her to a walk-in wardrobe in the bedroom and left her to pick out something 'a little smarter'. An outfit suitable for post-sailing drinks in the afternoon, which, Annabelle assured her, was the only point of joining a yacht club.

Astrid went through the rails of summer dresses. Nearly all were designer. It took her back to a time when she had a wardrobe crammed with the latest fashions. The dresses were all gone now. The flat, though – that still needed sorting out. To finally get Simon off her back. She picked out a light summer shift dress – magenta, with small yellow flowers. Then she took off her hiking shoes and slipped into a pair of strappy sandals.

Annabelle was waiting for her on a teal sofa in the living room, scrolling through her phone. She looked up from the screen.

'Much better.' She reached into a glass bowl on a coffee

table and picked out a pair of black sunglasses. They had round lenses the size of small saucers. 'Pop these on.'

Astrid put them on and gave a twirl.

'Perfect. Pure Audrey Hepburn.'

'Thanks.' She sat down next to Annabelle and glanced at the phone. 'So what have you found?'

Annabelle explained that the BYS had a committee who oversaw memberships. They were nearly all men. All some way into their sixties. Annabelle held up the phone and slowly scrolled down the committee members' headshots. 'Okay, let's see if we can bump into one of these lovelies this afternoon.'

'Then what?'

'And then we...' Annabelle focused on an imperious-looking man in full naval uniform. 'No, they're not going to tell us anything. Are they?'

'Probably not.' Astrid shuffled to the edge of the sofa. There was a stack of glossy magazines on the coffee table in front of her. She picked up the top one – an edition of *Vanity Fair* – and idly flipped through the pages. 'Unless, of course, I say I'm a society journalist.'

'Ooh, that's good,' said Annabelle.

Astrid clipped on an airy tone to her voice. 'Hi – I'm Astrid Swift. Society reporter for *Vunnity Fur*.'

'Mmm... I'm not sure about the accent.'

'Yeah – it's not the best, is it?' said Annabelle.

'The reporter idea might work though.'

'It might... and let's face it...' She got up from the sofa and smoothed her dress down at the hips. 'We've got nothing else.'

★★★

The first part of the plan went without a hitch. Annabelle was right. They peeled off from the road alongside the harbour, through the open metal gates with the initials 'BYS' in gold in the centre and past the gatehouse. And nobody batted an eyelid.

There was a steady flow of guests coming in and out of the front door. Some had clearly spent most of the day out on the water. There were younger crew members in dark blue fleeces, sailing trousers, and mirrored sunglasses on straps. For the older crowd, it was blazers and chinos for the men, with classic Ray-Bans perched above wind-rosed cheeks. For the women – light and floral, with big sun hats. Annabelle squeezed Astrid's hand and whispered in a half giggle, 'We made it.'

'I know, let's keep going,' Astrid said from the corner of her mouth.

They both glided into the foyer. A man in a black suit sitting in a chair raised an eyebrow. He might have said something. A weak, raspy 'Scuse me', maybe. But they were gone. Weaving through guests, some with luggage at their feet. Over the worn Persian carpet. Past the mahogany dressers against the wall. Past the black wooden boards with long lines of names of past trophy winners. Past stiff portraits of elderly members – blur of walrus moustaches and sailing caps, hands stuck in pockets and 'how long is this going to bloody well take?' expressions.

Astrid kept her eyes dead ahead on the door to the garden. A few more yards and they were through, out into the sunshine. Her heart settled. Annabelle plucked a couple of glasses of champagne from a table set off the gravel path and handed one to Astrid.

'Told you.' She clinked glasses.

The garden dropped in tiers down to the ramparts. At the back was a white marquee with some round tables laid out in front. All taken. The other guests milled around on the lawn or sat on the banked slopes, drinking beer or champagne and gazing out at the sea. Waiters in three-piece suits weaved between them, taking orders on white notepads.

Annabelle said something. Astrid wasn't listening. She was staring at Tranter's yacht, which was moored in the harbour. There were a few people in uniform wandering around on deck. It was too far away to make out if one of them was Tranter. Annabelle followed Astrid's eyeline and realised what she was looking at.

'Tranter's boat?' said Annabelle.

'Yup.' She took a sip. 'It's not fair, is it?'

'It's not.' Annabelle stood next to her. 'He killed two people. Tried to kill you. And he's going to get away with it because he's untouchable.'

'Nobody is untouchable,' said Astrid. 'I saw that film as well. Now, let's check those photos again.'

Annabelle brought out her phone and went through the headshots of the memberships committee again. She scanned the crowd and tables. 'It's like a posh person safari,' she muttered. 'Ah, here we go.' She pointed slyly to a table in front of the marquee. 'Tim Featherstone. The social secretary.' A man in a blue blazer, white shirt and pink tie was sitting on his own. His white peaked sailor's cap pinned down a wave of grey hair that spilled over his ears. 'I'll be here for backup if you need me,' breathed Annabelle. 'Good luck.'

Astrid took a deep breath and strode towards the table. In front of him was a tall glass. No liquid, just two half-melted ice cubes and a lemon wedge sitting at the bottom. Next to it was a digital stopwatch on a string, a pair of binoculars and a clipboard with rows of numbers and names.

'I'm so sorry I'm late, Tim,' Astrid gushed.

He looked up. He had a narrow tanned head that reminded her of the Easter Island stone statues. Tim had spent a fair amount of time gazing out to sea as well. There were deep crow's feet at the corners of his eyes, which twinkled from deep sockets. 'Sorry… I don't understand.'

Astrid sat down next to him and placed her phone on the table. 'It's for the interview we arranged for three o'clock. Francesca Smith. *Vanity Fair* magazine.' *Smith?* thought Astrid. It wasn't brilliant, but nothing else sprang to mind. And she was so tense she was amazed to get any words out.

'I'm afraid I don't know anything about this.'

'Oh, it was arranged through your press office. I guess with Cowes Week being so hectic.' She searched the phone, looking for the feature to record an interview. Again, something she could have practised. 'Now where is…'

'Listen, Francesca. I have to say. We don't court a lot of publicity here at the club. I mean—' he swept his hand out across the packed lawn '—it's not as if we're begging for new members.'

'I know, but I'm sure our readers would love to hear about how this club is at the centre of this year's Cowes Week.'

'No, I'm sorry to be so coy, but really. I'm going to have

to politely turn down your offer.' He pushed back his chair and stood up.

'I knew it.' Annabelle appeared at the table. 'It *is* you.' Annabelle leant down and gave Astrid an air-kiss. Then she turned to Tim. 'I'm so sorry to burst in. But I just had to come over. This, she...' Annabelle floundered.

'Francesca,' Astrid interrupted.

'Of course, sorry. Francesca,' said Annabelle. 'Francesca interviewed my husband and I in Bermuda about our yacht club there.'

'The Royal Yacht Club in Hamilton?' said Tim, stony-faced.

'Uh, hmm. That's the one,' replied Annabelle.

'I know it well. I'm surprised I've never met you before.' He eyed her up and down. 'Were you a guest?'

'A guest, yes.' Annabelle didn't miss a beat. 'Both of us were guests. Staying with the Crombies.'

'The Crombies?'

'That's right. Richard and Minty. You must have heard of them. Everyone knows Minty.' And with that, Tim's guard melted away. There was no way he was going to admit not knowing someone everyone else knew.

'Richard and Minty, of course.' He perked up. 'Yes, they're a riot, aren't they?'

'Anyway. I won't take up your time.' Annabelle gripped Astrid's arm. 'But thanks for such a marvellous article. I loved it. The club committee were delighted too. Good luck, Tim.'

Annabelle carried on down the path towards the drinks table. When Astrid turned back, Tim was back in his seat, his clipboard pushed to one side. 'Please, Francesca. Sorry about the confusion. Ask me anything you like.'

Astrid found the recording feature on her phone and set it halfway between them, which she thought looked professional. She'd considered being a journalist when she was younger. Someone from the BBC had visited the school and given them a talk. Now, wondering what first question she, or rather a journalist, might ask, she wished she'd concentrated. Ah, yes – she remembered. The three 'W's. All good interviews should ask them somewhere. Where. Why. What. She hit the record button.

'So, Tim. Tell me, *what* is it you like about being a member of the British Yacht Society?'

It proved to be a very good opening question. There were many things that Tim liked, no *loved*, about this place. Much of them to do with the food. Astrid was given, in some detail, a rundown of the best dishes of the house. Mostly comfort food that reminded him of his boarding school days. Crumbles. Shepherd's pies. Chutneys and marmalades, all of which, he told her reverentially, were made on the premises by a team of top chefs.

Then there was the clubhouse itself. The generous rooms for members wanting to stay over. A library. Private dining. Every luxury of a country house, but by the sea. Astrid glanced down at her phone. They were seven minutes in, and she'd yet to steer him to the yachting.

'And presumably you have to own a boat to be a member,' she asked.

'Not necessarily. Our membership rules only insist that

you are actively engaged in yachting. Or have shown great achievement in the sport in the past.'

'Right, so how does the voting for new members work?' she asked innocently.

'Ah, now that must remain a secret.' He reached out for his empty glass. Caught the attention of a waiter and jiggled it. 'Francesca, can I get you a drink?'

'No, I'm good. Thanks.'

When the waiter came over, he ordered the same drink. Double gin and tonic. Gordon's with Schweppes Slimline. Two wedges of lemon. Two ice cubes. Just the way he liked it. And here, it seemed, he got everything he liked.

The waiter backed away and Astrid said, 'Is Gabriel Tranter a member?'

'No, he's not,' Tim answered bluntly. 'Why do you ask?'

'A successful businessman like him. One of the island's favourite sons. I'd have thought he'd make an ideal member. I'm surprised he hasn't applied.'

'Who says he didn't apply?'

Astrid kept a straight face. 'Did he?'

Tim glanced down at the stopwatch. 'Hang on a minute.' He lifted the binoculars and trained them out over the bay.

Out on the water, a race was just about to get started. A line of forty small yachts chopped and turned, edging towards the starting line, as if an invisible force field held them back.

Below the ramparts, the crowds filled the boardwalk. On the sea wall was a line of small gold cannons, facing out to sea. At the end of the line, a man in a white peaked cap checked his stopwatch and, on his nod, one of the cannons blasted a plume of grey smoke out in the water. There was a cheer from the spectators on the shoreline. Way out in the bay, the yachts trimmed their sails and jostled out into the wind.

Tim put the binoculars down. 'Sorry, where were we?'

'Gabriel Tranter.'

'Tranter?'

The waiter arrived and laid down a triangular napkin on the table. Then he set a gin and tonic down on it. Tim lifted the glass to his lips, took a long sip, and smiled in satisfaction.

'You were telling me about Tranter's application,' Astrid said.

'Oh, yes. Right.' He put the drink down unsteadily. 'Gabriel Tranter has been rather persistent in trying to get membership at the BYS.'

'Really.' Astrid remembered how Tranter had told her he wanted nothing to do with the yacht clubs in Cowes. A killer and a liar then. No surprise.

'Yes. Offering to buy things for the club. Charity donations. But of course, it doesn't work like that.'

'How does it work?'

'It's all about…' he knitted his fingers together '…being a good fit for the club. You can't just buy your way in here. And it doesn't matter if you're famous either.'

'Tranter's father then. Not a good fit.' She copied his hand movement.

'I'm afraid he wasn't.'

'So what did Tranter make of you turning him down?'

'Francesca, between you and I…' He pushed the phone

over to her. Then made a zipping motion of his mouth. Astrid hit the off button on the recorder. 'The club committee is considering giving Gabriel Tranter membership.'

'Does he know this?'

'Not yet. You see…' Big gulp of the G and T. She was glad he was drinking doubles. He'd lost all his reserve now. 'Even though he's a rather, shall we say, abrasive figure, we do have to recognise his contribution to the world of yachting. We are at the epicentre of that sport, after all.' He paused. 'So tomorrow – if he wins the Fastnet Race, then we will grant him membership. But that must remain a secret.'

'Of course.' Astrid took her phone and put it in her bag. 'Not a peep.'

Tim checked his stopwatch again. Then picked up his clipboard. 'If you'll excuse me. Back in a minute.'

Astrid watched him cross the lawn towards the marshals on the platform down by the ramparts. He moved through the crowd with supreme confidence. A smile here. A pat on the back there. This was his world and he was completely at home. Everything in his life had come together to this point. The crow's nest of the greatest yacht club in the world.

A place where none of the discomforts that everyone else dealt with could intrude. No bills. No labour to wake up to. Cleaning clothes. Domestic details. All of that was taken care of with a gracious hand. Tonight, Astrid thought, he would be tucked up in his bed, his head sunk into two goose-down pillows. The chintzy curtains pulled tight to keep the moonlight out. Dreaming of a breakfast of toast with home-made marmalade served in a silver pot by a man in a three-piece suit.

It would be easy to despise him. For all the things he had. Easier still to laugh at him. But jealousy, they say, is a poor life companion. He'd got there by hook or by crook and he had what he wanted. Connections, status, legacy – there would be a wooden board on a wall somewhere with his name in gold and 'Social Secretary' written next to it.

In short, Tim had everything that Tranter wanted. She could see how that might drive Tranter to distraction. He had all the money in the world but not the approval of his peers. This was a place run by rich men, for rich men and their guests. And Tranter was on the outside. She looked out to his boat in the harbour. He was on the wrong side of the winning line for once. And it must be killing him.

Astrid got up from the table and threaded her way through the guests towards the main house. Annabelle saw her and followed close behind. Neither of them said anything until they were well clear of the gates. Then Annabelle gripped Astrid's hand and said, 'Whooo... we got away with it.'

'I know, you were right,' Astrid said. 'And hey, what was that Minty thing all about?'

'Oh, that.' Annabelle laughed. 'With this lot, there's always a Minty somewhere.'

'Anyway, you were amazing.'

'Thanks.'

'And I found out something very revealing about Tranter. Very revealing.'

They dropped into Annabelle's house so Astrid could change back into her hiking gear and to grab a strong coffee to settle their nerves. The news that Tranter wanted to join the British Yacht Society – desperately wanted to join – was a breakthrough. But how could they use it to bring him down? It felt like having a new weapon with no instruction manual. If he won the race tomorrow, he'd finally get his dream. He'd have everything.

The injustice of it all was still smouldering when Annabelle drew into the car park of Abbotsford Manor. 'What are we going to do about Tranter now?' asked Astrid.

'No idea.' Annabelle switched off the engine. 'Not yet anyway. It's like those crime shows. We're into the last part of the story. The bit after the ads for pet insurance and carpet shampoo. Something will happen.'

'You think so?'

'Yeah – it's like that episode of *The Coroner*. The one where the Punch and Judy operator is found dead. And the mayor of Lighthaven did it. Then *she* gets killed.'

'I know the one.'

'Then right at the end they discover that the mayor's daughter killed her. By hiding her mother's Ventolin inhaler…'

Astrid picked up the plot. 'And the daughter had actually smeared a prawn on her mother's scone. Which triggered a fatal asthma attack.'

They both sat there for a while, going over the episode. Then Astrid broke the silence. 'To be honest, I'm not sure how that moves us forward, Annabelle.'

'Yeah, maybe. But still, don't give up, Astrid.'

'Don't worry, I won't.' Astrid clicked the door open. 'Okay, I'm going to head back to the boat through the woods. It'll be safer. Will you report back to the group, if anyone is around?'

'Of course.' Annabelle hesitated. 'And before you go, I want to say something.'

Astrid took her hand off the door. 'You know you asked everyone earlier what they wanted?'

'Sure.'

'Well, today I got the one thing I've always wanted.'

'Really? I thought you had everything.'

'Yes – I did too. But there was one little thing, apparently. I didn't realise it until it happened.' Annabelle stretched back in the driver's seat. 'I have just stood on the hallowed lawn of the British Yacht Society with a glass of chilled champagne.' She closed her eyes, as if tasting the champagne again. Then she opened them and sighed. 'And nothing will beat it ever again. So, thank you, Astrid.'

'Why are you thanking me?'

'Because you made it happen. Without you, I wouldn't have had the nerve to walk in there.'

'Me neither,' said Astrid.

Thirty-six

Astrid followed the trail through the woods to the top of the valley and out into the sunshine. It was just after six and it was a beautiful summer's day. Blue sky. Puffy white clouds. It was too nice an evening to hunker down in the boat.

When she reached the high ground, she stopped to get her breath back. It was good to be here. On this headland. This island. But she had a creeping sense her time on the Isle of Wight was coming to an end. Cowes Week would be over tomorrow. Tranter would leave, if she couldn't work out how to stop him.

She'd miss the group, but it was time to move on. The tide was turning – and it was taking her with it. But where to? Hanbury, where there was Kath and Sheepdip, and Cobb? No. She turned to face the sea beyond the cliffs. To the south. Far south. To Spain to visit her father, as she should have a long time ago.

She set off again, but after a few steps she noticed that one of her bootlaces was undone. As she bent down to tie it up, she saw someone out of the corner of her eye stop abruptly. They were about fifty yards back down the slope. Black trousers, a black hoodie pulled over their head. It was as if they'd been following her from a distance and didn't want to shorten the gap between them. When she stood up and pretended to admire the view again, they hesitated. Then tucked in behind a high gorse bush. She was being followed.

Okay, she thought. Tranter had sent one of his spies. And she wasn't putting up with it. It was broad daylight, a trail of ramblers in both directions. Witnesses, if she needed them to be. It might as well be here.

She tightened the straps of her rucksack and strode down the path towards the gorse bush. About thirty yards from the bush, the person ducked their head out, saw her approaching and quickly retreated. By the time Astrid reached the bush, they were way ahead of her, hurrying down a narrow path that cut diagonally across the flank of the headland. Astrid quickened her pace. The figure in the black hoodie sped up. They glanced back now and then, to see if she was gaining on them, but not long enough to reveal their face.

At first, the trail plunged steeply over stony ground. Then it levelled out, running alongside cornfields and through pastures cropped smooth by cows. Then the trail dipped down to the road. On the other side was a car park for the theme park above The Needles. The person hesitated by the kerb, not sure which way to go next. Astrid had closed the gap – there was only twenty yards between them. Her hands were sweaty. Ready to get a grip of them. But they crossed the road, veered off down the hill and through the entrance to the theme park.

The theme park was proving popular. Hundreds of tourists were wandering past the white clapperboard shops at the entrance. Astrid fixed her prey in her sights. They were keeping close to a white picket fence, where there were fewer people in the way. On the other side of the fence was a funfair ride. Giant teacups, each with a handful of toddlers inside, rotated slowly in the sunshine.

A couple holding hands blocked the way ahead. The figure burst through their linked hands like a runner coming through the winner's tape. The man shouted, 'Oi, you mind?' as Astrid squeezed through the gap.

Next was a little racetrack. A bunch of kids were zooming around in little orange jeeps. Giant plastic dinosaurs loomed over them. Astrid ducked under the neck of a diplodocus and broke into a jog. In front of her, the figure slalomed round a sunburnt family of six and into a shop. Astrid followed them in, just managing to read the sign over the door that said 'Alum Glass Works'.

Inside was an open-plan workshop. A couple of furnaces glowed at the back. A man in a leather overall was standing in front of one of them, shaping a blob of molten glass round a metal pipe. A walkway ran round the room. It was blocked with people who had stopped to watch the glassblowing.

The figure in black had already shoved their way halfway through the queue. Astrid crabbed along the back wall, rubbing against bags and elbows. Apologising every second breath until she was shucked out into the gift shop.

Everything on sale was made of glass. Vases, ornaments, lighthouses in every colour were lined up on shelves. She scanned the room. She could just see the top of the person's hoodie on the next aisle.

Astrid swung round the corner. The person was ten feet

away. 'Yesss...' Astrid whispered. They were stuck. The way ahead was blocked by a couple who were admiring a paperweight in the shape of a teapot. Astrid stepped forward – the chase was over.

There was a crash of glass. With a single sweep of their hand, the person had knocked a bunch of glass lighthouse ornaments to the floor. Some other shoppers hurried over to see what had happened. In the confusion, the person dodged through. Sneaky, thought Astrid, backing away and taking another aisle out past a cashier, who mumbled, 'Someone's going to have to pay for that.'

Outside in the sunshine, Astrid scanned the park, her panic rising. There was no way they were getting away. Then she saw them. They were cornered by a wooden viewing platform that jutted out over the cliffs. The person pulled the hoodie down over their forehead casting their face in shadow and nodded calmly. As if appreciating how well she'd kept up. This was definitely the person who'd followed her that night on the boardwalk. The same calm arrogance.

Astrid edged slowly towards them, her hands slightly out from her hips. Like a cowboy shoot-out. If they ran at her... left... right – she was ready to tackle them. Ready to... and they were gone again. A quick swerve to their left and through the entrance to another ride. Above the door, the sign said 'Chairlift'.

When Astrid got there, they were twenty feet ahead of her at the pay booth. They rifled through their pockets. Pushed the coins through the grille. Now she had them. 'Ugh,' she moaned.

A dozen kids in the same light-blue T-shirts shoaled

around her and lined up in front of the booth. The figure in the hoodie barged through the turnstile. A woman with a beige bucket hat overtook her, apologising on the way. 'Sorry, we'll just get ahead. Thanks,' she said, getting in front of the kids.

'No problem,' Astrid said, checking he price board above the booth. It was £3 for a one-way ticket. The kids filtered through the turnstile. Beyond them, Astrid could see her quarry slide into a chairlift without looking back.

A minute later, Astrid stood on the painted square on the ground and waited for the next metal chair to scoop her up. The assistant flipped a safety bar over her shoulders and the chair rattled forward and out over the edge of the platform.

Astrid was okay with heights. Over the years she'd been on a few skiing holidays, so chairlifts didn't faze her. Which was a good job. This one was pretty basic. Two simple seats and a bar for the feet to rest on. The kids in front were screaming with delight as the chair bounced higher above the ground, then *gggrrrundled* alongside a pylon and out over the cliff.

Way below her feet, Astrid noticed a bunch of baseball caps on the cliff edge. They must have been blown off their owners' heads as the chair hit the updraught from the cliff. Six chairs ahead, her target's hoodie was still up. They were gripping the safety bar, eyes dead ahead. She had them now though. Definitely. To the west was a crescent of pebbly beach that ran up against the steep cliff. The same to the east. Next to the chairlift station was a wooden pier. A passenger boat, a sight-seeing tour of The Needles presumably, was just leaving. They weren't escaping that way then. She could relax now. They were trapped.

The cliffs down to her left were very different to the ones below the headland. Instead of hard limestone, they were made of dried sand. A wide stain of pink worked itself between the oranges and yellows. The bottom of the cliff was roped off. To stop people just digging up their own coloured sand instead of buying it up at the shop, maybe.

A few minutes later, the chair holding Tranter's spy shallowed out at the dock. A man stepped out to lift the safety bar back. But the person waved at him with a circular motion with their hand. The man stepped back. They were staying on. Their chair juddered round a big metal wheel, sending them back up the cliffs. Nice move. But not checkmate.

She dug out her phone from her pocket and quickly set it up to take a photo. They'd be facing head on to her in a few seconds. And they knew it. The person pulled the cord of their hoodie tight, and turned their back to her. When they passed each other, they were only ten feet apart. Astrid held up the phone and grabbed a couple of pictures. Shouted 'Hey!' But they didn't look round.

When she got to the bottom of the lift, Astrid waved to the man. 'I'm staying on,' she said. He grunted and stepped back.

On the way back up, she had a good view of the person ahead. The kids in the blue tops had got off at the bottom, so there were six empty chairs between her and them. She breathed deep and steady, letting her heart rate go down. The person was double tying their laces. They were getting ready to run for it.

As their chair passed the pylon, Astrid started counting.

She stopped when her chair passed the same point. Twenty-five seconds. It was a good head start. But she was in no mood to let them get away.

As soon as their chair levelled out, the person pulled back the safety bar and dashed to the exit. Astrid sprang out twenty-five seconds later and sprinted after them. When she rounded the corner, she saw them vault over the exit turnstile and dash out into the theme park.

Astrid sprinted up to the turnstile and pushed against it with her hip. It jammed. 'Come on,' she shouted.

'Can I see your ticket, please,' said a teenage girl from behind the booth.

'Uh? Yeah, sure.' Astrid slipped the ticket under the glass and pushed the turnstile. It jammed again.

'It's another three quid for a return,' said the teenager.

'What, I've got to—'

'This is a single.' The teenager pressed the ticket up against the glass. 'Return's another three quid.'

Astrid rooted around in her pockets, glancing over the park. Almost screaming. The person had melted into the crowd. She found the money and handed it over. But when she got through the turnstile, she knew she'd missed her chance. They'd gone.

She leant against a pillar and checked the photos she'd taken, although she knew before they came up that they were no use. Just a couple of blurred shots of the back of a black hoodie. Her heart sank. It had been so close.

'You want to buy your photo of the ride?' Another teenager, a tall pale boy, strode up to her. This island was run by teenagers in the summer, thought Astrid.

'I don't understand.'

'Oh, you probably missed it. There's a camera on the brow of the hill that takes your picture on the way back. Like a souvenir photo.'

Astrid burst out laughing. 'Fantastic.'

'Good news, huh?' said the boy flatly.

'You've no idea.'

He stood back and there was a video screen high on the wall. He sat down at a table with a laptop in the middle. As he scrolled through some photos on the computer, they appeared on the screen. He soon found Astrid. She was staring ahead with a determined expression.

'There you are,' he said. 'Number 1167.'

'Great. And listen…' She moved behind the laptop with her most winning smile. 'I don't suppose I could get the photo of another chair?'

'I guess.'

'It's my partner. He wanted to go back up on his own. He's six chairs ahead.'

The boy went back to the laptop and pulled up the photo of the person ahead of her. It was shot from straight on. And the photo was crystal clear.

'Is that her?' said the boy.

'Um… yes, that's her.' Astrid couldn't take her eyes off the screen.

It was Harlow Wade.

Thirty-seven

Astrid stood against the fence by the exit, the photo in her pocket. She took it out again, hardly believing what she was seeing. As if it were a faked Victorian photo of some ghostly apparition. It was almost impossible to believe – Harlow Wade was alive. That meant there was one person she had to tell straight away. The news had to be broken in person. Astrid took out her phone and found the contact number for Celeste.

It was getting late, but there was still enough light to meet up and get back to her boat. Astrid composed a text, all CAPS. It said they had to meet, right now – it was urgent. All would be explained when she saw her. Celeste instantly replied. She was always on her phone, so that was no surprise. They agreed to meet at the entrance of The Needles' Eye in half an hour.

Astrid waited outside the black iron gates. Eventually, Celeste appeared round the corner. She appeared flustered, hitching her bag up on her shoulder and rearranging her straw hat. 'I'm sooo sorry I'm late. My bad – I was hosting a drinks thing and couldn't drag myself away.'

'That's Cowes Week.'

'Madness… it's the same every year.'

Astrid wondered if she should just blurt it out. That Celeste's missing sister had miraculously appeared, alive and well. Maybe wait until Celeste had composed herself. 'You're almost through the week, I guess. One more day.'

'One more day.' She exhaled dramatically. 'Then I can relax.'

'Good, good. Now listen, I'm sorry to get you to rush down here. And to be so cryptic with my message.'

'That's okay.'

'The thing is…' Astrid hesitated. 'The thing is, someone has been following me this week.'

'Oh, no. Are you okay?'

'Yes, I'm fine,' Astrid said. There was no way of easing into the truth. It was like when police came to your door with bad news. At least Celeste would be pleased to hear this. 'Right, I'm just going to say it. The person following me… it was Harlow.'

'Harlow?' Celeste froze.

'Here, let me show you.' Astrid brought the chairlift photo out from her pocket and gave it to her. Celeste slipped her bag off her shoulder and set it down by the wall. Then she held the photo in her hands and focused on it. Her eyes began to fill with tears. The tears gathered into steady sobbing.

'That's okay,' said Astrid, leading her by the arm to the wall. They both sat there for a while, backs against the brickwork. It was true – the photo was of Harlow. Only a sister would be certain. Astrid didn't have any doubts when she'd seen it. The person on the chairlift had the same almond-shaped face. Same defined cheekbones. Harlow had barely changed in the three years since anyone had last seen her.

Celeste held out the photo to Astrid, who told her to keep it. It was hers. She clutched it to her chest then looked at it again, shaking her head. 'It's incredible.'

'It is.'

'Did you speak to her?'

Astrid explained that Harlow had watched her from a distance at the start of the week, although then she didn't know who it was. Then she'd followed her again today and managed to give her the slip at the theme park. It was beginning to dawn on them both. Astrid got there first. 'I guess she's back on the island and maybe ready to make contact.'

'I just have to wait then. Until she's ready.' Celeste dabbed at her eyes with her sleeve.

'I'm really sorry.'

'No, no... this is wonderful,' she said, pressing the photo to her chest with both hands Astrid had a strange thought. Had anyone, ever, been so excited about a souvenir photo of a ride on the Isle of Wight chairlift? 'Can I tell you something?' asked Celeste.

'Anything.'

'When we were growing up, Harlow and I didn't always get along. You know. Sisters... right?'

'Tell me about it.'

'It was only really when she was out of my life that I realised how much I missed her. My biggest fear was that she had died not knowing that...' she wiped another tear with the back of her sleeve '...that I loved her.'

Astrid gripped her wrist. 'At least you know she's okay now. And I'm sure you'll have a chance to tell her yourself.' She got up. 'I'm going to leave you to it, Celeste. Let this sink in.'

'Thank you, Astrid. And you know what I'm going to do?'

Astrid shook her head.

'I'm going to put this in her room.' She held up the photo. 'If Harlow makes contact with you first, tell her I'll be at the house.'

'I will.' Astrid knew that she had to tell Celeste about Tranter. How he'd been planning to cheat her on the development. 'Do you think you'll keep the house now? And not develop the garden?'

Celeste tipped her head to one side, unsure how Astrid knew about her plans for the environment centre. 'The development? Oh, no... I'm not going to sell the house now. It's our house. Mine and Harlow's.'

'I think that's a good idea,' said Astrid.

Thirty-eight

Now what was she going to do about Tranter? That was pretty much the main thought that had swirled round in Astrid's mind since she'd left Celeste at The Needles' Eye. On the bus back to the theme park, the long walk up to the headland and back down through the woods to the boat, all she could think about was how unfair it was. Tranter had his big race tomorrow, and then he'd leave the island. She was running out of time. Running out of ideas to get even.

It was high tide. She'd made a mark on the post with a penknife at the last high tide. The water was level with the mark. This is when she felt the most edgy. When there was still a way to sail in from the river.

She sat on deck in the failing light, a glass cradled in her hand, wine box at her feet. Watching the bend in the river downstream. She checked her watch. Another hour and the water would drop back enough to relax. The willow rustled in a gust of breeze. And then a boat appeared. 'Now what?' she said aloud.

She first saw the mast above the line of reeds. The boat was running slowly on the motor. Then the prow edged out round the corner and turned into the current. It was a

Bermuda sloop. About twenty feet. There was a dark-blue canvas awning over the drop to the cabin. Someone was standing behind it at the helm. Astrid stood up. She couldn't make them out just yet.

The boat took a line middle of the river. Then the engine cut, and it drifted alongside.

Astrid thought about where she'd put the penknife. In a drawer by the sink. There wasn't time to get down there. The person had left the helm and was walking inside the rail towards her, a line in her hand. She pushed the hoodie back from her head. 'You mind if I come aboard?' she said.

'Sure, Harlow.'

Harlow threw the line out and Astrid tied it up at the cleat at the prow. Then she tucked the fenders over the side as the Bermuda sloop was pushed up against Astrid's boat by the current. Harlow fixed another line at the stern, hopped over both rails and strolled up.

'Drink?' said Astrid.

'I think so.' Her voice was deeper than her sister's. A bit less refined. More of the expensive education had rubbed off somewhere.

Astrid went down to the kitchen and brought up another glass. A large one. It wasn't often you got to speak to someone who'd been missing at sea for three years. She was about to hear the answer to one of the biggest sailing mysteries of recent years.

Harlow had drawn up a chair and was sitting facing her own boat. Her hair was cropped to half an inch and dyed a dark auburn. Astrid sat down next to her and filled the glass from the wine box. She handed it over.

'Cheers,' she drawled, bringing the glass to her lips

Astrid topped up her own glass, then drained it down a couple of fingers. 'So,' she said. 'Where the hell have you been, Harlow Wade?'

'How long have you got?'

Astrid did up her fleece and sank back into the chair. 'As long as it takes.'

It was, Astrid felt, a story that Harlow had been waiting a long time to tell someone in full. It had been rehearsed in her head so often, for this moment, that it tumbled forward in perfect order. The story started a couple of months before Cowes Week three years ago. Harlow said she'd woken up and seen another article about her in the local paper. Yet again she was being feted as the Isle of Wight's next great sailing champion. Maybe England's. She read the report and it felt weird. As if part of her was being taken away. To be sold and traded. The pressure to live up to everyone's expectations, especially her father's, began to build.

This was the only pause in the conversation – when she first mentioned her father. She finished the wine and put the glass down by her feet. Waiting until she had the exact words – to be fair to him. He was a good man, she said. But driven. A workaholic who set impossible standards – for himself and her. He desperately wanted her to win at Cowes Week. The reputation of the family was at stake. It was too much of a burden for Harlow to carry. Along with juggling exam revision, a 'deadbeat boyfriend', and everything else that comes along with being a teenager. A fuse had been lit. If she didn't do something about it, she'd explode. She had a solution though. A few days before the race, she planned it all. She'd fake her death, and sail away.

'You could see no other way out?' said Astrid.

'Not then.' She sighed heavily. 'Now, of course, I can see how I could have done it differently. Back then... something had snapped. There was just this dark cloud and I had to get out from under it.'

'Did anyone else know?'

'Silas.' She looked tearful. It was clear she knew that he'd died. If not Tranter's hand in his death. 'Silas was my friend and he understood.'

'I'm sorry about your friend.'

'Thank you,' she said, gathering herself. 'Between us, we worked it all out. The day before I left, he got some provisions for the boat. Charts. Water. A few hundreds in euros. He'd found someone who could fake a passport too. Though I never asked who did it. Then that evening, I sailed out towards The Needles without looking back.'

'They found your baseball cap on the mainland three days later.' Astrid topped her glass up from the wine box. 'Did you throw it in the water?'

'Yeah, I did. Just before I sailed out of the Solent. I figured they'd need to find some piece of clothing if they were to believe I'd drowned.'

'Smart...'

Harlow carried on with her story. 'I sailed past The Needles just as it was getting dark. Then I switched off the instruments. It was foggy and the lighthouse was on – but I managed to reach Freshwater Bay round the coast. That's when Silas came out on the inflatable to modify the boat.'

'Modify?'

'Yeah, we changed the name. The sail. New fenders. I was across the Channel, heading to the Bay of Biscay, before they managed to put out an alert to international ports. I was clear. Home and dry.'

'Where did you go?'

'South of Spain. I picked up some work in the harbours. Cleaning boats. Bar stuff. Nobody asked to see my passport and after I dyed my hair, nobody recognised me. As far as everyone was concerned, I'd disappeared off the face of the earth.'

Astrid had so many other questions. And Harlow was happy to answer all of them. For the first six months she'd avoided reading anything about herself. Then she'd found an English newspaper and seen that her disappearance was still a big news story. That's when she discovered her father had died. The shock left her 'in a bad place, emotionally', she said. Wracked with guilt, unable to work out how she could ever return to the island. But then, after a couple of years, she began to realise she couldn't hide forever. So she came back. When Cowes Week was over, the sailing world would move on. It would be the quietest time to come home.

'And why are you telling *me*?' asked Astrid.

'Because I'd been watching the house and seen you working there. I thought I'd take a gamble and confide in a stranger.'

'Well, I'm glad you did. I'm so pleased you're okay.'

'Thanks.'

There was a coolness in the air. The rushes behind them clattered in a gust of wind. The willow shook and a handful of leaves twirled down and settled on the water. The first whisper of autumn. Astrid found her phone up on the control cabin and went back to her seat. Harlow had her feet tucked up on the seat. Astrid could sense she knew what was coming next.

'And when are you going to tell the world you're back?'

'I dunno… soon, I guess.'

'You should tell Celeste first.'

Harlow exhaled slowly, her breath forming as mist in front of her. 'I do feel bad about it – not telling her sooner. But I was never sure if she missed me. We didn't see eye to eye all the time.'

'Listen.' Astrid swivelled in her chair to face her. 'I've spoken to your sister. And she misses you so much. I know you guys didn't get on all the time, but she does love you.'

'I'm not so sure.'

'Harlow… after you followed me at the theme park, I worked out who you were. I told Celeste and she said it was a miracle. She told me that she'd be at the house, every day. Waiting for you. When you're ready.'

'That's good to know.' She gave a half smile. 'Hey, I don't know your name.'

'Astrid.'

'Okay, Astrid. I have a question for you.'

'Go on.'

She looked round at the reeds. 'Why are you hiding?'

Astrid told her how she'd ended up here. Hiding in a bend in a river. She didn't like to think of it like that. That she was hiding – it felt cowardly, and she knew she wasn't a coward. Harlow listened to the events of her investigation. How she'd found out that Gabriel Tranter had killed both Victor Leech and Silas, or at least his assistant had. And how Tranter had tried to kill her when she discovered his plans to build a yacht club in the grounds of The Needles' Eye.

Harlow took it all in. And when Astrid finished speaking, she said 'He can't get away with it. Can he?'

'Maybe.' Astrid folded her arms and sighed. 'I'm still planning to bring him down. But all I have is this one piece of information – that he's going to be allowed to join the British Yacht Society. If he wins the Fastnet Race tomorrow.'

'And he will. He's spent too much money on that boat.'

'I know.' She paused. 'So, I have that knowledge... and it's a weapon – except I don't know how to use it.'

'Hang on,' Harlow said brightly. 'He doesn't know this yet?'

'No.'

'Then that's your weapon.'

Before she went to sleep, Astrid lay in bed for a while listening to the scrape of the fenders on both sides of the boat as it rocked on the breeze. The old jetty on one side and Harlow's boat nestled alongside her on the other. It was good to know she was there. To have company. Harlow had left a teenager and come back wiser than her years. Astrid ran over the last things she'd said, about Tranter. Then she got it.

She reached for her phone on the ledge, found Tranter's number, unblocked him and typed in a message.

We need to talk. Just you and me. You owe me that.

It didn't take more than a few seconds for his reply to come in. Digital detox, my arse. He was such a hypocrite.

There's nothing to say. I'm leaving after the race. Just get on with your life.

She typed:

It's about your membership of the British Yacht Society.

She waited, imagining him sitting upright in the lounge of that big boat of his. Stroking his goatee beard. This had to get him. It had to... Yes.

Okay. Where and when?

She told him they should meet tomorrow on safe ground. Just him and her. The entrance to the Yarmouth pier at 9 a.m. There would still be time for him to get back to his race in the afternoon. He agreed with:

OK.

When Astrid switched off her phone, she realised something. She'd never given Tranter her number. He must have found it out somehow – one of the perks of owning a media company, no doubt. *Not for much longer,* she thought, pulling her sleeping bag up to her chin.

Thirty-nine

Astrid left the boat in the morning as quietly as she could. She didn't want to disturb Harlow, who was somewhere below deck on her boat.

He was already there when she arrived at the pier at nine. He stood just beyond the entrance, leaning on the rail with both elbows and staring out over the water – no doubt eyeing up the conditions for his race in a few hours. He was wearing a long-sleeved black top. The *Mistral 2* logo down one arm. He must be going straight to the race boat from here. She stopped a few feet from him, and he turned and looked her up and down.

'No phone?'

She'd decided to wear a plain T-shirt and shorts with no back pockets, so he could see she hadn't brought it. She turned slowly through 360 degrees, hating his eyes on her. When she faced him again, he was nodding.

'Okay,' he said. 'What's this news about the BYS?'

'In a moment.' The pier was empty. But most of the tables were taken at The Chatterbox Café, so there would be witnesses this time – if he tried something. 'I've a few questions first.'

'If you must.'

'Yes, I do.' She came closer. Only a couple of feet from him. 'I want to know why you tried to kill me.'

'We've been through this,' he said wearily. 'There's nothing else to say.'

'I want to hear it again. A confession – in broad daylight this time.'

'Hah,' he snorted. 'You're so dramatic. A silly, dramatic woman. Nosing around in other people's business, then complaining when it comes back to bite you.'

'Who's complaining?'

'You are. That's why you're here. Trying to wring out some apology. I told you – it's nothing personal.'

'Nothing personal?'

'It's just business.'

'Okay then. I won't tell you what I know about your membership at the BYS.' She held her ground, watching him process it – she had something he wanted.

He bit his lower lip in frustration. 'Fine,' he hissed. Then he checked his watch and started his admission. All of it. He rattled through the details of the two murders, which was his idea. Although Cristo was responsible for carrying them out in his usual creative ways. 'That's another golden rule of business, Astrid. Surround yourself with people you trust and who can get the job done. Treasure them – they're gold dust.' He was deadly serious. She had got in the way of one of his plans and she had to be disposed of.

'That yacht club development. Was it worth killing for?'

'Oh, yeah.' He gazed out at the land beyond The Needles' Eye. 'It was going to be incredible. Exclusive membership.

Restaurants. Gym. Media suites to cover the races. It was going to be the hub of yacht racing on the island.'

'Jeez.' She whistled. 'If they won't let you join them, build your own yacht club.'

He tipped his head to one side. 'What?'

'It's all because they wouldn't let your dad become a member of the Royal Yacht Squadron. I'm right, aren't I?'

'Well done… you read my book.'

'Speed-read it.'

'They should have let him in that club. Me too. I don't forget those kind of things.'

'Hey, maybe it's just nothing personal?' She laughed. 'Just their business.'

He checked his watch. 'Listen. I've got a race coming up. If you don't have any information, then don't waste any more of my time.'

He stuck his hands in his pockets, fidgeting. As if he was going to walk away. But she knew he wasn't. He'd come down here just before his big race. He was desperate to hear what she knew. She let him suffer a little bit more. 'Yeah, I was up at the club the other day for a drinks party on the lawn. It's lovely there, isn't it?' She brought her finger to her chin. 'Sorry, you wouldn't know.'

'Just tell me,' he barked.

'Okay… okay. Well, the good news is the British Yacht Society are going to allow you to become a member.'

'Seriously?' His jaw dropped. 'Wow… I mean. Just, wow.' He paced off a few feet then came back, clapping his hands. Then there was a glint of worry. 'And you're sure about this? It's not just gossip?'

'No, no. I spoke to the social secretary of the club. They're going to give you full membership. But on one condition.'

'One condition.' His face fell.

'Yes. You win the Fastnet Race.'

'Is that all?' he said, matter-of-factly. Then it was back to the smug Tranter. 'Hey... I'm going to be a member of the British Yacht Society.' He said the name slowly. Letting it sink in. Then he checked his watch again. 'I better go.'

'Wait.' She put her arm out to stop him. 'Before you do, I want to tell you who you really are.'

'If you must.'

'You're a man-child, Tranter. An alpha man-child who never grew up. Who just got rich by luck and bought bigger toys. The kind of man who leaves notes on napkins for waitresses half their age. And you'll never be happy. I know, I've met your type before.'

He laughed. 'Astrid... hey, gotta dash. I've got a race to win.' Then he hurried off the pier and out into the town square. There was a black SUV with tinted windows parked up in the bays. He opened the passenger door and got in, and she watched it drive off until it was out of sight.

She'd kept calm all the way through, and now her hand began to tremble with excitement. Because she'd done it. They'd done it. She walked off the pier and when she reached the parking bays, she turned left down the slipway.

The tide was out and the gravel beach was dry. Ahead of her, emerging from under the pier, were Frank, Wren, Annabelle and Kabir. 'Hey, guys,' she called to them. 'Did you get that?' The all held up their phones in unison.

Kabir said, 'We all got that.'

Forty

'I don't know what more you have to hear, Jim.' Astrid hit the pause button on Kabir's phone.

Jim sat back in his chair behind his desk. A slow nod turned into a long sigh of defeat. 'Okay.' He got up. 'I admit it – you were right about Tranter. Sorry.'

'Ooh, that last word,' said Astrid. 'I didn't catch it. Must be the sea spray in my ears.'

'Yes, yes.' Jim tried not to laugh. 'Sorry, Astrid.'

'Excellent. Well, now what do we do?'

'You need to send me that recording – to this email.' He found a business card in his drawer and passed it over to Astrid. He glanced at the brass clock on the wall as she forwarded the recording. 'The Fastnet Race starts in about an hour. I'll give the police a call. See if they'll get a boat out to him to stop him setting off.' He got up from behind his desk and escorted her to the door. 'There's protocol about boarding a boat and making an arrest. We just have to hope he'll play ball and come ashore.'

Jim turned the door handle and there was a shuffling of feet on the other side. When he'd pushed it open the others were standing in the corridor, trying to look like they hadn't been listening to the conversation through the woodwork. Astrid introduced them quickly. Jim shook all of their hands and thanked them. He stepped back into the doorway of his office, then when they were a few yards down the corridor, he called out, 'Hey, Astrid.'

'Yeah?'

'You'll need to stick around. The police will want to speak to you now.'

'I will. Thanks, Jim.'

In the car park, Astrid gave Kabir his phone back. It was going to be close. The police would have to trust the recording of Tranter's confession. Then send a police boat out to him on the busiest day of the year for the island. The last day of Cowes Week, when every competitor and weekend sailor would be crammed into the bay.

They walked across the car park in silence. It was too early to celebrate. Too tense to go their separate ways. Frank piped up, 'Why don't we go to the Admiral's Arms?'

'What goes on there, Frank?' asked Wren.

'Nice little boozer off the high street. I know the landlord. I'll get him to put the telly on the Cowes Week channel. We can have a few beers and watch Tranter get busted live on TV.'

'Of all the ridiculous ideas and nonsensical things you've come up with,' said Annabelle disdainfully. 'And then you go and come up with that brilliant idea.' She laughed.

Frank swelled with pride. 'Right then. Follow me.'

★★★

The Admiral's Arms was only ten yards off the high street, but it appeared to get very little of the passing trade, marooned, as it was, down a gloomy alley blocked at the end by a couple of black wheelie bins. The welcome was warm though.

The landlord, who was as puffy-faced and characterful as the Toby jugs on the shelf behind him, greeted them as they came in. He saw Frank and beamed. There was a line of pewter tankards hanging from hooks above the bar. He picked one out and, without asking what Frank wanted, started filling it with foaming beer that had the words 'Wight Squirrel' on the pump.

The others had the same – largely because there didn't seem to be much else available. Except Annabelle, who was driving. The landlord managed to find a can of diet lemonade from a dusty cardboard box down by his feet. It had 'Multipack – not for sale individually' on the side. He blew on the top and passed it over without a glass.

'Lovely,' said Annabelle. She really was being a saint today.

They all took their pints and made their way over to a high-backed mahogany bench that curled round an alcove.

'This is rather quaint, Frank,' said Annabelle, picking her way over the worn carpet. Halfway there she hit a sticky patch that dragged one of her Superga pumps off her heel. She didn't react. Determined to keep up her running praise of Frank. 'It's utterly charming – like being in the prow of a small galleon.'

It was. Everywhere were seafaring antiques. Coloured glass floats, pennants in frames, tackle and blocks, and heavy rope that wound through beams. It was the car-boot version of the lookout in The Needles' Eye. It was a lot gloomier though. A yellowish light filtered through the dusty window panes, adding to the deep-below-decks vibe.

There was a television up to their right in the corner. The old type. As big as a cardboard box. Frank had a word, and the landlord reached up and switched on. The screen was dark, a single white horizontal line across the middle. The landlord cracked the side of the television with a flat palm, and it came on. He selected the Cowes Racing Channel on the box underneath and left them with the remote to sort out the volume. There was nobody else in the pub to complain. Frank drifted off to the bar to chat to the landlord.

On the screen was a live aerial view of the bay. It was full of boats at their moorings. Top-end racing yachts – single hull, mostly. All with their sails packed away. For the moment. Crews in the same colour outfits – black, red, orange – were scampering around on deck making final preparations. Along the side of the hulls were the names of luxury brands – perfumes, watches, whiskies, fashion houses. The two presenters, one woman, one man, gave a running commentary of the boats. Their size, crew, other trivia. The chances of each one winning.

The four of them had knocked back most of their drinks, and there was no sign of Tranter's boat. Then the coverage cut to a graphic showing the route of the Fastnet Race. It started through the Needles Channel. Along the south coast of England. Then it veered north-west off the tip of Cornwall. The halfway mark was the Fastnet Rock off the southern tip of Ireland. That's how the race got its name.

Competitors rounded the rock then set off on the home run to nearby Plymouth, on the mainland.

Frank came over from the bar, a grin on his face. 'You'll never guess what happened. I was just ordering some grub... hey, sorry. Did you guys want anything?'

They all shook their heads.

'Right, anyway...' he continued, 'I was talking to Derek and he's got a mate who wants to sell his hot tub.'

'Mmm...?' said Astrid, not taking her eyes from the screen. 'A hot tub?'

'It was up at the holiday park, so it's seen a bit of use. There's a bit of algae on it because the pump went. But Derek reckons if I run bleach through the system it'll come up lovely.'

'Well done, Frank,' said Wren. 'That great news.'

'I'm over the moon,' said Frank. 'I'd given up all hope, but then sometimes, the hand of Lady Fate steps in. Problem will be how to get it up to Totland...'

'Sorry, Frank.' Kabir pointed the remote control at the television, turning up the volume. 'It's Tranter's boat.'

The aerial shot lingered over *Mistral 2*, 'one of the biggest, most high-tech racing yachts in the world', as the commentators breathlessly explained. It was stunning. And not just in sheer size – just under one hundred and forty feet long, half as big again as anything else in the race – but the design. It was entirely black. A towering single mast was positioned ahead of a level control deck the size of a small car park. Slim, razor-sharp fins curved out into the water. It had all the elegance and angles of a military stealth fighter jet. Among the white boats and the wooden classic yachts, it stood out a nautical mile. A killer whale among seals.

'*Mistral*?' said Frank. 'They might as well call it Tosser!'

The others laughed, except Astrid who was scowling at the television. The helicopter camera was homing in on the deck. Around twenty crew, all dressed in black, were sitting on the edge of the boat, their legs hanging under the rail. Tranter was at the helm set in the back corner. He was dressed in the same race outfit as she'd seen him in on the pier. There was a crew member standing next to him, laughing at something he'd said.

They ordered some more drinks and kept watching the coverage. The race for the biggest class of boats was due to start in about twenty minutes, at twelve thirty. A thought began to creep up on Astrid. A clawing sense of injustice. Would Tranter get away with it? There was no sign of the police. She texted Jim and told him they were watching the race in the Admiral's Arms. Asked him if he knew what was going on.

With ten minutes to go before the start of the race, there was still no sign of the police. From the commentary, they knew everything about Tranter's boat, though – its sail area was the size of eight tennis courts. A cutting-edge carbon fibre hull. The perfect sailing machine equipped for every one of the six hundred and eight miles of the Fastnet Race.

'This is grating,' said Kabir.

'It's puke-worthy,' agreed Wren.

Derek came over with a deep plate of potato mash and sausages and placed it in front of Frank, who thanked him, then spent the next minute swirling the gravy into a well of mash, as if mixing concrete. Annabelle checked her watch. 'I'm getting worried now.'

'Come on,' said Kabir. 'He can't just sail off... can he?'

Then finally the camera cut to a wider shot of the bay. The screen wobbled into focus on a police inflatable that was coursing out over the water towards Tranter's yacht. There was a collective whoop from the table. Frank's voice cut through. 'Got the bugger!'

Astrid had kept tight-lipped. She knew it was too early to celebrate.

They watched the police inflatable weave between some of the bigger yachts in the main pack. *Mistral 2* was anchored up at the front. Champing at the waves. There were three uniformed officers on board. Two at the front, the other at the engine. The inflatable turned in alongside the stern of the boat. Astrid stood up and went round the table. 'Just arrest him,' she whispered.

A police officer stood up at the front of the inflatable and shouted up to a crew member on the *Mistral 2*. He was a good ten feet below the level of the deck. The crew member went over to Tranter and spoke to him. He left the helm and walked to the rail. Peered down, unconcerned.

The door of the pub swung open and Jim strode in. He noticed them all in the corner, Astrid standing to the side of the table, staring up at the television. He gave a quick 'hi' to the others, then joined Astrid.

She looked away from the television. 'Hey, Jim. You got the message through then?'

'Yeah, came straight here.'

Jim explained that it had taken a while to get through to someone high enough in the Hampshire Police. It was their busiest day of the year. As they'd guessed. But once he'd fired off the recording of Tranter's confession on the pier, the police sprang into action. They sent a boat out straight away. As Jim had also guessed, the rules of arrest at sea were complicated. They couldn't just climb aboard and handcuff him. And Tranter would know that. He was on a floating castle – and he was king. Astrid's heart sank as she watched the screen. Tranter shook his head at the police officer, then strode back to the helm.

At the table, the others groaned. They sat there, rigid. Baffled about what they'd just seen. It was how they all felt.

'Is that it, Jim?' said Astrid.

'I think it might be. But, you know… let's see.'

The coverage cut away from the bay to the front of the British Yacht Society, where a man was attaching a green flag to a rope at the base of a wooden mast. Next to him was a man with a clipboard. Then the row of gold cannons.

The first man squinted at his starting watch.

Raised a finger.

Nodded and…

Booom.

The nearest brass cannon coughed out a plume of grey smoke. The first man raised the green flag up the mast and the footage was back out on the bay.

Mistral 2 wasn't the quickest off the mark. A couple of the other smaller yachts had their sails up and had eased ahead of the pack. There was a close-up of *Mistral 2*. Slowly, its grey mesh sail rose in an expanding triangle that nearly filled the screen. The sail bowed out in the wind. The boat tipped a few degrees to the side and pushed the waves aside.

'Now what, Jim?' said Astrid.

He didn't say anything for a while. Just stared at the screen. They all did. *Mistral 2* had picked up speed. Tranter was at the helm shouting orders to his crew, who were dashing into position around the boat. The police boat stayed where it was – defeated. Then it spun round and roared back to shore.

When Jim spoke, Astrid could tell he was trying to sound as cheerful as possible. For her. 'For the time being, Astrid, I'm afraid... it's not looking good. You see – once he gets beyond twelve nautical miles offshore, he's out of British waters. The authorities can't do anything until he comes back into Plymouth in a couple of days.'

'But he won't, though, will he?' said Astrid.

'What are you saying?'

'He'll run away. You think someone like that – with all that luxury – is going to jail? No, no.' She shook her head. 'He's not coming back to face the music.'

'Maybe. We'll see soon enough.'

'I know.' Astrid turned away. Not wanting him to see how upset she was. She bought another round of drinks for everyone. Letting her anger boil down. When she was composed enough, she went back to the table and squeezed in to watch the rest of the race coverage. They all seemed just as deflated. Even Frank, who'd failed to polish off lunch. 'It's not right,' he muttered, pushing his plate out to the middle of the table.

By now, *Mistral 2* was well ahead of the field, its huge sails gobbling up what wind there was. The prow carved through the waves, the green water rolling down its hull. Then just as it drew level with The Needles, it happened. As Astrid had said it would.

The mainsail began to lower. The boat righted itself in the water and slowed. A few other boats overtook it on either side. The camera zoomed in on Tranter at the helm. He was talking to his assistant. Disagreeing about something. Even from a distance, you could tell from Tranter's animated arm movements that it was an argument. He stepped away from the helm and went to the far rail. For the first time in half an hour, the commentators were lost for words. Astrid filled the gaps for them. 'He's pulling out of the race.'

'Looks like you were right,' said Jim.

They all watched in silence as the boat came to a halt. It sat, bobbing gently in the water. The rest of the field swerved past it – except for one boat, which motored up alongside, then cut its engine. It was the familiar shape of the Hallberg-Rassy. 'He's going to swap boats,' she said.

'Seriously?' said Wren.

'Watch this.'

The camera zoomed in on Tranter, who waited until the Hallberg-Rassy's fenders bumped up against the side of the *Mistral* 2. He zipped up his jacket and stepped nimbly across to the other deck. Behind him, his crew had left their positions. They were wandering the deck, trying to work out why they'd been abandoned.

The camera swung over to the back of the Hallberg-Rassy. Cristo was at the helm. Tranter patted him on the back and headed down into the cabin. The Hallberg-Rassy's engines started, and it rounded the prow of the *Mistral 2*. Then it cut across the field of competitors and sailed on, diagonally, past The Needles.

Kabir broke the silence. 'Where's he going to go now?'

'Monaco, probably,' said Astrid. 'He has a house there. I researched it. He lives there for tax reasons.'

'But the police can arrest him there... right?' said Wren.

''Fraid not,' said Jim. 'They'd have to extradite him to the UK first, and that's going to be nearly impossible.'

'But hang on. He can't just...' Frank stuttered. 'Just bugger off.'

Astrid said, 'I'm sorry, Frank. I think he can.'

Forty-one

On the drive back to Abbotsford Manor – Annabelle at the wheel, Wren in the passenger seat, the others bunched up in the back – a sour mood settled in the car. This wasn't how it was supposed to end – the villain sailing off into the sunset, or midday sun.

Astrid watched the scenery drift past. Tranter would get away with it, in the end. There would be an initial scandal. He'd hole up in his tax haven in Monaco. Ride out the storm. Get his media outlets to run the fake news stories to get ahead of the real ones. As Beckett would agree – a lie can travel halfway around the world while the truth is still putting its shoes on.

They pulled into the car park and decided to visit the potting shed to get a coffee. Astrid went round to the boot to get Wren's wheelchair. Kabir said he wanted to swing by the reception – he'd catch them all up. Annabelle clicked the locks of the car and headed off with Frank through the gardens.

Astrid and Wren were about to set off when Wren's father's minivan drove through the entrance. It lined up in a space and Michael got out. He waved at his daughter to come over.

'I should go,' said Astrid, pushing her rucksack higher over one shoulder.

Wren faced her. 'No, you're coming with me,' she said sternly. Then she set off towards her father. He slid open the side door of the minivan but Wren waved him away and continued towards the exit at the car park.

They both caught up with her at the side of the road. Her father was about to help her across, but she'd glanced left and right and set off again. And she didn't stop until she was at the bench on the village green. 'Both of you... sit down.'

Astrid and Michael chose opposite ends of the bench. They both pressed themselves into the corner and crossed their legs, avoiding eye contact.

Wren lined up in front of them and wove her fingers together. 'Right, I'm going to talk to you about art college.'

'We should talk about this at home,' Michael said. 'Between us. This is a family—'

'No, Dad...' Wren cut him off. 'If we talk about this at home, you'll persuade me to do what you want. And I'll go to my room and play video games. Which I love. But I'll always be there. Playing video games.'

He was about to speak, but she intercepted him with a steely stare. 'Let's start again, shall we?' Her father nodded solemnly. 'We're going to talk about art college – but first I'm going to talk about you, Dad.' A beat. 'I love you.'

He squirmed deeper into the crook of the bench. 'Wren. Not here.'

'Dad, I'm Generation Z. We tell people we love them in public. It's fine. Nobody dies.' She got back on track. 'I love you, Dad. You've done everything for me since Mum left. You're my whole world.'

'You too, Wren.'

'Now, Astrid.'

'Um, yes, Wren.' Astrid smiled nervously.

'I don't really know you, do I?'

'I guess not.'

'We've had a few chats and stuff at the art club, and a coffee. But I don't really know you.' Wren came closer. 'But the thing is, Astrid. I do know who you are. You're a really good person. And do you know why I'm sure about that?'

'Honestly… I've no idea.'

'Because you've never seen this.' She patted the armrests of her wheelchair. 'You've only ever seen me. I say this is like my beacon. It attracts the kindest people out there. The odd nasty person – but hey, who cares about them? And you, Astrid… you only wanted the best for me. I appreciate it.'

'Oh, I'm off the hook. Great.' Astrid brightened.

'Not yet.'

Astrid slumped back in the chair.

'Because you came to my house to talk to my dad about college. Didn't you?'

'I thought I'd try and help.'

'But if I didn't ask you to, it's not helping, it's meddling.'

'Sorry,' said Astrid.

'So listen up, you two. I think you're both awesome. You know that now. But I'm going to make my own decisions from now on.' They sat still. 'Somehow, I'm going to art college. And that's my final decision.'

Michael shuffled towards the front of the bench and ran

his hands back through his hair. He did look so much like her. Especially when he was in a kind mood. 'Okay, Wren, I agree. You should go to college. But the problem is, we don't have that kind of money. You'd get a loan for the tuition fees. But there's the accommodation – it's too expensive.'

'Next year then,' she said quietly. 'I'll get a job. Two jobs.'

'It's London, Wren,' said Michael. 'I can't see how we'd do it.' He put his hand on her shoulder, and she tipped her head against it. Eyes closed in defeat.

'Hey.' Astrid got up. 'I've got a plan. Not long ago, my husband left me. I wish he'd evaporate into atoms and drift away on the wind, but unfortunately, he's still very much in human form. And he's insisting that we hold on to our rather splendid Thameside apartment.' She reached into her rucksack and scrabbled around in the bottom. Her grip closed on the bunch of keys. 'Now, here's what's going to happen.' She tossed the keys over to Wren, who caught them.

'What are these?' asked Wren.

'They're the keys to my apartment. I'm going to insist that you stay there, rent-free. My ex-husband will do what he's told. And so will you. I have my faults, I know, and I'm going to work on them. But I'm Gen X and we always get what we want. And I want you to stay in the flat. So that's what's going to happen.'

Wren's lower lip trembled so hard no words could leave her mouth. She held out her hand for Astrid's and mouthed 'thank you'.

Astrid squeezed her hand. 'Okay, then it's done.'

The village green glowed in the late afternoon sun. The gardens beyond the road fluttered with colours. It was a beautiful place. A beautiful island. That's why she had to leave it, she thought. Because then you knew you had to come back.

'Listen – I have your number, Wren.' Astrid put her rucksack on. 'I'll send you all the details about the flat when I've sorted it out.' She paused. 'I'm not good with goodbyes. So I'm just going to sort of wander off. See the others before I go. But we'll speak soon, right?'

Wren made a little comic 'peace sign' with two fingers. Then Astrid turned away from them because it was a moment for Wren and her father to share.

On the way to see the others she thought about Cynthia Leech. Her parting comment that the death of her husband had been 'so exhilarating'. Now it all made sense. The days after Victor's death had been a social whirl for Mrs Leech. Flowers. Calls. Cards. Complete strangers like her had turned up at the door. It had made her feel alive again. She would slump sometime later. Long after the funeral. Now, though, she was the centre of attention. Happy to talk to anyone who'd listen. And for once they were listening to her, not Victor.

In the potting shed, Frank was in his usual spot, sprawled in his chair, coffee mug balanced on the armrest. Annabelle was at her easel, putting her latest watercolour – otters at sunset – in a simple card frame. Astrid came in and made some more hot drinks for everyone, to chase off the beers from lunchtime.

Kabir came in, an expression of disbelief on his face. He held up a forefinger. On the tip was a small bright orange dot – a sticker.

'It happened,' he said.

'I don't understand,' said Annabelle.

'I went to reception to check on our art in the sale. Someone has bought one of my pieces – the watercolour of the house. They actually liked it and paid for...' He trailed off and turned to Astrid. 'It wasn't you, was it?'

Astrid made a crossing action over her heart. 'I swear on my life, it wasn't. You're a proper artist now.'

'Amazing, I got what I wanted.' He went over to a chair, the orange sticker still on his finger.

Then a thought struck Astrid. They had all got what they wanted. Kabir had sold a piece of art. Annabelle had her afternoon in the sun at the BYS. Frank's hot tub. Wren and art college. It felt good – to see them all so contented. It was something that Tranter would never be now. 'I've just worked it out,' she said. 'About Tranter. What happened is a good ending.'

'I dunno,' said Frank, 'I'd prefer to see him in jail.'

'Sure,' said Astrid. 'But this is a much better punishment. Tranter wanted one thing more than any other. To be a member of the BYS. Then he'd truly won. But you know – people who think they've won don't know where the winning line is.'

'I like that,' said Kabir.

'Yeah,' said Astrid. 'I can't remember who told me that. But it's true. Tranter will never be allowed to join the BYS now. He threw it away because of his greed and meanness. And he can only blame himself.'

'Doesn't matter where he goes,' said Kabir. 'People know there's something fishy about him. He'll be a social pariah.'

Frank said. 'Social piranha?'

'Pariah, Frank,' said Astrid. 'An outcast. He'll be turned away from every club and restaurant in Monaco. Wherever he goes, it will be the same.'

The other three agreed. Tranter had had his chance. To prove he was the best. To right the wrong done to his father. And he blew it.

'Yes, to feel the sheer joy of getting what you've always wanted.' Kabir held up his finger with the sticker on. 'Then to lose it. He's going to regret that for the rest of his life.'

Astrid nodded. 'Every, single, day.'

'Oh,' said Annabelle, 'sorry to change the subject. But did you notice if any of my art was sold, Kabir? I mean, not to overshadow your big moment, obviously.'

'I'm not sure, why don't we check.' They all got up and wandered to the door. Except Astrid. The others were expecting her to follow so they didn't look back.

She found the sketch pad in her rucksack and carefully tore out drawings she done of them. On the back she wrote the date and the words 'First case solved for The Art of Murder Club'. Then she left them on Annabelle's easel, where they were sure to find them. While she waited for them to reach the reception, she gazed up at the open skylight. The sky was pale blue.

People's lives aren't like jigsaws. That's what Simon had told her once – that there won't be a time when all the pieces fit together. He *would* say that, though, because he'd never committed to anything completely. She did believe there was something missing in her life now. A small blue piece of sky that needed slotting into place. Would that make everything perfect? Probably not. It was time to find out though. She needed to go, right now, and visit her father. To make things right between them.

The boat was still stocked with food and drink. The water tanks were filled, batteries charged. She had everything she needed to get a long way down the western coast of France without dropping anchor. She checked the bookshelves. Her uncle had sailing charts for the whole of Europe. They were well worn. Had he sailed around Europe? To Spain?

Astrid worked out a route. Sixty-five nautical miles to the Cap de la Hague, which jutted out into the English Channel. Then she could cut south-west, through the Channel Islands, round the craggy coast of Brittany and down towards Spain. It was best to sail overnight when there would be fewer of the big cross-Channel ferries around. She made a flask of coffee and brought it up to the control cabin along with the charts and her red head-torch. Then she went over to Harlow's boat.

The cabin door was open and she could see Harlow down there, listening to the radio. She knocked on the door frame and Harlow came up on deck.

'You leaving?' said Harlow.

Astrid told her about her sailing plan. Harlow approved. It's what she would do. There was nothing like sailing at night, she told her. Astrid untied the ropes at the stern. Harlow sorted out the prow. They met back at the well of the cabin, the flow of the river still gently pushing the boats together.

'You hear about Tranter?' said Astrid.

'Yeah, I listened on the radio. He bailed out of the Fastnet. They'll never let him back on the race circuit again.' Harlow wound the rope up over her hand and elbow, then dropped it on the deck. 'It looks like you won in the end.'

'It does.' Astrid tidied her rope on the deck. 'So, are you ready to let everyone know you're okay?'

'In a couple of days. I promise.' Harlow shrugged. 'I'm not looking forward to the press attention though.'

'It might not be too bad. And hey, when I was talking to people about you, so many people are still missing you. Complete strangers. It's like the island is still hanging on to this shared grief.'

'Is that right?' Harlow seemed shocked.

'Yes. Everyone will just be relieved you're okay. They'll understand.'

'You think?'

'Definitely. And you're going to see your sister first, aren't you?'

Harlow folded her arms. She smiled coyly. 'I will, Astrid. I'll make it right again with Celeste. Promise.'

Astrid stepped over the rail and Harlow started the engine. Her boat moved forward, the fenders rolling down the side. Astrid remembered something. She walked to the stern, keeping up with Harlow. 'One more favour, Harlow. Could you drop in and say hi to Patrick and Jane at the coastguard watchtower?'

'Patrick and Jane?'

'A couple of the volunteers. And say bye from me.'

'Sure, Astrid.'

Astrid waited until Harlow's boat was far enough upstream to give her room to turn her boat in the bend. She eased the prow into the current until it caught the flow and fell round slowly to face downstream. Harlow whistled to her. Astrid turned at the wheel and Harlow called after her, 'Safe sailing, Astrid.'

'You too, Harlow.'

The wind had picked up to a stiff breeze. Small waves. Numerous whitecaps – four knots on the Beaufort scale. The sails filled. The boat charged on ahead, eager to get some miles under the keel before dark.

There were no other boats on the water. She had it all to herself, clearing The Needles – the jagged rocks honeyed in the early evening light.

The red-and-white lighthouse, as bright as a seaside parasol.

The island – a green and pleasant diamond in a slate sea. Tide in. The smallest county in England. Getting smaller every minute, by every nautical mile, as the *Curlew's Rest* pressed on due south, neither of them looking back.

About the Author

M.H. ECCLESTON has had a fairly meandering career – starting out as a radio presenter for the BBC, then staying at the Beeb as a journalist and producer for six years. After that, it's a bit of a blur – he spent a couple of decades, at least, freelancing as a foreign correspondent, TV presenter, sketch writer, voice-over artist and film critic. For the last few years he's been a full-time screenwriter and now novelist. He lives in Ealing with his family, which is ruled by a mischievous Frenchie called George.